BLIPS
ON THE WAY TO
OBLIVION

BLIPS
ON THE WAY TO
OBLIVION

A Novel By

ARABELLA ARK

BLIPS ON THE WAY TO OBLIVION
By Arabella Ark
© 2020 by Arabella Gail Ark
TXu002189745
1-8656910311

Blips on the Way to Oblivion is a work of literary fiction. Most names, characters, and incidents are fictional, products of the author's imagination. Any resemblance to actual events or persons, living, dead, or in history, is fictional but may contain an underlayer of truth.

Arabella Ark
2376 Kamehameha V Hwy.
Kaunakakai, HI 96748

arabella@arabellaark.com
arabellaark@icloud.com

Other Books by the Author

Doggone: A Story of Loss
Pants on Fire! A Tale of Friction
Wet Dreams: A Novel of Crime
The Life She Didn't Live

Dedications

To George Henry Hoffman, a man of courageous loyalty, sporting a
silvered mane of moon-lit hair

To Cheryl McMurphy Joseph, a generous woman filled
with insights and love

To Linda Thorpe, a childhood friend and proof-reader of my dreams

Souffles

...

Those who are dead are not ever gone;
They are in a woman's breast,
In the wailing of a child,

...

The dead are not dead

...

Spirits inhabit
The darkness that lightens, the darkness that darkens,
The quivering tree, the murmuring wood,
The water that runs and the water that sleeps:
Spirits much stronger than we,
The breathing of the dead who are not really dead,
Of the dead who are not really gone,
Of the dead now no more in the earth

...

...Birago Diop
Senegalese poet, diplomat, and veterinarian,
voice of the Negritude literary movement in Africa

"…as much as I scrabble through the ruins of my memories,
I find that time, that other time,
fresh and untouched by forgetfulness…"

Ida Puik
Holocaust survivor

BLIP ONE

Blowing in the Wind

It began, though she could not have known it then, with a full moon of cratered shadows, darkening the surface of what had gone before and what was to be, reflecting a life perhaps not her own, yet a life that was to become her sorrow.

This was her first incarnation as a septuagenarian, and the sudden deterioration of her memory alarmed her. She was falling, falling, falling, losing the foundation she built her lives upon. If she lost her memories, how would she know who she was? She feared becoming lost. But, what she feared more was becoming lost to him

He hadn't come, and she was waiting. He had never failed to come before. But, she was older, much older this time around.

"Where are you?" she whispered as she looked from her bed through the window to the sea below her house. "Aren't you coming?"

Images of William Merrill flickered through her mind. He often sailed into her life, tall, a head of silvered hair rippling like moonlight across the sea that bore him, eyes laughing as they scanned the horizon, eyes which had seen much over the centuries. He was strong, and she needed his strength added to hers as she was aging and growing frail. His strength would help her gently down the unknown path of senility, for Lucky's mind felt like a dandelion bloom in the wind, its delicate network of lacy seeds blowing in every direction.

"Hello! I'm here," a woman's voice rang out. "I've got your mail. Want me to bring it up?"

Startled, Lucky wondered who this was? A middle-aged blonde with a disheveled ponytail came into the room, a bit out of breath from the stairs, holding out several letters and a few magazines. Lucky turned in her bed, still dressed in a white silk gown under equally white silk sheets, white being her favorite color. What time was it? Must be later than she thought by the stream of light coming through the window. Pushing herself up to lean her back against the pillows, she glanced at the clock. Eleven. She reached out for the mail with her left hand, and the old pearl held by the two, tiny gold hands on her gimmel wedding bands glinted in the morning sun.

She sifted through the pile of envelopes and stopped at one that had come from a DNA testing lab.

"What's that?" the woman asked looking down at her. "Oh! You're wearing your wedding g…" the woman began to exclaim before letting her voice trail off.

"I have no idea," Lucky replied to the question about the mail. She held the envelope for a while, weighing what possibilities it might contain.

"Are you going to open it?" the woman asked, straightening the bed-clothes, and looking at her mother's old wedding gown.

"It's probably junk mail," Lucky said and tossed the letter to the floor.

"Let's check," said the woman, picking it up, and to Lucky's displeasure, sat uninvited on the edge of the bed. The woman remarked, "Well, it really is addressed to you, and it is a DNA report."

"Ah, so it is," Lucky said, glancing at the paper.

"Did you order this?" the woman asked.

Lucky shrugged.

"Would you like me to read it? I see you've been translating," the woman noted as she moved a heavy, leather-bound Latin manuscript from Lucky's lap to the bedside table.

"Alright," Lucky nodded. "Go ahead. Read the letter out-loud."

The woman skimmed before reading, "Your DNA comes from every race and every locale in the world." Lucky nodded. "I thought you were Caucasian," the woman said in an accusatory tone. "You told me you were English and French."

"Did I?"

Skimming further, the woman paraphrased, "It says the tests you ordered for mitochondrial DNA identify genetic variations about your direct ancestral line for both males and females."

"I know, I know all that," Lucky interrupted. "They preserve information possibly lost from historical records about female ancestors."

The woman continued, summarizing, "It says because of the way surnames were passed down, your case shows too many variants for any detailed or conclusive information."

"Useless," Lucky said, disappointed that this latest quest failed to reveal what she wanted to know.

"Conclusive information about what?" the woman asked.

"Children. I want to know if I have children."

The woman gave her an odd look.

"In the past, my past," Lucky said, waving the woman away. "I want to find my children."

"Oh. Of course, you do."

Lucky wanted to know if she had ever smelled her own newborn. Would it be earthy and of her? Or antiseptic? Would their little cries and groans fill the room, the sounds of love itself? She wanted children, she needed children, to tell them the story of her lives.

She knew her own mind was fading. She sighed, knowing she was gently dozing on this comfortable bed, which was dangerous, because it was becoming a bed of forgetfulness.

She often forgot who she was and where she was. Was she on her beloved island? Or, was she in China? Or, Morocco, France, England? Was it now, was it then? Her memories bounced like a ball spun on a roulette wheel. Where they chanced to stop, she couldn't guess, and as the wheel spun round, she slipped in and out of her history at random. She felt frightened. Time was passing, leaving her behind.

She had lived often, died often, always certain she would resurrect. But, that certainty was eroding as William had not appeared.

"Would you like me to write down any memories you might want to share?" the woman offered.

"No," Lucky snapped, feeling suddenly protective. "They are personal. Memories are heirlooms. I want mine held in my children's hearts and minds."

The woman sighed and got up. "I'll do some tidying downstairs. Call, if you need anything. Lunch at twelve."

Perhaps, Lucky thought when she was alone again, she was not even alive. Perhaps she had never lived, not her own life nor any of the other lives she thought she remembered.

She lay back on her bed wondering not if there were children but rather if she ever wanted children. Maybe not. Maybe William or Vassilios had not. Maybe she wanted but did not conceive. Maybe she conceived but failed to carry. Maybe she had children, and they died. Or, were killed. How to know, how to know when her mind floated this way and that on its own watery dreams?

Was she dreaming a life within a dream? She relished dreams so much that perhaps she encouraged them to become memories, memories of an altered state she willed to return to her intact when she was awake. Her mind undulated over faces of people she once knew and places, places far from her bedroom, far from this time, from this day. She experienced moments of deja-vu, the paranormal, even out of body experiences like astral traveling, which felt more real than life and certainly more real than dreams. She was familiar with such out of body experiences from her youthful practice of kriya yoga.

She glanced across the room to the corner facing Mecca where she kept her prayer rug. She unrolled it for afternoon idles or evening meditation, allowing her dreams to become prayers and those prayers to metamorphose into reality. Despite not being religious, she liked to pray. Even on her travels, she packed this small Moroccan prayer rug she had chanced upon in a French flea market once, quite ragged from misuse.

She worried that if she traveled back, would anyone know her? Had she kept records hidden somewhere in her homes? Diaries or journals? If so, where? If she traveled back to Athens when she lived there with Vassilios... Oh, when was that? Three hundred years before Christ? Then she worried about traveling forward again. She understood time travel was not as easy as shifting a gear on a car as she had gotten stuck in the odd century a few times on previous trips.

She was uncertain where to begin. She had lived many incarnations. She long forgot how to speak or write the tongues of Greek, Cantonese, Arabic, French, and more from the lands where she lived and loved. She could scarcely understand the Olde English of the texts from the library at Rufford, she was trying to decipher. She was at Rufford, wasn't she?

She wanted to keep her mind sharp. She found crosswords tedious, loathing pencils whose erasers she used too often. Sudoku was beyond her. She found working with languages challenging enough to hold her interest without exhausting her. She leaned over to retrieve the book she had begun to translate a few weeks earlier from the bedside table where that woman put it. Some portions of its text were from manuscripts preserved by an order of monks who established a monastery at a place in England called

Rufford in the twelfth century. Latin, written by them, remained easy for her to understand, and she was glad she took two years of it in school.

At just the moment Lucky read that her English family estate was built atop a Cistercian Abbey, a shadow darkened the page. By the shadow's shape, she saw it was a hooded figure though she could not see a face. She pretended to continue reading without moving, though her skin chilled as it rose in goose bumps.

"The Abbey was founded on twelfth July 1147 by Gilbert de Grant," she whispered aloud, "during The Great Anarchy and housed an order of Cistercians called The Black Monks." There, the monks grew vegetables, or tried to grow vegetables, in the salty soil, soil almost too soft to bear the weight of the sandstones for the Abbey walls they built. They dug deep, making a cellar first, thinking a cellar necessary to hold the summer's harvest which was to feed their small colony through the months of winter. The summer proved so cold that little grew, and, despite their months of labor, they did not need the cellar.

"Above the cellar and to the sides north and south, naves grew, then arches lifted to soar across the naked space, and soon the monks enclosed the church with sides and a roof which lay atop the arches as they seemed to march toward the heavens. It was a simple building meant to house simple men living simple lives in prayer and abstinence and hard work in the name of the lord…" Oh, she thought, in the name of survival. Rufford, apparently, was the poorest of Abbeys.

She read that one of the monks during Medieval times came into possession of a forbidden manuscript, a Grimoire of Black Magic. It gave instructions into the Necromantic arts. Possibly Sumerian in origin, the Grimoire detailed how to raise, summon, and command Demons, Devils, and the Dead. This monk was more secretive and daring than the others. He attempted to translate the foul book into Latin, from its original language, though he knew even owning such a book, let alone trying to translate it, brought the death penalty. The monk, his original name not known, was careless, got caught, and was executed. He became known thereafter, or rather his ghost became known thereafter, as the Black Monk, a malignant spirit who roamed unhappy and unhampered at Rufford. Although the Cistercians were long gone, their Abbey demolished during the Reformation, and the land sold to Lucky's ancestors, this, its darkest ghost, lingered on.

This mountain in shadow loomed forward chilling the air. Lucky dropped the book.

"I brought lunch," the woman said, jolting Lucky from her work. "Teriyaki salmon bowls," she announced coming into the bedroom with a tray. "Need help getting dressed?"

"I want to stay in bed today. I am translating," Lucky said imperiously though she was trying to calm herself. "You can set the lunch tray here on my lap. Put it on this Latin book you almost made me drop."

The woman looked at the leather binding before squaring it on Lucky's lap as instructed. "What is it about?" the woman asked.

"Spooky stuff," Lucky replied.

"Really?"

"Yes, ghosts and such." Napkin between her chest and the tray, Lucky removed the plastic cover from the bowl. Steam from the still-warm salmon fogged her glasses.

"*Whole Food's* finest take-away!" the woman announced, who seemed rather pleased with herself or perhaps pleased with her shopping.

"They have a *Whole Foods* now in Rufford?" Lucky asked. "I thought you shopped at *Tesco*." The woman gave her a quizzical look before sitting on one side of the bed and taking her own bowl from the bag she set at her feet. Without responding to Lucky's question, the woman began to eat.

After a long pause, the woman asked, "Isn't Rufford that place in England where you made sculpture once?"

Despite enjoying her first bite of the savory salmon accompanied by rice and broccoli, Lucky felt irritated by the question. She let her eyes roam the photos on the wall as she chewed before answering, "Of course, Silly."

Pushing the tray from her lap, she added, "I thought you were bringing a roast chicken from *Tesco* for lunch."

The woman shook her head. An uncomfortably charged silence fell between them.

After clearing lunch, the woman came back upstairs, this time carrying a large cardboard box. From it, she took out several framed photos. She began to rearrange photos already lining the white bedroom walls and to hang some new silver gelatin prints from the box.

"What are you doing?" Lucky asked, rather flummoxed by the third, or was it fourth, intrusion just when she was drifting off.

"I thought you might like some of the photos from Kuwait I took."

"Animals or war?" Lucky asked, rousting herself. The war photos made Lucky contemplate death. She was over the cusp: no longer dallying in middle-age, she had crossed into old age, tiptoeing closer to death and into an unwanted caducity.

"Mostly war. A couple of dogs."

"Let me see the dogs," Lucky demanded, holding out her hand. She liked dogs.

"Those don't look anything like my Woofie or Molossus," she commented. The woman hung them on the wall anyway.

"Here's one of Turkey you might like," she said, handing Lucky a black and white photo in a silver frame.

"Oh yes, I remember him. Such a good dog."

Turkey was, in fact, lying on the floor right next to her bed. On hearing his name, Turkey let his tail thump the bamboo plank floor, but he did not rise. The woman looked at Lucky, then away, giving Turkey a few soft pats on his head. She was wiping a tear at yet another marker of Lucky's quiet descent.

"I must find him," Lucky said urgently.

"Turkey?"

"No, no, not Turkey. My husband. I must find him." Lucky suddenly felt compelled to ask her husband if they had children together. She must find him, them, rather, her husbands, as there were many, although he was always the same. The mixture of time and distance in her fragile mind did little to still her heart. Did she have to take that fearsome trip through time now? Maybe she had a husband in this life? O, why hadn't he come? Where was he?

She remembered then that her husband left going to the east, she left as well but in the opposite direction, skirting the pinkened tops of gray clouds, drizzling tears, going west. She always went west, following the sun like its rays, hoping to meet again somewhere on the far side of where they started.

She leaned back into her pillows and remembered when she was Hiza, a child, and Ibn left, heading east from their Moroccan *dar* to Egypt, then Damascus, finally to India and China. She remembered being Arbella, fearful of James, fleeing west to Kent, as her husband, William, sailed east to Flanders where they planned to join. She shuddered at the memory, for James caught her. That time, she was the first to die. From China, Merrill left, forced to sail east to England with Jardine; she sailed west up the Pearl on her junk as far as she had ever gone and met him there again when he was reborn as the Muslim Sultan, Du. Those were but a few of the partings from him she remembered, her timeless love, her husband. Guillaume, Vassilios, William, Merrill, Ibn, Du.

"Where would you like this photo?" the woman asked, holding a portrait of a man with wavy, maestro-like white hair and a broad grin looking across an isthmus to a blue sea.

Taking it, Lucky said, "My dear, this is my husband. Where is he?"

"You mean Dad?" the woman asked.

When Lucky heard the woman close the front door and start the engine of her car, Lucky threw back the bedcovers and got up. She was a bit tangled by her gown, twisted as it was between her legs ready to trip her feet. Pulling the gown to the side, she went carefully to the rattan bureau and took the silk bag from the top drawer. Merrill wrote on a stiff sheet of Italian velum what he wanted in their marriage, a precious sheet she kept next to a red silk bag containing a braided lock of black and white hair. Together they rested inside a slim cinnabar chest at the back of her lingerie drawer. Gently, she loosened the cords and took out the braid, just as she remembered it: one-part white, the other black, woven together as one and alongside it, the sheet. Then, returning to her bed, she opened the sheet and read:

"It is not what the poets tell us about love."

She whispered, though she knew it by heart.

"It is, after all, my darling, my Lady Luck, the little things that make a life together work. No matter who baked the bread or didn't make the bed, who forgot the groceries or didn't walk the dog, I want us to care for each other with the same kindness as the day we met, and do the little things for each other with patience. If we are to make it on this journey for the long run: the one that lasts through all eternity, may we share respect, understanding, kindness and patience."

She pressed the letter to her chest before refolding and returning it to the cinnabar chest, as she didn't want the ink to blur with her falling tears. She replaced the chest in the recess of the drawer, not thinking it the least bit strange that events, people, emotions, and their conjunction followed orbits like the planets did with their moons, creating ellipses that crossed out of time.

She lifted the window and filled her lungs with noon-day air. Looking to the soft white clouds, she vowed huskily, "I'll find you, my love. Haven't I always found you, or you me, in the strangest of places and circumstances, predestined as we are to love one another? Why are you taking so long? I am getting old! Please, please hurry back to me!"

A radio was playing on the beach below a song she remembered from another life. Old songs carried on the wings of melody and lyric held life in them. They nourished her, as they revived faraway pieces of her memory. She attempted a small pirouette, holding the gown's train at arm's length.

She thought she heard Merrill sing "Home sweet home" or was it "Auld Lang Syne," singing as he did when he returned from a day or trip away. And, now, as if she heard those songs, his face, his name, his scent came back to her. And, lying back on her pillows once again, her heart rejoiced even though it was too often a grave, well-watered by tears.

She played the virginal and lute once, while he, at another time and place, plucked the frets of a tembor and sang the Uyghur songs of Xinjiang. The love she longed for was their duet, though to her it seemed symphonic, vibrating like a full ensemble, orchestrating the heavens, its music rustling the stars, creating a harmony as ephemeral and ever-changing as clouds, yet constant. They—she and Merrill, Guillaume, Vassilios, Ibn, William, Du--drifted lazily over continents and seas and centuries like a melody on the wind, sometimes scraping mountainsides, losing one another and mourning in terrible thunderstorms of loss, a cacophony of cymbals clanging and oboes wailing; other times evaporating in the heat of passion, the light of their love a parabolic mirror catching the sun to burst into flame, whether newly reunited or in stages reborn, flying like high flute notes sustained by conjoined breaths or gliding on currents of air like the glorious plucking of harp strings sounding a sonata. She found him, she always found him, or he her, resuscitating their love before losing each other in the last agonal breath of departure like the lingering note of an oboe, the losing the agony she suffered in each lifetime, only to find in the end, the hope of resurrection to be the reason for living.

On the nights she remembered him best, she knew it was the moon, perfect in its porcelain opalescence, which painted the ceiling of their time together an unexpected blue, when he made her want to smell the stars and savor the Milky Way. Gazing at the moon perfect in its purity, she thought she saw his shadow there, lying quiet as a sheet across the bleached, lunar surface. Her husband's white hair, luminescent like the moon, was to her a refreshing cone of ice before the sugar syrup was poured over, and his voice was sweet as the syrup, cherry flavored, perhaps with a hint of azuki bean, his hum soft, satisfying, and soothing, always soothing, melting away any roughness from the day as it traveled from her ears through her throat down to her heart.

BLIP TWO

Hunger for His Touch

She married him on more than one occasion. Perhaps first was in China, no, it was second, as the first was against King James' orders in London, when she was Arbella, heir to the throne, and he, William. No, that was not the first. The first was in Morocco two centuries before, when he was Ibn, the scholar and she, Hiza, a dark-haired child, under his protection. This first, she was remembering was not the first nor the second, no, nor was it the third. The second was to William in London after James assumed the throne. The third was to Guillaume, who came to her as a tutor, in France. The fourth, the one she was desperate to remember, was on a junk on the Pearl river near Canton, when each wore a jacket, a *ru*, of indigo blue standing on bamboo planks in the mid-morning sun. Or, perhaps that was second, the first having been in Morocco. No, wrong again. The first was in Greece in its Golden Age when she masqueraded as a boy in that misogynist society to enjoy the freedom of a male in thrall to the actor, Vassilios. Oh, did it matter? She knew they were merchants, whether of olives or rugs or ceramics; they were pirates trading in opium and pearls; they were actors, sculptors, vintners, musicians, weavers, doll-makers, royalty, and above all, lovers.

He was older, too, and carried the gentleness that comes to some with age and experience. That gentleness was why she married him throughout the centuries and across the continents. It was the way he made her feel: encouraged. She knew she could do it all: become wealthy, have children, lead people, see the world. But, throughout the centuries it was nigh impossible for her, no matter how talented or wealthy or clever, to be her true self without a man. With a husband at her helm, she could do and create anything.

With a mane of white hair waving above his leonine features and demeanor, he remained fifty-six in most of their encounters, while her age varied from thirteen to well over seventy. Called by many names, his name, like hers, changed depending on the culture, language, or century. In France, he was Guillaume, in England, William and Merrill, in Morocco Ibn, in China, Du, and again, in the Pacific, Merrill, her Merrill again, his names implying royalty, a golden helmet, a king, and a bright sea. Hers merely Lucky, like the rolling of dice in a game of chance. He manifested as Caucasian, Arabian, Chinese, bearing eyes of glittering, gold-flecked hazel beneath trim white brows, inside a long, diamond shaped face, always clean shaven, an unremarkable nose above broad lips drawn thin in a smile across straight, chalk-white teeth. He was a big man, neither athletic nor bulky, simply large, manly, soft curling reddish hair on his strong forearms and chest, and imposing in the most elegant and leonine of ways.

Despite the beginnings of dementia, she did not forget everything. Her thoughts drifted to her life as an opium smuggler on the Pearl; he a consumptive about to return to England with that horrid man called Jardine. That Jardine infuriated her, forcing her love, who was so ill, to return to England without her; Jardine petitioned Parliament to shoot the *la shi* out of her people, because her emperor forbade the import of opium. What trouble that greedy Jardine started. Ah, yes, another infamous trade war, infamous because the better armed foreign power took the day even though it was doing the devil's work addicting her people to opium.

She remembered marrying Merrill a second time after he died when he returned to China as the Sultan Du and took her Muslim faith, well, her old Muslim faith, the one she clung to in her time in Fez four hundred years earlier. Together, they rebelled against the Chinese emperor to protect their chosen Muslim community which straddled the western edge of the empire.

Again, she married him when he was her tutor, Guillaume, her much older tutor, at her father's home in the Dordogne, their millhouse of sandy, chamfered limestone and climbing roses in the south-western cave region of France, the floors covered in Moroccan carpets some relative collected long before. Over her russet curls, she wore a wide brimmed hat with a veil tied under her chin, a long beige afternoon dress in the style of the 19th century, and he, oh, she could not remember how he was adorned, only that she adored him. They walked on the pavers flanking the house, meandering through the gardens, her father painfully absent, angry at her willfulness to marry his employee, a man too far her senior.

And, then there were the tropics, this tropical isle, where she lay abed. The air-conditioned shade of their first hotel room, blindered against the sun or perhaps the light of the full moon, a fan or breeze cooling their bodies above the sheets, her head at his groin, his soft moans punctuating the silence.

His hands were large and fleshy, strengthened by fingers thick like the pads of a lion's paw but sensitive enough to fasten the clasp of her pearls beneath the curls at the nape of her neck, or pull a bougainvillea splinter implanted in the sole of her bare foot from a careless step in the garden, or to float a Dvorak composition from the keys of their piano. Best, they knew how to play her, how to touch her naked skin like a feather on the breeze, to slide into her moist folds to rouse her interest and desire, to pinch the lobes of her ears at just the right moment, and to pull her hips into his to make their bones one.

It was the little things, as he wrote, that held their love over time: the way he loosened her braids before placing his lips softly upon her neck to whisper endearments, his lips brushing a beauty mark on the left below her ear; the way his eyes twinkled as he lifted his glass to toast her before an evening meal; the way he sank to his knees in front of a beloved dog to seek its face as he stroked its head.

For him, it was the way each morning she rolled on her side to spoon her back into his arms; the way she beckoned him with her eyes and the turn of her head to close the buttons on her clothing she could not reach or to pull the stays even tighter on her tiny waist; the way she kept their kitchen stocked with aromatics and delicacies, preparing them effortlessly for his famished tongue. Little things, little things made them hunger for one another. The daily morning rose set in the tiny yellow Chinese cloisonné vase she brought from Jingdezhen. Next to it sat a green jade dragon which held a gold pearl in its jaws, a gift from one of her trips he considered his good luck charm. The table set with her favorite blue and white, willow pattern plates. Her aged Moroccan prayer rugs stacked by the fire. The pillow cases freshly pressed on the bed each evening. The lips ever ready to smile or open in laughter. Her attitude of appreciation. Their mutual pleasure in silence or music.

He was tall; for life in Morocco, China, Greece, and France, he was tall; for life in the Pacific, surrounded by Polynesians, he was of average height. She was neither tall nor average. Perhaps diminutive best suited her. Her breasts were perfect orbs rising like clouds of starched white linen, each crested by a soft rosebud of pink. Her hips were ample for bearing children and lovers, although she could not remember ever bearing a child. Her legs were short and while not her best attribute, were not her worst, either. Her hair and face, never the same hair and face, held a classic beauty, whether perched atop a Chinese, Arab, or Caucasian body.

It was her vibrant spirit that dominated her entire being and set her apart from other women. She was curious about life and wanted not only to taste but also to eat, chew, and swallow as though never sated. She created: acting in the theatre, sculpting from porcelain, plucking the lute, cooking over a wok, or weaving designs into carpets.

His hair remained the same despite the century, thick, white, long on top, rising in endearing curls near his ears and the nape of his neck. His eyes were kindly, gentle in watching, and his voice soft spoken yet deep. His unthinking kindnesses.

Her hair changed. Sometimes it was straight and black, hanging in a single braid down her back, as she bent over tea or the worn prayer rug on the junk where she practiced *qi gong*. She remembered cutting part of her hair and snipping a lock of his white to plait together as was the custom in their Chinese wedding, the black and white looking like the yin/yang symbol. She tucked the hair into a red silk bag and placed it like a treasure in a red cinnabar chest in a compartment of a teak cabinet.

Other times, like in France, her hair was russet and bounced in long ringlets to dangle at her slender waist. And, in the tropics, her hair was golden, matching the rays of the sun in yellow brilliance, before it turned a silvered gray like the waning moon as her age approached his and went beyond.

Her favorite of all the places they co-joined might be that home on the island, filled with tropical blooms, fruiting trees, and a remarkable vista of the deep blue Pacific stretched out below. The property had a waterfall and pool; water they watched tumbling into a mirrored spatter of sunlight through the forest of rain. She called it *Jannah,* their Garden of Eden. Its power invigorated her, its chill pool excited her, the foliage all round hid lichen and toadstools where they took barefooted forays along muddy jungle trails and over the blackened rocks.

In their island life, she courted the danger of the volcano, from the threat of its sulphurous fumes to the might of its fountaining explosions. There on days of "vog" the horizon lay as a white shroud, and behind it, back lit as behind a theatrical scrim, loomed the active volcano, a strange and desolate mound where sea and sky merged into this ghostly shade. Pumice dust fell as detritus from the air, nicking unshielded skin, burning the eyes and throat. Lava oozed silently from fissures in the earth and cooled in thick, smooth puddles; its counterpart fountained high and fell back in sharp, jagged pinnacles covering acres in deadly, black needles which cut their naked feet as they attempted to hop-scotch over its hardened crust. Something was about to happen, yet nothing did. There was no big event, but there lingered an omnipresent threat, a foreboding, despite their enjoyment of many benign, sunlit days.

It was not his favorite. He did not enjoy mud or stones beneath his tender feet. He did not enjoy the myriad insects feeding on dropped fruit, the mosquitos swarming his legs and bare arms or stinging his sleeping face, sporting swollen red and itchy welts by morning. Worst, he did not enjoy the fecund humidity.

His favorite of all their seasons of love was winter, with its long dark nights spent not far from Hampstead at a cottage down a hedgerow under snow. It was not hers. He loved the whistle of the kettle over the fire, the chill, the warmth of eiderdowns, her nakedness beckoning him to cover her with his body beneath the sheets. He liked to dress sitting on the rumpled bed in the morning gloom, yesterday's clothing scattered on the floor quite forgotten beneath their well-used bed, pulling on two pairs of socks, an undershirt, then a tartan plaid Pendleton, long underwear, trousers, preferring suspenders to a belt. He liked looking over his shoulder at her still, supine body, soft, not yet concerned with the trivia the day might bring along with the usual toast and tea on a tray. He could have electric blankets, he could have heating pads to warm the sheets, he could have central heating. But, he didn't. He wanted the coals from the fire to linger faintly glowing by morning, he wanted the weight of the quilts, he wanted the cold of the sheets warmed by his love, his adoration, of her.

And so, they compromised, living part of each year throughout the centuries on various islands—in the Pacific, in Asia, and on land in Northern Africa and Europe—both in love, in cold, in humidity, and in the semi-discontent each place brought to one or the other.

None of his physicality mattered except that it acted as a road map home, making him easy to recognize on each new journey. Yet, this very physicality also drew her to him like iron seeks a magnet, as he knew every motion of making love as though he had invented the art himself. In each resurrection, she felt haunted by that magnet, drawn toward what was unknown and needed discovery anew, a compulsion in her bones to find the missing, the absent, the life-giving, ferrous-rich marrow that completed her, allowing her to be whole once again.

Driven by zest and lust, they dove headlong into whatever time or place they landed. For him, it was a recognition not of her body but rather of her soul, the spirt that enlivened her and took her beyond that mortal body, whatever body she currently inhabited, young, old, sensual, feeble. He recognized her in every incarnation. Not by her looks, her age, her dress, her speech: as sometimes she was a child, sometimes a septuagenarian; sometimes she was blonde and Caucasian, sometimes brunette and Muslim; twice, Asian; sometimes donned in pantaloons and bustiers, other times wearing a mini-skirt or a caftan of silk. She could wear a veil, a sack over her head, and he would know her, because he recognized her by what his heart saw and saw anew until the end of time. No earth jacket hid her essence from him. He could be blind, and he would know her as she came near. Neither by her scent nor her gait, but by her energy, by the radiant play of her soul, by the light of her being and joy in living.

Joined as a key in a lock, they allowed themselves to live in whatever time and place they chose. Like the left hand knowing what the right played in a piano concerto, they fit, creating music, splendid cadences elevating the ear and the heart, lifting to soar as though no finale was possible. They joined as one like the mad mating of two birds in flight. They had no need for stardust. They loved on the earth, and that love shot sparks to the heavens, creating stardust of their own.

She often mused when looking at other people: why bother with anything short of eternal love? Why put up with the quibbles and quirks of fussy, mismatched souls? Why settle for less, for so much less?

O, he loved her. He loved her for centuries. He could not get enough of her, the sweetness of her breath, her operatic cries in the ecstasy induced by him, her wit, her intelligence, her kindness, and open heart.

But, he failed her. In every incarnation, he failed her. Normally, by dying, whether of old age or disease or accident, once by disillusion. He was generally the one to die first or to depart. And, she the one to mourn and to long and to await her own death, so that they could begin their dance anew.

Was it a glance? A slim smile? A suppressed giggle? Or bending to pet and whisper comforting words to a stray dog? Or, an aroma from her wok of sizzling duck or any of the foods shared over many lifetimes and tables? The slant of her hips as she watched a child at play beside the myrtle bush? Or simply her own eternal playfulness, the nymph in her come to splash him and swim away, leaving a froth of bubbles and gaiety like champagne freshly poured to overflowing from his fluted glass?

She remembered sharing that earthly, carnal love, sensual and rich. "We must have begat many a child," she said as she picked up the photo of the maestro-haired man, "although I cannot remember a single one. Where are they?"

BLIP THREE

Wrap Your Love Around My Finger

The babe slipped out sheathed in liquid red, eyes ablaze from the fire within, fingers stretching to hold onto what they had just lost. The day slipped out as well, as the dawn parted her lips, spreading warmth across the belly of the world.

Miracles do happen, small and oft unnoticed, like the coming of the day, like the arrival of the child.

No dogs lifted their necks to howl, no sudden wind gusted through limbs, as the mother's limbs were supple encircling the child. Nothing ominous stirred the air. Yet, the day was not normal. Not by any means.

Men disappeared. Not that morning nor yesterday nor the day before. Slowly, over time, they left like water seeping through sand, not noticeable, unlike water taking time to pool.

She was feverish, always feverish, with longing and love and unquenchable hope. He must return. Her man must return.

In her arms fidgeted the babe, still reddened by blood, silent, not a cry spilled from its mouth which opened and closed like a fish gasping for air on the shore. Perhaps it sought a nipple, though she did not suckle it. Not yet.

She lay out of time, neither dreaming nor melancholic, in a mood without descriptive, somehow deep, and very, very quiet.

The home fronted a pond, whose waters were shallow yet muddied. Her quiet was like the pond, cool and opaque, perhaps even muddied with the silt of memory, little islands of time, like the continents seen from the heavens, bobbing up to the surface now and again to remind her of a precious love she had known.

She couldn't help wondering, "Did he simply die, and I failed to notice? Did I kill him? Is that why he is gone? Or, was it the other woman? If so, which "other" woman? There were so many." She was old enough to laugh, to laugh about all the betrayals, about the loss of innocence that happened not only once, but each time she forgave and began to love him anew. Everything turned in her memory, and every memory into the lyrics of her lives, balanced equally in poetry and pain.

The visitations came unexpectedly on a sudden inhalation, a prickling of her eyes and a rise of her skin. Were they memories, phantoms of her imagination, or ghosts? Whatever they were, she learned not to resist, to accept, rather, whatever was reaching out to her. It might take a few seconds or more, and then she knew, not through sight or smell, but rather through skin and memory of touch, who was there. Perhaps, it was one of her daughters, if she had any, on occasion, her son, if she had a son. Years before, it was no one she knew, at least not from this world. Her dog sensed them and emitted low growls to ward these entities off, coming as they did unbidden and unwelcome; entities that exuded hostility and want, consuming her like a dust mote into some vacuum of timelessness and eternal restlessness.

Her mother helped her back then in Greece, her mother the Pythia. She lit the purple flame and taught Tyche, her daughter, to recite the incantation: "I see you. I have nothing for you. Go in love." She said the entities sought love and sucked it from the unwary like vampires to ease their exhaustion of spirit. Lucky was her girl then, Tyche.

"You must send them away," her mother admonished, "but do it with a blessing of love."

Tyche wanted them to leave her alone. She was too open, open to the realm of the unseen, the realms without the barricades of time, like the Pythia, a conduit to psychic realms. The appearance of the entities made her nervous. At first, even remembering the incantation was hard as these entities interrupted her, bombarded her, attempted to gnaw their way into her soul. Gradually, she would regain her composure and was able to recite it line for line, emphasizing each word, eyes closed, whispering. Later, eyes open, she took a broad-legged stance and said aloud, in her deepest attempt at a baritone, word by word, "I see you. I have nothing for you. Go in love." She knew they had left when her big dog, Molossus, quieted. Visitations from these phantom strangers grew less frequent, while visitations from those she loved increased. To those, she spoke, she whispered, she prayed, she praised, she cried, she moaned, she demanded they come back.

Then the babe was born.

No name was chosen. She didn't look to see if the child was male or female. Gender was of no consequence. Still, the child did not cry.

Arbella, its mother, was hungry, ravenously hungry and looked about for something to eat. Where was she? What was this place?

Gray light shrouded the room, its stone walls gray, its windows curtain-less. It was elevated, perhaps a second floor from the height of the deciduous trees she could see from its paned, single window. She glanced about the room. A wooden chair sat in the left corner. A smock hung from a hook on the door.

She pushed herself higher onto the pillow. A gasp of pain escaped, emanating from her torn gut. Her hand rose to press it, almost accidentally slapping the babe beside her. It shocked her to see this child. Was it hers? How could it be?

She heard a clanking like pieces of metal colliding. She turned her head to peer out the window and saw in the courtyard below—what courtyard was this with its cobblestones and clock tower? —two maids dressed in garb from long ago carrying metal milk pails which clanked upon each other as the women walked side by side into the square. The clock-tower struck five harsh notes. Was it morning or evening? Arbella didn't know. The general gloom outside gave no clue. The maids' chatter drifted up but she could not make out their words. She tried to call down to them but her voice made no sound.

Wet spread through the blanket and sheets. She returned her gaze to the bed. It was not blood from the birth. Yet, moisture was seeping every-where as though a bucket of water spilled onto the mattress, which now sagged, depressed by weight, whose weight? The bedclothes felt clammy. Her nightdress, the child's swathing, the sheets. The walls ran with moisture.

Someone she could not see sat on the side of the bed, making it list slightly to the right. She did not gasp. She did not grip the babe, the silent babe. She sat still, and she waited.

When the clock tower stuck six times, the weight lifted. The smock on the door hook shuddered as the latch clicked open then shut. She and the babe were alone once again, shaking, and thoroughly wet.

The sun came up, and she realized it was morning. Lucky tried to rise. Failing that, she sat straight in the bed and scrutinized the scene out the window. She was indeed on a second floor. Across the cobbled walkway stood a red brick, single story edifice leading to a tall clock tower fronting a roofless two and a half story, Georgian mansion. Its triangular portico was intact, but its walls were not. The mansion, or what remained of it, in turn connected to a brick wall and gateway leading to a grass-filled meadow dotted with clover and wild flowers by a lake, shimmering in the distant morning light. The wall then turned to connect to her building, completing the square. A stone cherubim spat water from the center of a small fountain in the courtyard where two men stood dressed in blazers, trousers, ties, normal late twentieth century business attire, drinking coffee from paper cups. The clock tower struck eight.

Baffled, she rose. Placing her hands on the mattress to push herself up, she found it dry. Looking down, she saw no baby. No blood. Only rumpled sheets. Her jeans and shirt hung from the hook on the door where a smock once hung. Her computer sat on the wooden chair. Her suitcase lay open on the wooden plank floor beside it.

She dressed, brushed her teeth and hair, grabbed the keys, ran down the winding staircase of the old carriage house, lifted the wooden bar from the heavy oak door, unbolted the latches, and stepped outside onto the cobblestone walkway. She ran into the courtyard, interrupting the two men who were engaged in conversation.

"Did you see anyone? Did you see two maids come through here? Did you see anyone at all?" she asked, quite frantically.

"No, no one," one of the men replied.

"There was a baby," she gasped, "and two maids and someone very, very wet."

The men looked at each other.

"I'm the artist, Lucky. I'm in residence. There was a baby on my bed this morning, and now it is gone!"

The men began to laugh.

"I am not a crazy American! I saw it!" she yelled, beside herself with anxiety and confusion, and dumbfounded by their bemusement, or perhaps it was their boredom.

"Of course! That's the clammy baby," the man in the blue blazer with the bad haircut remarked, in a tone nonplussed by her discomposure.

"The clammy baby?"

"Haven't you visited the undercroft?"

"What undercroft?"

"Rufford is famous for its ghosts. All the stories are displayed in the undercroft below our offices in the main house. You'll find the clammy baby story there."

They chuckled and walked to work in the council offices up a flight of stairs in the only intact section of the manor, leaving her red-cheeked and quite confounded below.

She walked slowly behind them to the main house, found the steps and signs to the undercroft, and descended. There, indeed, were several wooden figures standing beside stories written for tourists of the hauntings of Rufford from centuries past and present. As she read the tales, she rotated the pearl ring on her finger, as was her habit, and shuddered.

There was speculation that the clammy baby was born to a laundry maid, who, shamed, had drowned it in the pond. There was further speculation that it was the child of Arbella Stuart and her husband, William Seymour, a child who died shortly after its birth when its mother was imprisoned in the Tower of London. Arbella, only child of Charles Stuart, First Earl of Lennox, by his marriage to Elizabeth Cavendish, was once an heir to the crown after Elizabeth I died.

"Ah," Lucky wondered, "was it William I married?" Yes, she felt sure it was William, her husband and resolute protector.

Oh, the love they shared almost four centuries earlier swam slowly, on almost severed neurons, back to her. She did remember cutting a lock of her hair to give to him as a keepsake. It was after their first meeting at the Tethys Festival, when the gold glinting off the large seashell throne where she sat made her glow and lit William's heart with desire for her. Her cousin, James, newly crowned king was jealous, worried that she, Arbella, cousin of the now dead Queen Elizabeth I, would take the crown in his stead.

To ward off James' fear of usurpation, William sought permission to marry Arbella. Not receiving a warm welcome at the palace, William determined a secret rendezvous.

"This pearl, my dearest, my Lady Luck," William said, presenting Arbella with a gimmel ring made of two interlocking bands, "is as pure and fair as you are to look upon, for it is an emblem of your modesty and purity of heart." He placed the band with the pearl on her venal finger. The other band he placed on his own finger.

"We'll each wear one of bands until we are united in marriage," he explained. Aware of James' possible wrath, William set careful plans. They married in secret on 22 June 1610 at Greenwich Palace.

"Are we truly escaping to France?" she asked.

"We must go separately as not to rouse suspicion," William admonished. Indeed, William had cause to be fearful, as he knew a plot was already forming against the paranoid James.

"Go with your handmaid to Exeter. I'll arrange a boat. Sail to the Channel Islands. Another boat will take you to Brittany where I'll be waiting."

"What will you do?" she asked, stroking his cheek while searching his gold-flecked eyes for answers.

"I'll take a few of my men and sail from Dover. I'll begin preparations as soon as I leave you. No one must know." And, before he departed, they kissed.

Did they consummate their marriage? Did she bear his child? And, if so, did it die of natural causes, or did James kill it, or, worse, did she?

But, the William she remembered seemed a young man, not fifty-six with a shock of white hair like her husband, rather each of the husbands she married over the centuries.

Filled with curiosity, Lucky inquired at the Council office if there were any gravesites on the estate.

Estelle Cummins, the Council's purser, answered, "Why yes. There are quite a number."

"Where would I find them?" Lucky queried.

"Oh dear, the estate is so large. Let me sketch you a map. I'm rather busy now. Come back day after tomorrow, and I should have a map of sorts for you."

"Thank you!"

"I say a map of sorts because I haven't walked the whole property. There may be more gravesites than those on the main concourses. You might take a look in our library," Estelle suggested.

"Library?"

"Yes. Second door on the left past the stairs. Loads of books and manuscripts from medieval to present day. The Cistercian monks here kept meticulous records, if you can read Latin or Olde English."

Lucky knew she only had time to explore in the late afternoons and possibly at dusk due to her teaching schedule; she was there to teach an afternoon workshop to elderly residents of Nottinghamshire newly enamored of clay, which didn't leave much time to explore. To do so felt a bit daunting as the estate closed at five, and she would be there alone. After the ghostly visitation, she felt uneasy about this delving, uncertain of what she might find or of what might find her.

Late in the afternoon, she took a public path by the lake, which spread below the broken brick walls of the main house. The lawns shone a velvety deep green, luxuriant from their nightly baths under the wet English sky. She sat looking at the lake, tranquil in the windless evening, sat for quite some time on a wooden bench on which she failed to note a bronze plaque coincidentally engraved "W&A." It was October, and the leaves on the sycamores and oaks were changing color. A few of the early leaves, recently fallen, lay dying on the concourse which meandered through the grounds. She mused, wondering where to bury a child if she lived here as Arbella or as one of the unfortunate servants from the past. Rather than burying it, perhaps she or a servant tossed it into the lake? Hence, the clammy baby?

To her right were the formal gardens, beyond which lay an herb garden. She had taken a quick walk through them on arrival the first week. The formal garden held roses set in square beds, both purple and white iris, day lilies, tulips, and many other northern flowering plants she couldn't readily identify as she had grown up in the tropics. Behind, stood a large labyrinth she hadn't dared enter on her own as she needed companionship for that tour, one on which she feared getting lost.

The centre's director, Ian, showed her the herb garden, taking care to point out the section of poisonous plants, warning her not to touch or even brush them with her clothes.

"These plants were cultivated for hundreds of years as weapons to be used surreptitiously against enemies come to dine," he told her. "That one is hemlock. When eaten, it paralyzes the lungs. That's Queen Anne's lace, often used to induce miscarriage. Over there is monkshood, some call it wolfsbane, probably the deadliest of all. Causes terrible stomach pain and heart problems, or so I'm told."

"They really used these plants?" she asked.

"Oh, yes, indeed. Deadly nightshade there produced hallucinations and rashes. My wife, Maggie, takes care of this area. You'll meet her later at lunch."

Signs posted along the edges of this section of the garden warned parents to hold their children's hands and not to touch the plants.

"Perhaps this area should be cordoned off, if it is so dangerous," Lucky said.

She recognized many herbs like the basil plants gone wild through lack of pruning, and the dill, fennel, and parsley.

"Don't the cooks use these herbs in the restaurant?" she asked.

"I'm afraid not," Ian said. "Our English diet goes heavy with cream and cheese, our cobblers served with clotted cream, our vegetables boiled until yellow. Not your *cuisine nouvelle* or health conscious preparations, I'm afraid. Not a vegan entrée on the menu. But, we've found it's what the locals who visit the park desire." She tried the restaurant once. The menu was quite unappetizing. She chose a meat pie assuming it was standard British fare. The level of grease and gravy appalled her, and she found only a few bits of meat, a couple of carrot slices, and a few withered peas beneath its thick crust of flour and lard.

As Lucky walked the pathways at Rufford in the late afternoon light, she found plaques nailed on tree trunks commemorating marriages, births, or deaths. She soon came upon short, wrought iron fences surrounding a few headstones. Some of these enclosures housed graves for favorite family pets: dogs, cats, caged birds, rabbits. One for a best beloved riding horse. Others for people. The headstones dated over several centuries and were in varying states of decomposition, some of the writing impossible to discern due to heavy overcoats of moss and lichen. She made notes of every headstone marked for an infant who had died within the first year of life. Small angels or wings sat atop those, sculpted from stone. Often, she found a mother buried next to the child, having succumbed herself to childbirth or disease. She heard the beating of wings in this tiny world watched over by marble angels, angels on tombs, on bridges, on churches, and tears surfaced as she thought about the soul of her own son, riding on the cusp of a new moon in the heavens. No headstone there read "Arbella." No headstone read "Stuart" or "Seymour."

In the library, Lucky read that Arbella was the only child of Charles Stuart, first Earl of Lennox, by his marriage to Elizabeth Cavendish. Her father's brother, Henry Stuart Lord Darnley, married Mary, Queen of Scots. Lord Darnley fathered Arbella's cousin, James, the same James later favored by Lord Burghley to lead the country when the childless Elizabeth I died.

Arbella didn't remember much about James as he was nine years older than she. They'd not played together as children. Her father died when she was an infant. Her mother, Countess of Lennox, raised her at first before herself orphaning Arbella when she was seven. Fortunately, Arbella became the ward of her formidable grandmother, Bess of Hardwick, who adored her and set about preparing the child to be queen.

Arbella was a great-great-granddaughter of King Henry VII and stood prominently in line of succession to the English throne. Bess refused to let Lord Burghley, the Master of the Court of Wards, raise Arbella, as expected. If Arbella was Lord Burghley's ward, history might be very different, as he would most likely have chosen her to rule, rather than James.

Talk began at her birth about whom she might marry. As a young child, she dressed as lavishly as any princess and studied all the arts, in the event she might one day rule. Of the arts, writing was her favorite. During most of her childhood, she lived with her grandmother, Bess, hidden in the protective isolation of Hardwick Hall in Derbyshire. Hardwick was but one of Bess' houses. Each of her four marriages brought her greater wealth. She became the richest woman in England after Queen Elizabeth I, and she conceived Hardwick as a conspicuous statement of her wealth and power.

She situated the house on a hilltop overlooking a large swathe of the Derbyshire countryside. She chose a daring design by the architect, Robert Smythson, an exponent of the renaissance style of architecture at a time when great homes no longer needed fortifications against invading forces. The windows were exceptionally large and numerous, when glass itself was a luxury, leading to the saying, "Hardwick Hall, more glass than wall." The internal walls of the structure held the chimneys to give scope for the huge windows without weakening the exterior walls.

The house's design demonstrated a new concept of a more modern way in which life was to be conducted within a great house. Hardwick was one of the first English houses where the great hall sat on an axis through the centre of the house, rather than at right angles to the entrance. Each of the three main stories had a higher ceiling than the one below, the ceiling height indicating the importance of the rooms' occupants: least noble at the bottom and grandest at the top. Bess desired a wide, winding, stone staircase to lead to the state rooms on the second floor which included one of the largest, long galleries found in any English house and where young Arbella ran free.

Arbella loved these spacious galleries filled with ornate furnishings and art, the figures in bronze and marble her favorites. She often made up stories and games, talking to the sculptures as though they were friends, as her only companion was a small spaniel gifted to her by the Queen. There were no other children in the huge manor; her only true companions the spaniel, the sculptures, and the doll. Her world was large, rich, and lonely. Bess admonished the girl to take care with the furnishings; a sea dog table being especially precious. She warned Arbella not to touch it, but where the child set her dolls anyway. The eglantine table with its inlaid top was another place forbidden to her but where her playthings oft lay forgotten, although Arbella never left a doll behind on her adventures, even though her favorite doll was quite fragile, fashioned as it was of papier mache, paint, and cloth. It was small enough for her young hand to grasp about its waist. Its dress was an exact replica of her own, fitted with a stiff ruff about its neck and tiny farthingale beneath its skirt. As the child didn't know a mother nor was she ever babied, she treasured her dolls and Woofie, showering on them all the attention and love she did not get for herself.

Arbella and Woofie, as she named the black and white, curly-haired spaniel, raced each other through the corridors and chambers, up and down the wide staircases, through the kitchen and out to the courtyards. Pretending to be a wild goose, she flapped her arms in the air and made ridiculous honking noises as Woofie chased her. Or, she hid from him behind one of the nineteen-foot high Gideon tapestries that stretched down the hall for over two hundred and thirty feet; the tapestries hung below a spectacular plaster frieze illustrating hunting scenes.

Perhaps she lurked behind a heavy oak door. He sniffed along the baseboards until his nose brought him to her feet. Jumping with excitement, he barked and barked until she cooed, "Good boy, Woofie. Good boy!" thus quieting him with a hug.

Hardwick Hall contained a fascinating collection of embroideries. Bess expected Arbella to become proficient in this skill, and she watched her grandmother's deft needle sign her monogram, "ES," on each piece. "ES" in fact stood atop each side of Hardwick's roof with a crown between each initial signaling Bess' aristocratic Derbyshire reign.

As Arbella matured, she filled the air of the house with music, practicing pieces on the virginal, passed down from Henry VII, and the lute. She had a sweet voice and learned to sing madrigals. Her grandmother often let her stay up to entertain her many guests, pushing the entertainment prior to the meal rather than after, so both Arbella and the guests were fresh, and the child could retire after dining.

Bess proffered her talented granddaughter lessons in several languages, drawing, sewing and embroidery as well as in a variety of musical instruments. For Arbella's sixteenth birthday, Bess gifted her with a precious copy of *My Ladye Nevell's Booke,* from which she learned to play the best virginal compositions.

"My dear," Bess began, "*My Ladye Nevells Booke* has forty-two pieces for keyboard by William Byrd. He is considered by everyone at court to be the greatest composer." Arbella responded joyfully with a huge smile and embrace.

Arbella played the lute, often older scores from as early as 1540, the virginal, and the flute. The viol and virginals were popular, as music was an important aspect of most nobles' education and entertainment. Henry VIII had had double virginals, a sort of spinet that had two sets of keys.

Nearly all the keyboard music of the renaissance sounded equally well on harpsichord, virginals, clavichord, or organ. Few composers had an instrument in mind when writing scores. Byrd's compositions elevated the keyboard.

The heavy and oblong folio retained its original elaborately tooled Moroccan binding, stamped with the title and an illuminated Neville family coat of arms was on the title page, with the initials "H.N." in the lower left-hand corner. There were one hundred and ninety-two leaves, each consisting of four six-line staves with large, diamond-shaped notes. At the end was a table of contents.

"Byrd is best loved for his madrigal," Bess enthused. "Your voice is so lovely, Arbella, I want you to learn these quickly to sing for our guests." Madrigal was a part-song for several voices, typically arranged in elaborate counterpoint and without instrumental accompaniment, a great favorite, she knew, of the palace guests. Arbella practiced solo songs with lute, singing to her Woofie for as long as her voice held out. In addition to Byrd, she liked English composers, John Dowland, and Thomas Campion.

Hardwick had a fine garden, including herbaceous borders, a vegetable and herb garden, and an orchard. To one garden, however, Arbella was forbidden entry. It hid behind a high hedge of mock orange, and its front was a locked wooden gate. This garden, all the servants warned, contained plants cultivated specifically for their poisonous leaves or seeds, plants like Queen Anne's lace and nightshade.

Once, William, or perhaps it was Merrill, found her when she was a child. She was swinging alone in her English garden, an older woman, perhaps a grandmother or nanny, seated on a bench close by. A spaniel chewing on a bone paid the man no mind. The man stood under a large yew for a time, watching. As Arbella let the swing slow to a dawdle, he approached. She was humming a nursery rhyme, "Goosey, goosey gander, Whither shall I wander?" when he interrupted, "Upstairs and downstairs, And in my lady's chamber."

She giggled.

The grandmother or nanny quickly sprang up and shooed him away, worried that this white-haired gentleman did not have her ward's well-being in mind. He was too friendly, too intimate, too intrusive.

"Don't speak to that old man," she warned the girl, who just giggled and continued to sing as he bowed and withdrew, aware that she, his Lucky, was yet too young.

The extensive grounds also housed Hardwick Old Hall, a slightly earlier manor used as guest and service accommodation once the new hall was completed. Ambitious schemes of plasterwork, notably above the fireplaces, decorated many of the Old Hall's rooms. There, Arbella enjoyed private childish adventures with Woofie and her doll.

Woofie lay at her feet under the table, or occasionally rested in her lap, while she dined. Arbella slipped bits and pieces of the meats from her plate at breakfast like beef, pork, lamb, mutton, and bacon. At supper, she dropped bits of veal, deer, and fancy fowl such as peacock, swan, and goose

into his panting mouth. Arbella favored duck best of all, whether cooked
and on her supper plate or alive, swimming on the pond.

The kitchen at Hardwick was a hub of activity like those of the royal
courts. Food for hundreds of people, including the staff, was prepared
every day. This work required a multitude of servants, and the kitchen
had several master cooks, each with their own workers. Arbella frequented
her grandmother's kitchen only by standing at the threshold of the large
door at the base of the stone steps. She waited there quietly until someone
noticed her. Then, one of the master cooks brought a small treat of some
sort to her delight. For birthdays, Bess ordered the dessert master to create
animals, birds, fruits, and baskets made of sugar and marzipan, known as
"marchpane."

Bess, enamored of sugar, ordered the staff make wine glasses, dishes,
playing cards, and trenchers out of a crisp modelled sugar called "sugar-plate."
Those who could afford to buy sugar were very fond of sugary desserts, so
much so that their teeth turned black. Having black teeth became such a
status symbol that people deliberately blackened their teeth to appear that
they were rich enough to buy sugar.

"Arbella," Bess would order, "remember to brush your little teeth with
burned rosemary wood to make them white and drive out the worms!"

"Worms!" Arbella shrieked. "Might worms live in my mouth?"

"Oh, yes," chided Nanny. "Worms cause holes and toothaches."

One morning, Arbella chased Woofie outside to one of the large ponds.
Some were stocked with salmon and trout, others with eel, pike, and stur-
geon. She liked to visit the ponds, throwing bread crumbs to the fish, and
waiting for them to lift their gaping mouths to the surface to suck in the
morsels. Ducks rushed over quacking in groups to noisily crowd out the fish.

"I am so tired of fish!" Arbella complained one mealtime to her grandmother.

"Ah, my dear, we must eat the creatures. You know, the Queen has
made a law that everyone, even the poor, must eat fish on Wednesdays,

Fridays and Saturdays."

"But, why?" Arbella sulked.

"Elizabeth wants to support the fishermen. And, if she learns we are disobeying her," Bess warned, "she could put us in jail for three months! Imagine that! I wouldn't care to be locked up in the Tower, would you?"

Arbella ate her fish, very small portions, without another word on the prescribed days, frightened as she was of imprisonment in the Tower. The servants and the poor in the villages also ate fish, the fish they caught, anyway.

Woofie was one for outdoor adventures. When outside, the plucky spaniel wiggled from Arbella's arms to race about the grounds, chasing any birds he could find. One morning, Arbella heard loud honking from behind Hardwick's large kitchens. Woofie raced to where young servant girls sat plucking the down from geese which were honking in great distress. Woofie joined in the chorus barking at them with all his might.

Breathless from running, Arbella stopped. She asked one of the girls, "Why are ye hurting the goose?"

"Oh, miss, we need to make new ticks, ye know, beds for the house." The girl looked at Arbella out of the corner of her eye, saying, "Ye sleep on a nice soft bed of feathers, don't ye?"

"Yes, but, you're hurting the goose!" Arbella persisted, her face growing hot.

"The down should grow back. If m'Lady orders goose for supper, then we kill the goose and pluck it after."

"What about the swans and the ducks?" the child asked, afraid of what the answer might be, as she adored ducks with their funny waddle and shiny feathers.

"Ye like their eggs, don't ye? We don't use their feathers for much," the servant spoke continuing her plucking over the screams of the goose. "Now the peacocks! There's a bird for ye! Their plumes are beautiful, don't ye think?"

"My grandmother has a fine peacock fan…" Arbella's voice trailed off as she worried what torment the peacocks suffered for the making of that fan.

Arbella marched into the large kitchen and pulled on the sleeve of the head cook.

"If you cook a goose, I won't eat it!" Arbella announced and dashed out again, crying. The cook sent a scullery maid after the child who was quickly found and brought back.

The cook asked, "Would ye like to keep that goose for a pet?"

Arbella wiped her eyes and nodded yes.

"The girl will put a tie about its neck and bring it to your chamber. It may take a while before it takes a liking to your dog," she warned. "And now, would ye like to see what really goes on in this fine, big kitchen, young lady?"

Curiosity triumphed over sorrow, and Arbella happily agreed. The cook grabbed a handful of freshly shelled hazelnuts from a nearby counter and dropped them into Arabella's small hand.

"Let's look at desserts first, shall we?" The cook knew Arbella was fond of desserts, thriving on pastries, tarts, cakes, cream, custard, crystallized fruit, and syrups. The cook regarded fruits with a bit of suspicion and rarely served them raw. She preferred baking fruits like apples, pears, plums, cherries, lemons, raspberries, blackberries in tarts or pies, or boiling them to make jams. Melons, and strawberries she stored near the doorways, allowing the cold English air to keep them fresh, far from the heat of the enormous ovens.

"Do you like this?" Arbella asked, holding up a peach.

"These peaches, oranges and pomegranates are only for m'Lady's table," the cook said, "not for me."

"Why not?" asked Arbella.

"They are costly, they are. Can only be eaten by the rich, just like those hazelnuts you're having a go at and walnuts."

"Oh," said the child. "What about the pies?"

"Pies are popular with everyone, even those in the village," the cook said. "Preparing meals for this great house takes a lot of time and many hands. Look, we make pies from scratch. Over there on those shelves are the spices and sweeteners like honey and sugar." She took down a jar, lifted its lid and allowed Arbella to smell its fragrance.

"What is it?" the girl asked, taking a second sniff.

"Nutmeg. It is the most expensive spice of all."

As they walked toward the table where a pastry chef rolled dough, the cook warned "Watch ye! Don't go close to the open fire there! Broth is boiling in that big pot, and ye mustn't get near it! Look there at Sarah," the cook ordered. Young Sarah was basting the roasts with a long-handled ladle. Her sleeve sat high on one arm which a bandage covered. "She went too close to the ovens," the cook cautioned, "and got that nasty burn on her arm."

"Here?" Arbella asked.

"No, in the village at the communal oven. The village people cannot bake at home. Their houses would go up in flames if they had ovens. Their houses are not made of stone like this fine house. They have walls of wattle and roofs of thatch. Sometimes they use the baker's ovens for their pies. Sarah was helping her mother, taking her breads there for baking and got her arm burned on the door. Not everyone here in Derbyshire is employed by your grandmother," the cook went on. "Sarah's family like every other eats bread. They might have a bit of butter, maybe some cheese, an egg or two, and pottage."

"What is pottage?" Arbella asked.

"Ye never had pottage? Course not. It's a vegetable soup thickened with oats. I don't suppose you eat many vegetables, but most families do, as we cannot afford meat."

"We eat what we can catch," Sarah chimed in, "like blackbirds, pigeons, and hare. My mother raises chickens. We use rabbit droppings to fertilize the gardens. In my garden, I grow lots of things like turnips, parsnips, carrots, lettuce, cucumbers," she took a breath and went on, "cabbage, onions, leeks, spinach, radishes, garlic, peas, beans, lentils and skirret, I grow them at least until the rains and ice harden the ground."

What Sarah didn't say was that she regularly snuck some of the Hardwick hens' eggs into her large apron pocket to take home at the end of her long day's work.

"Oh, look!" Arbella cried, "Love apples!" These were tomatoes from Mexico.

Many foods Sir Walter Raleigh introduced from Mexico and Central America lay scattered on the cooks' tables. Red kidney beans from Peru filled glass cannisters. Plucked carcasses of turkeys hung on hooks over a large marble counter. Arbella watched the new turkeys with their unattractive red wattle, caruncle, and snood pecking in the yards along with the chickens and ducks.

"Yes, your grandmother's acquaintance has brought a great many new foods to the kitchen, but I do not know quite how to use or cook them. I doubt they're very tasty anyway."

"My grandmother says they are special delicacies. I tried the potatoes at the palace brought by Sir Walter. But, I didn't much like them. I found them mushy like porridge."

Two maids walked in the doorway from the cobbled yard side by side carrying metal pails of milk which clanked upon each other as the women chatted. The metal made quite a racket, startling Arbella. Her skin suddenly prickled as though she'd heard that clanking sound in a dream just remembered or as a moment of *deja vu*. Such moments, jarred out of time, unsettled her. As she turned to look, she saw Sarah returned to basting the meat on spits at the huge hearth. The meat was turning slowly to ensure even roasting. But, Sarah wasn't turning it. Next to the spits were several wheels with little dogs trotting inside. Arbella looked up at the cook with a questioning expression.

"Why are the dogs trapped in the wheels?" Arbella asked.

"Those are turnspit dogs," the cook told her. "We breed them here at Hardwick. They can walk for hours inside the wheels."

"But, the dogs look tired and hot," Arbella protested.

"The wheels slowly rotate the meats you like so much for your supper," the cook remonstrated.

Arbella stepped away, feeling abashed.

Just then one of the young boys walked to the hearth and slid a fiery coal onto his shovel. Then he dropped the coal into one of the wheels. The dog inside jumped and ran faster to keep the coal from burning its paws. Horrified, Arbella ran to the counter where a pitcher of water for washing-up sat. She doused the coal and amid her own tears and cries.

She turned in her distress to flee the kitchen and saw more wheels with dogs. These wheels were pressing fruit and churning butter. The dogs in them wore collars that choked them unless they kept walking. She ran from the kitchen. She looked everywhere for her doll, and when she found her, held her tightly to her chest. She found Woofie and took him to her room.

She was dreadfully upset and thirsty. She asked her maid for ale. She never drank water as it was known to cause illness and was quite unsafe. Everyone drank ale, and some liked the stronger wines like claret, malmsey, and sack, a costly type of sherry, for which she was too young. Sometimes she drank milk, usually before bed, sheep's as well as cow's, and milk made butter, cream, and cheese.

When she slept that night, she dreamed Woofie was running in a wheel with red coals singeing the long black fur on his tail. She woke exhausted. She became greatly afraid of the grand kitchen and the meals prepared there. She ate less and less, a habit that stayed with her into adulthood when she perished of malnutrition in the Tower.

Even though a child, Arbella wore cloth of gold and silver, tinseled satin, woolens embroidered with gold and silver like Bess, who was grooming her granddaughter as a princess. In winter, sables and other furs were abundant in Bess' closets. Elizabeth I very much enjoyed the softness of sables. She got hers from an unexpected source, Ivan the Terrible, Tsar of Russia.

Elizabeth had laughed to Bess, "He sent two ermine gowns along with a proposal of marriage. I kept the furs but refused his proposal. I am pleased to accept presents. I received a pair of sleeves embroidered with pearls and a ruff with matching cuffs."

Bess confided to Arbella, "The Queen may be jealous. She issued a proclamation against 'excess of apparel.' She doesn't want any of us to outdo her!"

"I wish my subjects to know their place and dress accordingly," Elizabeth told the court. "I have decreed that only earls may wear cloth of gold or purple silk." And, indeed, after that, no one lesser than a knight wore silk long stockings or velvet outer garments. A knight's eldest son wore velvet doublets and hose, but his younger brothers did not. A baron's eldest son's wife wore gold or silver lace, but these luxuries were forbidden to women below her in the pecking order.

Bess' personal wardrobe was complex. She wore her bodice stiffened to lie flat across her bosom; her skirts split in front to show an underskirt, the hems adorned with valuable jewels. Sleeves, bodice, ruff, skirt, underskirt – all came as separate pieces held in place by pins and reassembled with other elements to create another look. Arbella liked to watch as servants outfitted her grandmother. Tailors measured her and servants dressed her, tasks taking several hours in the morning and again in the evening when she changed her attire for an outing, dinner, or a ball.

Fascinated by the dark opportunities proffered beneath the layered skirts held on a 'farthingale' frame worn over the hips, Woofie dashed under the hems to bite the tassels on her shoes, annoying Bess greatly and almost knocking her off balance. Those afforded the few times Bess lost her temper and ordered Arbella and her little dog from the room.

The clothes worn by the rich made the poor feel poorer still. If a lady could not afford a farthingale, a 'bum roll' tied round the waist under the skirt did almost as well. The breeches of a working man were baggy and knee-length. Working women wore fitted bodices and long full skirts.

Elizabeth's proclamations regarding dress did not change anyone's behavior. Prostitutes flaunted themselves in rich garments. Young apprentices who were supposed to dress in modest blue, as were prostitutes, often burst out in colors, such as popinjay or lusty-gallant red. She forbade over-long swords, but men wore them defiantly. In fact, both men and women wore ruffs, old and young, courtiers and working people. They began as a simple frill at the neck of a full-cut shirt gathered into a neck band. But, they sagged limply, until someone copied the Dutch and starched them. But, if the starched ruffs got wet, they too collapsed.

Although invited often to stay at Elizabeth's court, Bess feared treachery. Arbella preferred living in Derbyshire with her grandmother, who by that time had married George Talbot, 6th Earl of Shrewsbury. When Bess finally took Arbella to London for a royal visit that lasted a year, the weather confounded them. They did not have proper garments to protect against the English rain. A hooded cloak kept off the worst weather, but unless made colour-fast by that elusive alum, they risked arriving at court in a puddle of leaking dye. Bess most certainly did not want to appear ashen-faced with dye dripping from her cloak.

After the five-day journey from Hardwick with a stopover near Rufford, Bess asked, as they neared the palace, "Arbella, dear, how is my complexion?"

"You look pale," the girl answered honestly.

As cosmetics were in fashion. Bess used ceruse, a thick, eggshell white and quite toxic paste containing mercury to smooth her complexion. Unfortunately, the toxic paste often melted, giving the face a shiny gray appearance. It also smelled. Bess retrieved a small gold cosmetic case from her tiny velvet bag and dabbed vermilion on each aging cheek. "Should be alright," she murmured. "I hear the Queen relies on ceruse as well these days."

The servants carried the ruffs – also known as 'bands' – in a bandbox, which they pinned on their mistresses' clothes when once out of the rain and safely inside the palace.

Gazing at the great portraits lining the halls, Arbella asked, "Grandmother, why are the ruffs painted white in the Queen's portraits? Didn't you say she wears pink or yellow ones?"

"I suppose the painters take some license. They never paint the staggering amount of jewelry she wears, either. In the portraits, they only show only a few pearls besides her crown. See there? They only painted the six ropes of pearls she purchased from Mary."

"Those are from Mary, Queen of Scots?" Arbella asked, surprised as she knew of the terrible strife between the two queens.

"Yes, indeed. She bought them off her rival. They are beautiful Chinese pearls, hard to find. Imagine. But now, pearls are coming to us from the New World like fish from the sea and are quite common. They need only boring and polishing to be ready to wear."

"Why doesn't the Queen wear diamonds instead of Mary's pearls?" wondered Arbella.

"Diamonds need careful cutting and are never as prized. My dear, at court you must take notice that some of the ladies wear charms."

Arbella shook her head and asked, "What is a charm?"

"You'll have to look. You tell me how many you count. It will be our little game, all right? Do you know they believe sapphires and unicorn's horn avert the plague?"

"Do they?" Arbella asked, amazed.

"I doubt it. That awful red coral they string they think is useful against witchcraft. The ugliest charm I've seen is the bezoar."

"What is a bezoar?"

"It is a stone formed in the intestines of a Persian goat," Bess replied, "It is believed to protect against poison."

Arbella gasped.

Bess went on, "It is hardly attractive strung round a woman's neck, though many a superstitious woman wears one."

"I prefer your pearls, Grandmother," said Arbella. Bess wore five long strands of gold pearls almost daily and when seated for her portraits.

On seeing Elizabeth's courtiers in the throne room, Bess whispered with a grin, "Except it were a dog in a doublet, you shall not see any so disguised as our countrymen."

Arbella covered a wide smile of her own with her hand as she surveyed the silks, ribbons, pleats, and puffs which looked like wildly colored bubbles worn as shorts over tights covering the courtiers' buttocks and hips. Pinking decorated the nobleman's doublet and hose, which was a series of patterned slits cut in the fabric with differently colored lining pulled through the slits in little puffs. A short cloak completed the ensemble with a feathered hat and jewels. When Arbella spotted pheasant feathers in a nobleman's hat, she felt a sudden pang for the birds.

"Grandmother," she whispered, "it looks like we have entered a garden of fantastical flowers and ill-formed birds!"

The great days of the codpiece were declining, giving way to a modest buttoned or lace-up opening; but they were still useful as somewhere to keep pins-- as they were heavily padded-- or a purse. Arbella turned away when she saw a courtier pull an orange from his and eat it.

When the queen was not busy with matters of state, she filled the evenings at her court with entertainments. The nobility loved to have a good time and she knew exactly how to proffer it. On their extended visit to the palace, Bess and Arbella attended great banquets of rich foods, wine, music, and dancing. Arbella saw the queen drink from a unicorn horn, which was the tusk of a narwhal, nearly six feet long.

"I've never seen such a cup," Arbella whispered.

"It's magical," said Bess. "It is an antidote to poison. The Royals live in terror of poison. There are so many jealous of power and position. In fact, the queen often eats theriac."

Arbella looked questioningly at Bess.

"It's a mixture of parsley, carrots, wine, honey, pepper, and cloves. Some eat crushed bezoar, that stone from the belly of a goat, to ward off death."

What Elizabeth did not know was that she was poisoning herself by wearing lead-based cosmetics on her skin.

Arbella watched the Queen drop a stone into the unicorn horn.

"What is she putting into her drink?" she asked her grandmother.

"An emerald, I suppose."

"Why? Won't she choke on it?" asked the girl.

"Many put gems into their cups. They believe they act as an antidote to poison," Bess explained. Arbella learned much about the perils of life and death at court.

During their visit, they watched Elizabeth and Robert Dudley, her Master of Horse, ride together almost every day. Bess commented, "Dudley is probably the most accomplished horse-man in England. Look at him match the Queen's speed and vigor."

Early in Elizabeth's reign, Dudley brought over some new horses from Ireland, as the Queen complained her own horses were not fast or strong enough.

"Grandmother, I want to ride! May I?" Arbella begged, only to have Bess caution,

"Only if you do not compete with the Queen."

Elizabeth loved horses, spending many an hour riding fast through the Palace grounds. Her love for the sport terrified her Councilors, who feared that she might seriously injure, or even kill herself, from a fall. Some of her ministers bewailed that the Queen was neglecting matters of state. But, Elizabeth was undaunted. She tired her ladies by riding hard. At sixty, she rode ten miles, which she did quite willfully to prove her expertise to a courtier who had advised the aging Queen to take the carriage.

She hunted stags, deer, and hawks. She kept beagles for hunts. Riding her favorite steed with her courtiers, when an unfortunate animal was caught, she was the first to cut its throat. A French ambassador reported that she killed "six does" with her cross bow. Hunting parties took several hours, as the Queen and her courtiers rested and picnicked in the forest. She also went hawking. The Queen watched as a trained hawk took to the skies in search of prey and waited for it to dive for the kill. Then, she spurred her horse to recover both the hawk and its prey.

Elizabeth had no concept of animal cruelty and enjoyed a whole manner of violent animal sports, such as bear baiting, cock-fighting, and dog fighting. She was particularly fond of bear baiting, in which a bear was chained in a pit and tormented by dogs. Yet, she kept pets, such as her much loved spaniels and greyhounds. In fact, a little spaniel went with her everywhere just as Woofie went with Arbella.

Elizabeth supported a culture of literature and drama, music, and chivalry. As they were in London, Bess took Arbella by boat across the Thames to the Globe theatre to see William Shakespeare's *Antony and Cleopatra*. The acting and rich language mesmerized the girl. She left the theatre whispering favored lines to herself, committing many to memory.

"Grandmother," Arbella asked on the way home, "Shakespeare must have written some of the lines for you!"

"Oh? And what would those be?"

"I like this one a lot: 'Age cannot wither her nor custom Stale her infinite variety,'" Arbella quoted. Bess laughed aloud at this.

"I do believe he meant to flatter the Queen."

"Grandmother," Arbella asked, "might I act one day?"

"Oh, never, my dear! Only men are actors!"

"But, I saw Cleopatra," Arbella corrected.

"Yes, yes, but that was a man dressed as a woman. The stage is no place for a woman. You have a very different and noble position in life, as one day, I hope, you will be queen."

Shock and disappointment tore at the girl's heart on hearing this rebuke.

"Usch," Arbella bit her tongue and did not say what she felt, which was "I'd loathe be queen!"

Owing to Arbella's status as a possible heir to the throne, discussions of appropriate marriages for her began in her childhood. Arbella, considered by many as a possible successor to Elizabeth, knew she did not herself aspire to the crown. When she came to marriageable age, she danced at a masque-ball held in honor of Prince Henry's investiture as Prince of Wales. The

Tethys Festival celebrated the titan who fed the waters encircling the earth. Arbella followed, in order of precedence, Anne of Denmark, who appeared seated on a raised throne shaped like a silver scallop shell and draped with gold cloth. Lanterns set around the throne made it blaze like jewels. Second came Princess Elizabeth who sat at Anne's feet. Arbella, dressed as a Grecian water nymph, came next.

Inigo Jones costumed the nymphs with head-attire that looked like shells and coral beneath diaphanous veils. Arbella's upper garments were of sky-blue taffeta embroidered with maritime motifs. She wore a half-skirt of silver cloth worked with gold and a longer underskirt in the blue. Around the hem of the skirt was a meander of lace like a river with sedge and sea-weed banks in gold. At the ruffed shoulders and sleeves, the embroidery shone in the candle-light; gold embroidery sparkled on her satin shoes.

On either side of her, in caves or niches, stood five women masquers who represented the other nymphs or guardian spirits of various rivers. They came down from their caverns one by one and marched in a wandering path towards the Tree of Victory with Tethys where they offered flowers to the Ocean King. The nymphs then chose men from the audience to dance. Arbella took the hand of William Seymour, Lord Beauchamp, member of the prominent Seymour family, clearly besotted by her loveliness.

William dressed stylishly, showing off his fine legs right up to his crotch. Next to his skin, he wore a white linen shirt, which supported his starched ruff. His doublet had a skirt, of varying length, under which were points, or hooks, onto which the breeches were tied or hooked. This fashionable Elizabethan opted for short breeches padded at groin level, so that they looked like melons. Arbella wondered how he could walk, let alone dance. That was not all; his breeches were cut into narrow panels, joined at the waist and hem, with a colored lining showing in the spaces between the panes.

Of course, they danced. Of course, they fell in love. Of course, she fell into trouble for wanting to marry him. William's touch was light, gentle. Theirs was a time of sighs and rare sightings, tenderness, and gentility. Until they kissed, that is. She did not so much as inhale his breath. It came into her heated as though expelled through the open-mouthed roar of a lion in rut. The hot air shot through her lungs and down to her womb, speaking in an animal tongue of love and desire such as she'd never known but which remained in her marrow for eons to come.

She wrote lengthy descriptives and many letters of love to her beloved, William who stood sixth-in-line to the throne. He was grandson of Lady Katherine Grey, a younger sister of Lady Jane Grey and a granddaughter of Mary Tudor, younger sister of King Henry VIII and Arbella's ancestor, Margaret Tudor. William's grandfather reported their courtship to the Queen. The influential Cecils –Lord Treasurer, Lord Burghley, and his son, Secretary of State Sir Cecil, then turned their attention away from Arbella's candidacy for the crown. To her great relief, they looked instead toward her cousin, James, preferring him as successor.

On Elizabeth's passing childless in 1603, James ascended the throne. But, Henry Brooke, Lord Cobham, funded by the Spanish government, plotted against him. They invited Arbella to participate in his overthrow. In the version of the "Main Plot" presented at trial, Cobham admitted negotiating with the Count of Aremburg to contact the Spanish court for a very large sum of money. He intended to travel to Brussels and then to Spain to collect the money, and go back to England via Jersey, where Sir Walter Raleigh was governor. Raleigh and Cobham planned to divide the money and spend it in furtherance of sedition. Instead, Arbella, loyal to the crown, reported the plot to cousin James.

Although Arbella and William at first denied that any arrangement existed between them, William gifted her with a ring. It was a gimmel, consisting of two interlocking bands, wonderfully symbolic in that each band was free yet fit with the other to create the whole. Gimmel rings housed beautiful cut stones and ornate carved features highlighted with colorful enamel. The ring William presented not only had fede hands of gold holding a pearl, but also included a touch of *memento mori*. On the inside of one band an infant was scribed as a symbol of life. On the inside of the other, its interlocking mate, a skeleton lay as a symbol of death. Worn together, the bands symbolized everlasting love.

"The pearl held by the hands," William told her, "can only be given in love by a pure heart such as mine." He slipped the band with the pearl and infant onto her finger and the skeletal band on his. They wore them thus leading up to their wedding day, when the two bands met on her finger, the joining of lovers.

Yet, King James grew fearful, wondering if Arbella's marriage to William was the prelude to yet another attempt to seize his crown. His mother, Mary, Queen of Scots was a Stuart and her second husband, Lord Darnley, murdered a year after their wedding, was a Stuart, as was Arbella. Mary led a turbulent life and her dogs, Maltese terriers, were one of her only comforts in the final nineteen years of her life while held in prison by her cousin, Queen Elizabeth I. At Mary's execution at Fotheringhay Castle, she concealed her beloved Maltese beneath her skirts, which no one realized until after her beheading.

James issued a royal warrant for the arrest of Arbella, now the Lady Beauchamp and William. James imprisoned Arbella in Sir Thomas Perry's house in Lambeth and Lord Beauchamp in the Tower of London. The couple had some liberty within those buildings. Arbella wrote often to Beauchamp and to the King. When the King learned of her letters to Lord Beauchamp, however, he ordered Arbella's transfer to the custody of the Bishop of Durham. But, Arbella feigned illness to postpone her departure.

William used that delay to plan their escape. "Go to Lee in Kent," William urged. "Dress as a man. I've brought clothes." She did as he said. But, William was detained. Her ship set sail for France without him. Beauchamp did manage to escape from the Tower, but by the time he reached Kent, Arbella was gone.

The channel was rough and the crossing brought on strenuous bouts of nausea. She did not suspect she was with child, but thought rather the nausea came from the roiling waves. Sadly, moments within sighting Calais, King James's men overtook her ship, forcing its return to England. The Channel waters were rougher yet on the return, and she was not only nauseated, but she also hemorrhaged. Once onshore in England, she fell seriously ill. When her health was somewhat recovered, Arbella was taken to the Tower. There, she was allowed a serving maid, proper food, and furnishings paid for by her estate. Sir Walter Raleigh was imprisoned there as well, where his wife and sons kept him company and his own personal furnishings surrounded them. He had known Arbella since childhood and was very kind to her.

Unaware of her plight, William caught a ship to Flanders. He inhaled deeply once onboard and out of the harbor. For him, the sea came alive. It rolled beneath him, carrying him, he prayed, away from England and prison and onward to freedom and to his love.

Though she wrote over one hundred letters to William, Arbella never saw or heard from her husband again. After Woofie died, Arbella was thankful to Sir Walter as he gave her one of his pups to have by her side to curb her loneliness, as no one knew what might become of her, least of all herself.

"What will you name the little thing?" Sir Walter asked. She remembered being at court when Sir Walter's company's expeditions to Virginia came back from the Americas with caged turkeys, love apples, tobacco, and potatoes.

"I think," she replied, playfully, "I'll name her for you and your exploits."

"How so? Would you name the pup 'Roanoke' or 'El Dorado? Love Apple, perhaps?" he teased, adding, "It's a male. And, he's got a lot of gold on his chest," he said petting the pup. "I'd be pleased enough with El Dorado.'"

"No," she laughed, "I think I shall call him Turkey."

In the end, she languished in the dank tower for fifteen years. Arbella Stuart Seymour, Lady Beauchamp, refused to eat and died of malnourishment in, of all places, the ironically named, Beauchamps Tower.

They interred her body in a lead coffin and placed it in the vault of her aunt, Mary, Queen of Scots, placed it directly on top, in fact, of the queen's coffin. Arbella now rested eternally above the mother of the very king, James I, who had torn Arbella from her beloved William, punishing them for their love, a love which was hardly an act of treason.

Lucky returned the borrowed books to the council library at Rufford. She felt tired. The effort to translate texts--diaries, really--written by a great, great aunt on her mother's side proved exhausting. The language seemed stilted, the script archaic with f's and s's cloned and a great many words misspelled. Tears fallen long ago blurred some of the words into illegible cakes of dried ink.

Her distant relative wrote of the children buried along with the family dogs and horses beneath the yew tree in a little wrought-iron, gated yard near the lake.

"Ms. Cummins," Lucky said, "I think I've read enough for today about my family. I only wonder now if you suppose Arbella returned to Rufford on any of her trips to London? From what I read, Hardwick Hall is to the north in Derbyshire, and Rufford would have been on her route to the court."

"She may have. Are you wondering if the clammy baby was her child?"

Lucky shrugged. "I have no way of knowing." She picked up the map Mrs. Cummins had drawn of the estate for her. "What do you think?"

Ms. Cummins thought before replying. "Even if Arbella didn't visit on those trips, it's said around here that after death, a soul often returns to the place it was born." She sighed. "Perhaps the clammy baby really is here."

Then, as Lucky opened the door to go out, Mrs. Cummins added, "Me? My opinion? I suspect it may be Arbella wandering hereabouts."

She wore white, her favorite of the colors, for it was at once both all colors as contained in a prism of light and no color at all from any pigment. It was the color of clothing for baptisms, for virgins, for western weddings, for Oriental funerals. It was the color of peace, waved like a flag of surrender, or wrapped like a bandage over a treated wound. It was the color of bones bleached by death, age, and decay into something other-worldly. It was the color of luminescence, and a color spelling purity...no spoilage, no soiling, no dirt. As ivory and pearls, white was coveted. Holding all colors like fragments, if broken apart, white became the story of her many lives. And, white was also the color of her dirt: a nearly translucent clay, when fired, called porcelain, a clay she one day sought.

She cleaned the child and wrapped it in strips ripped from parts of her white gown not soiled by blood. She bared her breast and hooked the little fish onto her nipple, allowing it to suck for more than she could ever give. She stroked its head, now dry and coated with a fine misting of white down reminding her of the belly of a goose she once had kept as a pet before it grew big enough to eat. She breathed. And, perhaps her breathing became a hum. And, perhaps her eyelids lowered. And, perhaps she heard that rhythmic ingestion of honeyed milk and felt the fish babe swelling on a river of fat in her arms.

She wasn't thinking of the child; she was thinking rather of its father. Gone. She wanted to find him, and when she did, she wanted to kill him for leaving her, again.

O memory. Where was hers? On clear days, she worried she had lost her mind already before finding her history, her progeny, her past. Her mind was fragmenting, puffing, and popping away from the heat of her lives like dried kernels of corn in a pan, scattering to times gone by, salted by tears dropped for people and places she missed. She felt an urgency to collect her memories as she was fast approaching her eightieth year. Yet, memory was but dandelion fluff. She remembered dreams, lots of dreams and wondered if her life was a dream within a dream as Poe once wrote:

> Take this kiss upon the brow!
> And, in parting from you now,
> Thus much let me avow:
> You are not wrong who deem
> That my days have been a dream;
> Yet if hope has flown away
> In a night, or in a day,
> In a vision, or in none,
> Is it therefore the less gone?
> All that we see or seem
> Is but a dream within a dream…
> …Is *all* that we see or seem
> But a dream within a dream?

The lines between waking and dreaming for her blurred like a watercolor dampened too many times, its colors losing their edges, blending, each indistinguishable, one into the other. She no longer knew what had happened. And, when what happened had happened. And, precisely where it happened and with whom. Was she to know her husband: Merrill, Guillaume, William, in her next life? Was this death, the death of memory, final and there was no other life to follow? Was she inching closer to the edge of the diving board, perhaps one or two, at the most, steps away, before the last plunge, the plunge into the dark water at the deep end of the pool? Is that why she was seeing those others, those earlier selves, and husbands: Vassilios, Ibn, Du Sultan and the rest, why they came floating, unsummoned to mind, did they come to take her with them, back to… oh, where? the other side? Wherever it was they went? Was she ready to go? Did she even have a choice?

She remembered the dress. It was white, of course, but soiled. She tore it off when she got to the lake, or was it the mill stream, and watched it float over the ford like a bridal veil thrown back from the face. She stood naked in the cold rush of water and rubbed her thighs and knees rhythmically with her hands, her fingers from the icy river stiff like bristles on a brush. She carefully scraped under each nail with a twig, letting her fingers drift and soak, rubbing again to remove the clotted stains.

She had no reason to worry about her nakedness; there was no one to see. There was no one. That was the problem.

BLIP FOUR

Haunted

Lucky tried to remember some of that time as La Chanceuse with Guillaume, yet a vague, dream-like memory of England overtook her effort. Intrigued, she concentrated on it instead. Of course. England was coming back into a focus of sorts. Yes, she had lived and traveled there many times. Ah, who was she there, then? She knew she wasn't Chinese in these incarnations. She was English. And? American. And, what?

H's flooded her mind. So many H's. She shook her head, putting the H's in place. There was the great house, Hardwick Hall. Yes. That was it. There was another H. What was it? Yes, Hampstead. And, another H flew by: Haunted. One journey was brief she remembered, yes, to a haunted place called Rufford, another blip in the great randomness of cosmic irony. But, she was British, too, once long ago, in another of the lives she recalled, fourth in line to the throne, in fact.

Bloody bones. Oh, yes, bloody bones. Fractured memories surfacing, horrors, some her own. Babies dying, women dying. All that fecundity, those juices allowing egg and sperm to create life as quickly as it took it away by breeding bacteria, which spread green lightning through the openings, the openings that birthed, the openings leading backward on liquid veins to the core, soon slaying, martyring the mother, then perchance the baby.

People met on the way flowed to her. Mothers, fathers, sisters, brothers, friends, co-workers. The people with whom she had played, loved, loathed, worked. And, her dogs, lovely dogs, all. They were blips, like stones on the path, embraced or tripped over, during her lives.

"Let go of the past, let go of the past," friends advised. It was that woman who advised her to let go, that blonde woman who kept coming to her room with the mail or lunch, annoying her. What foolishness, Lucky mused. The past shaped her, shook her, tossed her out, whether onto hallowed ground or quicksand, never predictable. She watched death at work. She saw death arrive in childbirth, plague, war, famine, solitude, cruelty. She didn't like it, death, not one bit.

That was not true. That was a lie. She didn't like the death of her loved ones. But, she frequently wished death would take away like a punishment many of the blips in her life, those people who had made everything harder, more painful, costlier, like Jardine, James I, and Ma Rulong. She imagined their deaths often. She even conjured the Furies once, the Greek Eumenides of old, to respond to her call, to open Pandora's jar and let loose its imprisoned evils upon her enemies. The neighbors she wished dead, the liars she wished dead, the lawyers she wished dead, the men she wished dead, and the women. Any who had betrayed her with lies. And, herself. Yes, for she had betrayed a time or two, betrayed with lies of her own, lies, mainly, of omission, like little abortions.

She flew to England to lead workshops on figurative sculpture. The art center in a converted stable, north of Nottingham, stood atop an old Cistercian Abbey. There had once been an old brick manor house built over the foundation of said crumbling twelfth century Abbey, but it had burned in a fire. The roof was gone as well as some of its walls.

She didn't find its bombed-out ruins charming. Normally, ruins drew her to them, like those at Mycenae near the ancient theatre at Epidaurus.

How she loved wandering in those Greek theatres, where Clytemnestra, the sister of Helen, lived with Menelaus' brother, King Agamemnon, before Paris stole Helen away, and the long Trojan War began. She loved the worn lions' gate lintel leading to what was the palace shortly past the grave of Agamemnon and the treasury of Atreus. A classic betrayal. Ruins like Stonehenge where guesswork played at why the stones were circled there at all. Ruins like the Acropolis where democracy began. Ruins like Teotihuacan with its long avenue of the dead and its pyramids to the sun and moon where Aztecs worshipped and sacrificed. But, this English Abbey? Its manor house vandalized, its brick walls riddled by practice bullets fired from guns of World War II soldiers, bored while billeted there with far too much time and too many guns on their hands?

Rufford Abbey had been a grand country estate of one hundred and eleven rooms and twenty staircases located near Sherwood Forest. Prior to the first world war, King Edward VII had regularly enjoyed fox hunting there with his mistress and friends, using Rufford as a base when visiting Doncaster races and shooting parties. But, by the time Lucky arrived, close to one hundred years later, it was a "has-been." Fire had consumed almost all the interior rooms, and little of its roof remained intact. The clock tower, walls, carriage house, and stables remained relatively unharmed. What was left behind of the house itself was brick rubble, partial walls, dressed stone and ashlar with ashlar dressings, and plain tile roofs. It was Grade I listed and scheduled as an Ancient Monument. Its remains, standing in a one-hundred-and-fifty-acre park and woodland, were open to the public as Rufford Country Park, part of which was a local nature reserve. The stable had been converted to the ceramic's studio Lucky was to use, while she was to reside in a loft above the carriage house with a restaurant below.

She officially checked in at the centre's office with Estelle Cummins, who held Lucky's stipend check and dispensed some local information.

"You might find this tiny bit of history interesting," Estelle said, handing her some tourism brochures. "You can find more detailed information about Rufford's long history, if you like reading, in our small library to the left," she added, pointing to a door on the left.

Originally, a Cistercian Abbey founded in 1147 by Gilbert de Gant, Rufford was populated with monks from Rievaulx Abbey in Yorkshire. The English Pope, Adrian IV, gave the blessing for the Abbey following which its lands expanded, and the nearby villagers were evicted to make way for it. A new village called Wellow, just outside the estate, housed some of the displaced people and their descendants. But, the monks could barely feed themselves much less make any revenue to give to the church. And, the Abbey failed. After the Dissolution of the monasteries in the sixteenth century, Rufford was converted to the grand country house that crumbled in disrepair around her now, gaining a reputation over the centuries of being haunted. People said unsettled souls crowded the undercroft of the Abbey chapel on whose foundation the manor house stood in a shamble of its former self. Ghosts lurked outside on the spacious and forested grounds as well. Visitors said that they heard a child crying in an area of the grounds near a ditch close to Broad Ride. Two ladies claimed that they had heard that crying noise one afternoon whilst out walking their dogs in the park. Locals said they saw the spectre of a giant monk walking the grounds carrying a skull.

A housemaid at the Abbey drowned herself and her child in the lake behind the manor after an unwanted pregnancy. A guest of the Savile family claimed she was woken in the middle of the night by a clammy sensation, like cold skin brushing against hers. When she related this incident to other house guests, it transpired that other lady visitors to the house said they also were bothered by a so-called clammy baby or what they felt was the ghost of a dead child trying to snuggle up to them in bed! The infant phantom was thought to relate to the old legend of a child being murdered in the house. Of course, the bedrooms and salons of the great house were demolished years before, but stories of a ghostly child kept cropping up, keeping alive the tale of the clammy baby.

Estelle Cummins, the Nottinghamshire County purser whose office was in one of the Abbey's intact sections, organized tours, collected fees, and documented visitors' tales. Mrs. Cummins wrote multiple reports of voices, strange balls of light drifting in the air, footsteps, chanting, and smells of horses. A gentleman tourist claimed he was hit by small stones apparently being thrown at the group. A woman told about seeing flying balls of red light. There was the White Lady. Some speculated that she was the spirit of the unhappy Arbella Stuart, a lady who due to her royal connections might have become Queen of England after the death of her cousin, Queen Elizabeth the First. But, Arbella died instead a prisoner in the Tower of London. Her mother, Elizabeth Cavendish, and father, Charles Lennox, had met and secretly married at Rufford Abbey. And, their child, this Arbella, was born there. Some believed her unhappy ghost returned to the place of her birth. Others thought the White Lady was a bride, jilted at the altar, left alone to drift like the cool evening mists over the lawns and lake in an eternal purgatory of heartbreak.

There were at least three known Ghosts. In addition to the White Lady, some saw a diminutive Victorian woman who wore a long black dress, name not known, wheeling an old-fashioned pram around the grounds. Some thought perhaps the clammy baby was wrapped inside. Third loomed the devilish Black Monk. A local woman said her husband had seen this ghost in the form of a misty grey figure one snowy January day whilst delivering parcels to the Abbey offices.

But, Lucky did not know any of these stories before she arrived at Rufford Abbey to work in its modern Ceramics Centre. She came to the estate to create art. They offered a residency in a large and airy studio where she received a stipend, meals, housing, assistants, and the use of a large art studio, equipped with kilns, brassiers, and more. In exchange, she was to offer two public workshops. Lucky flew to London from the Pacific half way around the world, excited to research new materials and firing methods for her large figurative sculpture of mothers and children. She was internationally recognized for setting such figures in abstract postures. A prestigious gallery in Hampstead commissioned any figures she created at Rufford for a later exhibition. How much simpler it was to create them in England, she reasoned, rather than encountering the expense and logistics of shipping from her studio in the tropics. And, so she arrived at Rufford one splendid October day when the leaves hung golden on the trees and lay red as dried blood on the grass.

That first day, Ian, the manager, toured her through the village and estate before introducing her to her quarters. They took a late lunch at a small pub so that his bride, Maggie, could join them after her work. Ian was very much enjoying showing Lucky the highlights of the village and its surrounds before Maggie arrived. Maggie was tall, almost matching Ian's height. Both were dark haired and fit, in their mid-forties, this a second marriage for each. She brought two teenaged daughters into his home, which he and his son maintained after his own divorce. Tweeds suited Maggie and looked hip on her in a British sort of way. Her hair was salon cut, blunt, one side falling just below the ear, the color of a raven's wing. Her conversation was engaging. She was a self-styled biologist, with no formal degree, said she volunteered in the lowlands to eradicate invasive species and helped in the gardens at Rufford.

Maggie liked being tall and reminded Lucky of Snow White: the raven locks, white skin, red lips, and innocent look. Maggie did not think herself beautiful though her prince, Ian, adored her and gave her his heart. But, she mistrusted him, imagining he loved others, as he couldn't possibly love her, as she didn't feel she measured up. She saw every woman of a certain age as her rival. After all, in her mind's eye, the mirror on the wall asked over and over who was the fairest one of all.

When her prince spoke to another woman, Maggie toadied up, made fast friends, kept the woman under the closest of surveillance, certain that the woman or the Prince formed an alliance or dalliance or whatever which was upsetting and proved Maggie's deepest fear that she was nothing, less than nothing, a woman of neither value nor import.

Her first husband lied to her, adeptly. She didn't realize it until she had sunk up to her neck in depression. Then she met Ian and for a moment felt safe, until she began to believe her own unjustified fantasies of betrayal.

Lucky, Maggie, and Ian climbed the hill road to the old castle, now a museum, on a crest where they stopped to enjoy the view overlooking the valley.

Turning to leave, Lucky noticed Maggie wore an unusual pendant. "What a unique necklace," she remarked.

Maggie put her hand to her throat where the pendant cradled and smiled.

"Yes, it is a bezoar. It is a lucky charm. The ancients said it protects against poison."

They headed down the hill where Maggie parked her car and saw her off. And, so passed Lucky's first afternoon at Rufford, Lucky quite oblivious to Maggie's scrutiny and rising insecurity.

Ian drove Lucky back to the estate where he showed her the carriage house where she was to stay. It was a two-story building of red brick with large oak beams between the floors and supporting the joists. He carried her travel bag up the stairs. Her ceramic tools were shipped to the studio weeks before. He showed her a tiny kitchen overlooking the rectangular court with the clock tower rising above the red brick manor wall, the bedroom with a double bed and a single chair, the bathroom across the hall. A locked door to a room he said was unused stood to the right of the landing.

"You can take breakfast after ten downstairs in the restaurant. You'll probably hear the cooks banging pots and pans before then. You'll have students in the afternoon. Handing her a variety of keys, each with a label—one for the studio, one for the carriage house and so on, Ian said, "Alright, then. Have a good evening. By the way, in the morning you should meet our purser, Estelle Cummins. She's got an office just below the clock tower. As she's in charge of your stipend, best to let her know you're here. I'll be off now."

"Wait," Lucky said, stopping him. "Where does the caretaker stay?" she asked, "over there?" pointing to a Rapunzel like tower beyond a high hedge.

"No. That's a water tower. I don't suppose you have any of those on your island. To answer you, we don't have staff or caretaker living here."

"No staff? What do you mean? Who is here at night?" she asked, taken aback.

"No one, I'm afraid," he said, clearly embarrassed by her shock. "Don't worry," he added. "The main gates get locked at night when the staff finishes work. That's at five. You'll be fine here on your own."

"So, you're saying, the staff is locked out, and I am locked in?"

"I suppose that's right. Don't worry," he repeated. "No one has ever reported an intruder."

"This estate is huge," she gestured widely. "Is it fenced all the way around?"

"There are fords…"

"Fords?"

"Ah, yes. Rufford is a ford. It means a shallow place in a river where it easy to cross. Today we have bridges. So, I suppose someone could enter by any of the fords as they are not fenced."

She was not happy with this news, yet she didn't know what she could do. She had not rented a car or made provisions for any other place to stay. She had her laptop but the centre shut down the wi-fi when the staff left at day's end. And, she hadn't seen a telephone in the carriage house where she was to stay.

She accompanied him down the twisting stair. He took an enormous brass key ring holding several medieval looking keys from a hook on the wall. Two of the keys fitted locks on the door. An oak bar stood at attention in the corner. He lifted it and dropped it in place onto two hooks on either side of the door.

"Quite effective, don't you think, to keep out any intruders?" he quipped. She did not find it funny.

She went to bed hungry, their lunch at the pub being the last food she'd eaten that day. Ian pointed out a pub across the highway at the roundabout, but if the estate was locked, she would not be able to get a meal there. She determined to find a way to get into the village the next day to get some provisions. She liked to snack and was a night owl. There was no television, no internet, no cell phone. She was glad she had packed a few books for the plane. She wanted them now and wished she had brought some chocolate bars in her bag. She hung her smock on a peg behind the door and set her computer on the single wooden chair before crawling between the very chilly sheets on a less than comfortable bed.

It was the middle of the night. Blown sideways by the wind from the north, rain slashed the upper floor leaded windows. Lucky woke to thudded banging. She thought a shutter had come loose. As she rose from the bed, she realized the banging was coming from downstairs. It sounded like fists beating on the large wooden door below her bedroom, the entry door on the ground floor of the carriage house where she was staying, quite alone. But, that was not possible, as high iron fences and gates surrounded the grounds and were locked every evening when the staff departed for the day.

In any case, she had barred the door, dead bolted it, key locked it before climbing the winding stairs to her small quarters above the park restaurant. She knew she had barred it. In the day, a heavy two by four length of aged oak stood to the side of the entry. Heavy iron arms bolted to the wall on either side of the door remained eternally at the ready to hold the length in place barring entry from the outside at night. She had to squat to lift the substantial length of wood into place and often grunted as she did so, quickly pulling her fingers away lest they get pinched as it dropped between the iron arms.

The place, the grounds, the buildings, the lake, and pond altered so at dusk. The staff left at five, locking the tall, ornate wrought iron gates at the two ends of the property behind them. The one hundred and fifty acres were fenced all round. She was the only person on the property from dusk to past dawn. No one had told her it was to be so.

It was late that first night when the heavy rain began followed by loud banging on the oak door downstairs.

The main gate stood a quarter mile from the carriage house. How could anyone get onto the grounds at this hour? How could they have found their way to her door? No lights were on anywhere, it was raining steadily, and there was a fierce wind blowing.

She called out, not one to readily submit to fear, "Who's there?"

The banging continued unabated. She got out of bed, put on her robe and a light, opened the bedroom door, and stood at the top of the landing.

"Who's there?" she called out again. No answer came, and the banging continued.

Slowly, she walked down the treads to the bottom of the stairs, gripping the handrail for support.

"Who's there?" she asked for the third and, she hoped, final time.

"It's me, Maggie! Let me in!"

"For god's sake! Maggie? Ian's Maggie?"

"Yes! Please hurry! Open the door!"

"What are you doing here?" Lucky shouted through the door. She flipped on the entry light and squatted to lift the oak bar from the door. She unlatched the deadbolt and pulled the brass ring from the hook on the wall and fiddled with the many keys to find the right ones to unlock the door. Maggie rushed in. She was wild with—what? Lucky didn't know. Maggie's hair looked done up by egg beaters then flattened by the rain, water flowed from her eyes, one swollen and beginning to blacken, snot dribbled from her chiseled nose, and lipstick lollygagged lopsidedly across her right cheek.

Lucky pulled Maggie's cloak from her shoulders and dropped it to the ground; water wept from its folds to puddle on the stones at their feet.

"Come, come up," Lucky commanded, pulling Maggie by the hand up the stairs. She grabbed a towel from the bar in the bathroom and wrapped it around Maggie's shaking shoulders. Once she seated Maggie in the tiny kitchen, Lucky filled a pewter kettle with tap water. She got out a box of oolong tea left in a drawer. She set two stained King George VI cups with mismatched saucers on the small, cracked vinyl cloth over the table. She found some packets of sugar; there was no milk in the refrigerator. She glanced at the clock; it was well past midnight.

"Maggie, what's wrong?"

Maggie stared at the cups, shaking, stared at the kitchen wall, stared a long while at nothing, while fingering an oddly shaped bezoar charm hung around her neck.

"How did you get in?" Lucky asked. "Weren't the estate gates locked?"

Maggie continued to shake. She made no effort to dry herself. Water dripped from her clothes. Like most people not from the tropics, she wore her soaked shoes into the house, where they leaked red stain, leached from the dyed leather. Lucky set the kettle on the stove and took two packets of tea from a tin, placing one in each cup, before Maggie spoke.

"Ian and I had dinner across the way. At the small pub at the round-about. We had a row. I had to come to you."

"Me? But, why? I don't understand. We don't know each other!" Lucky protested.

"I said we had a row!" Maggie repeated. Her lips were swollen making her mumble.

"Your face is bloody. And, your eye? Did he hurt you?" None of the husbands Lucky could remember ever hurt her, as violence was not their way.

Maggie didn't answer. She sat shaking and staring at the stove behind Lucky where steam shot from the kettle.

"Ian is about control," Maggie said. "It's subtle but pervasive. What I can wear, where I can wear what I wear, the cut of my hair, the color of my hair."

Lucky didn't know what to say or why this stranger came to her. "I'm sorry. You didn't know this about him before you married?"

"I didn't pay attention. He is clever. He masked his control through compliments. He said things like 'Darling, you are so beautiful with that straight hair, I love it swinging below your shoulders. But, when we go out tonight, wear it up, he ordered. Not a pony tail, just a bun at the nape of your neck, okay?'" Maggie's hair clung to her cheek and she brushed it behind her ear. "Or, he said, 'Darling! Pants suit you. They make me want to grab your gorgeous, tight derriere! But, not outside the house, please. Okay? I don't want anyone else getting ideas about my dearest treasure!' Or," she went on in a monotone, holding her head in her hands, "'No, no, my dear, not the tangerine. Don't you have something in navy? Navy draws much less attention, don't you agree?'

"His jealousy flared if the false flattery wore thin, and I challenged him. But, I was jealous, too. I felt insecure." Lucky poured boiling water into the cups and pushed the sugar toward Maggie. Lucky sighted a dish with packets of dried creamer on a shelf. She passed it to Maggie.

"He started commanding me in bed," Maggie confessed, "or withholding, leaving me untouched. Ian doesn't seem to care about my pleasure. Sex for him is about him," she cried. "Period."

Lucky had only met Maggie that afternoon, and she was providing far too much unwanted, intimate information. Lucky sat and blew on her tea, before sipping it quietly. Putting down her cup, she asked, "And, tonight?" she ventured, "How did you get that black eye?"

"He's been hitting me for some time, Ian. I get through it by taking pills."

"Pain pills?"

"Yes. I have a prescription."

Opioids, Lucky surmised. She's probably addicted. Maybe, Lucky thought, those pills account for this bizarre visit and confession. "Maggie," Lucky asked again, "how did you get in?"

"I have keys. Ian gave me a set when he became manager of the estate, in case he had to work late and I wanted to get in. Cell phones don't get reception here."

Lucky sat still and waited. Patience was one of her qualities. What she wanted to know was why Maggie and Ian had fought. She wanted to know why Maggie, whom she did not know at all, sought her out. But, she remained quiet and did not ask these questions.

Maggie blew on her tea, ripped four creamers into it, stirred loudly, then downed the drink. Putting down her cup, she opened her bag and took out a knife, placing it on the table. It was large, the type used to carve a roast.

"I came here to kill you," she said.

It took finishing her own, cold cup of tea in silence before Lucky grasped that Maggie was serious. Here to kill her? Why, for God's sake? And, how naïve was she to let this Maggie in late at night and in a deluge?

Maggie whispered, "I told Ian to stop flirting with you. He said he wasn't. I got jealous. Crazy jealous."

"Right, Maggie, Ian wasn't. Ian wasn't flirting with me," Lucky responded with deliberate caution, her attention focused on the knife while watching Maggie's eyes intently. "Your husband isn't interested in me. Nor I in him. I don't know either of you. I have a partner of my own." After a pause, Lucky added, "I am most certainly not on the make as I'm in love with someone myself."

They both looked down at their empty cups with bags grown quite cold.

Then Maggie began to apologize. "I am sorry. So sorry. This is embarrassing. Ian was effusive when you agreed to come to the center. He couldn't stop raving about your resume, your current work. That was okay. We host many artists here. But, he went on about your beauty. Your beauty. Not your work. So, I had to meet you. I couldn't let him spend the afternoon alone with you. That's why I joined you for the castle tour and lunch."

Lucky did not add another word, not wanting to add to the crazy suspicions. The knife sat on the table next to Maggie's hand. The woman needed to be calmed and gotten rid of. Maggie reached for the towel and patted her head and face. Then she flung it violently to the floor. She began to shudder and gasp for air.

"My first husband cheated on me. I cheated on him. With Ian. Ian cheated on his first wife. With me. Now I'm suspicious of every little thing that could be a clue to infidelity," she confessed, pushing back her chair. "I suspected he was lying and sneaking about with other women. You came along and fit the bill."

Lucky had known women being jealous without cause. How many supposed friends had she lost over irrational jealousies? She had never slept with a married man, yet some of her married friends wrongly accused her of dalliances with their husbands, a behavior totally against her principles. "We are our brothers' keeper" was her motto, and that included treating other women as she wanted to be treated: with respect. She was flirtatious, highly so, but her flirtations originated from interest and curiosity rather than sexual desire. She loved to laugh. Flirtation and the delight in conversation probably triggered women's ire, making a few of them fiercely insecure and possessive.

Lucky didn't say a word. She sat very still. The knife remained on the table next to Maggie's hand. Lucky's mind raced. What to do? She didn't have a phone, she couldn't run, as there was no place to escape. She thought of the cast iron frying pan hanging on a rack behind her head. Could she get it off its hook quickly enough to hit Maggie if she grabbed the knife to strike?

"What did Ian say to you?"

"About what?"

"Me," Lucky said.

"Things like you were beautiful and from an exotic island, and, I don't know, he just upset me. I told him to just shut it, just shut it, I was his wife and he just couldn't go on and on about another woman. He said I was crazy. And, I said, 'Crazy? You think I'm crazy? I'll show you crazy! And, I grabbed the knife off the joint platter at the pub. He jumped back. He must have thought I was going to stab him. But, I threw it into my satchel, and stormed out. I didn't care that it was raining. I just thought I'm going to find that woman and put an end to it right now!"

"Maggie," Lucky said, without missing a beat, "would you like another cup of tea?"

As she picked up her cup, she swept the knife to the floor and kicked it under the table. Maggie didn't seem to notice, saying, "No, no. I've bothered you enough. I should get home."

"Where did you leave your car?" Lucky asked.

"On the road, outside the main gate."

"That's a long way. Do you have a cell phone? You might call Ian to tell him where you are and perhaps he'd come to help you."

"No, no. I don't want Ian to know I've been here. I told you there's no reception. Promise me, you've got to promise me, you won't tell him!"

"Not to worry," Lucky assured her, who was very worried. She walked behind Maggie down the stairs.

"This has to remain between us," Maggie insisted before stepping onto the pavement and into the rain's onslaught. Without hesitation, Lucky spun round, shut the door, bolted it, knelt to lift the bar into place, and turned one of the enormous keys in the lock. Then she rose to lean her back against the door.

"My god," she said to herself, "what just happened?"

It turned out that Lucky soon learned she was not the first woman Maggie tried to kill, or rather, perhaps had killed, if one was to believe the local gossip.

There was Katie. Katie was a biologist, hired by a conservation group to clear the wetlands near Rufford beyond Sherwood Forest of infestations of non-native plants. Giant hogweed was a problem as it was especially abundant by lowland streams and rivers, but also occurred widely on waste ground and in rough pastures. It grew on moist fertile soils with partial shade. Himalayan balsam was well-established and extremely invasive throughout most of the lowlands. It also thrived in moist and semi-shaded damp places on banksides by slow-moving watercourses. Two other species offered great potential to become invasive in certain habitats. Skunk cabbage was planted for ornament beside ponds and swampy streams but readily escaped into the wild. Its normal habitat was wet woodland, where it grew on bare or partly-vegetated nutrient-rich mud.

Katie's was a cushy government grant job, paying well, affording a semi-detached rental near the river and few actual work hours, mainly spent supervising the manual laborers. Tall, pale, and reedy, Katie kept in tow a non-descript boyfriend and a father who was Maori from New Zealand, shriveled from his former stature by age and very dark. She was devoted to them, her studies, and this project.

Maggie, a good twenty years older than Katie, possessed a talent for twisting truth into damaging lies, a trait as bad as her penchant for jealousy. Maggie was jealous that Katie got a position so near Rufford which she considered to be her turf. She wanted Katie's lucrative contract for the wetlands. She was paid a pittance by the county council to upkeep the poisonous herb garden at Rufford, a position Ian had secured for her. As soon as she could, she befriended the younger woman, boasting false credentials of being a biologist herself, which she most certainly was not, and volunteering to help clear the invasives from the lowlands.

Maggie managed to get on the team by saying she could recognize poisonous plants. She got a tiny small private sector grant to protect wetlands for the propagation of native birds. What she really did was little for the birds, aside from banding, and much for herself by building a glass conservatory at Ian's house with the grant funds. Jealousy infected her work. She wanted to be number one though she had no credentials to place her at the top. Her unbridled need for attention and praise made her ruthless and cunning.

In the realm of poisoning, Maggie was an expert, quite like the Black Monk was centuries before her time at Rufford. He planted the poisonous herb garden she so carefully tended. In his day, most non-violent killings were by poisonous brews. Political rivals, mismatched lovers, unwanted pregnancies, heirs to the throne oft were dispatched by poisons. Estelle Cummins warned visitors to avoid the garden and to fear touching any plants or allowing the plants to brush their clothing. It was Estelle who told Lucky about the director's wife, Maggie.

"Maggie is proprietor of the garden," Estelle said. "Best to avoid it, you know, stay on the side of caution. She doesn't take kindly to visitors there."

At home, in her small glass conservatory, Maggie grew five of the deadliest plants known in England. She cultivated purple-flowered monks hood and wolfsbane of the aconitum family in five-gallon buckets, nourished monthly with fish emulsion. Wolfsbane, if ingested, caused heart failure as did another of her favorites, foxglove. The cuckoo pint festooned with its clumps of poisonous orange berries stood in one corner and in another, hung the deadly black berries of nightshade, which were known for causing convulsions. Hemlock flourished in the glass hot house, even though it grew readily enough in waste ground and near rubbish bins. It bore purple spots on its stems and sported white flowers. Ingestion of the stems and roots caused paralysis of the lungs.

Yet, Maggie's true area of expertise was neither her gardening nor her birding. It was, rather, her trouble-making, which she created at every turn. This time, she contacted the funding foundation. She wanted to get Katie's laborers fired. She falsely accused them for failing to work full shifts. She laced Katie's water flask with a tincture of hemlock and wolfsbane. For good measure, she dropped in the opioids she herself took when she was in pain and often when she was not. She had gotten a prescription after the first beating from Ian, a prescription she renewed regularly. Maggie bided her time to see the results, noting with pleasure the changes in Katie, and adding more deadly tinctures and addictive opioids whenever and wherever she could.

Katie's dad liked to join her on field trips. One outing, he tripped, breaking his left leg, and was medivac-ed to a hospital in Doncaster for care. Katie couldn't leave the job, so her boyfriend, the non-descript one, accompanied her dad. It made for a perfect opportunity.

A few days later, on their return, they discovered Maggie alone in Katie's house.

"Who are you?" asked her dad. Maggie did not answer.

"What's going on here? Where's Katie?" demanded the boyfriend. When Maggie ignored him, he shouted, "Hey! Who are you and why are you here?"

"I'm cleaning up," Maggie said, bagging the girl's belongings in zip lock bags.

"Why?"

"Oh, you don't know?" Maggie asked, smiling a bit.

"Know what?" both men asked.

"I don't want to be the one to tell you," Maggie demurred, adding, "I'm sorry for your loss."

"Sorry for what loss?" the father asked.

"Your daughter. She died."

The old man slipped and might have fallen to the floor, but his cast held him upright, though it scraped loudly on the linoleum. The boyfriend bent to steady him.

"Died? Katie? My Katie?" the father stammered.

"Yes," Maggie said. "I heard she overdosed."

The father looked at the boyfriend questioningly.

"What? Katie doesn't do drugs," the boyfriend protested. "Neither do I!"

"The ambulance medics told me she overdosed on medication," Maggie reiterated. "They found opioids in her blood."

How Maggie relished this encounter, loving to mislead. It gave her pleasure, almost sexual, like the first moist stroking of her clitoris, whether from her hand or Ian's. Lying excited her. And, the more she lied, the more excited she became. Particularly, if her lies were believed. She could soar with belief, telling even more fantastical tales until she soared in ecstatic waves, oblivious to the harm she was causing. Insecure, jealous women like her hurt themselves and everyone dear to them.

That day, instead of her usual chic attire, Maggie wore a black sleeveless man's tank top, loose over her unsheathed breasts flopping under a plaid Pendleton wool shirt and long mountaineering pants. Her hair hid tucked under one of Ian's herringbone flat caps, her disguise for this work. She looked old without make-up and toughened, with a few untidy hairs slipping below the hat.

Again, the boyfriend protested, "Katie doesn't take medication." After a pause while he got the old man got situated in a chair, the boyfriend asked, "Who are you?"

Maggie didn't offer an immediate response. Then said, "A friend."

"Who told you, you could come here and touch her things?" the boyfriend persisted.

"I'm just helping," Maggie smiled.

"You have no business being here in our Katie's place!"

"This place smells funny!" the father muttered.

"Yes, I disinfected it. Chlorox," Maggie said smugly, "to be on the safe side."

"Safe side? What are you talking about?" the boyfriend asked.

Maggie kept the semi-smirk on her face as she closed a zip lock bag and dropped it to the floor, before silently picking up a gallon container of bleach and walking out of the house.

She got hired in Katie's stead the following week. The workers, never fond of Maggie, suspected foul play. But, as neither the father nor the boyfriend, too taken by grief, had pursued an investigation, neither did they.

Lucky worked hard and in ten days left Rufford with its strange inhabitants, living and dead, behind. She sold the sculpture she made at a London exhibition in Hampstead before booking a ticket on the *Eurostar* bound for Athens that winter.

BLIP FIVE

Moon river, wider than a mile...
Oh, dream maker, you heart breaker
Wherever you're goin', I'm goin' your way
...Andy Williams

Quiet days on the Yangtze, she lay with her head and shoulders over the bow of the *kakam*, letting a hand twined in her long, black hair finger-trail in the water. She loved water. Floating, drinking, bathing. She immersed fully dressed, and after, letting the cotton of her indigo pants called *ku* and her shirt called *yi* cling to her body for hours slowly drying, leaving her cross-collared jacket called *shan* to lay open, soaked as well. She didn't mind washing laundry or filling buckets to boil rice or soup. Water, to her, was always soothing, refreshing, rejuvenating. In China, the only place Lucky knew by heart was the river, the Pearl, whose water was never clear, always a rather unpleasant, opaque shade of green.

A wet life, a floating life like her dreams, Lucky--Ying Yue, as she was known there--undulated in and out of memories.

Her guardian dog, Foo, could not protect her from the river. Water terrified Foo, who knew instinctively that if he fell overboard, he would drown. The loyal Shar Pei had no body fat and no webbing between his toes. He was unable to swim or float. Foo adored his mistress and, on shipboard, warded off any strangers who came near. He was rust in color with so many loose folds he looked as though he was a small lion, his wrinkles piled high on his head like a full mane. The wrinkles protected his body from bites, being solid muscle underneath all that loose skin.

Like her dog, Ying Yue did not know how to swim, yet she was unafraid. To bathe, she tethered her waist with a rope carefully knotted to the railing of the *kakam*, the small vessel some ill-informed foreigners called a junk. The Chinese had three kinds of vessels: *jonouq*, junks, the large ships having up to twelve sails, made of bamboo rods plaited like mats; middle-sized boats called *sao*, zaws, and small ones called *kakam*.

Sometimes, her *kakam* held steady, other times it pulled her behind as though it was the horse and she the cart. She liked the thrill of the water passing swiftly over her skin. She clamped her mouth tightly shut as the least intrusion of river water could bring unwanted parasites into her digestive system, aiding an earlier than desired death, a death she met much later after her migration to Kunming.

Ying Yue's father and brothers lived comfortably as *Cohong* on the river. The family owned many ships which carried a slew of their agents to foreign places for trade. They oversaw the building of their vessels in Zaytong, Quanzhou, or at Sin-Kilan, Guangdong. As *Cohong*, they enjoyed high status, overseeing trade at their warehouses that sat on Lintin Island near the mouth of the Pearl. Nowhere in the world were there to be found people richer than the Chinese, she thought. The *Cohong* were particularly powerful in the Old China Trade, as they were tasked with appraising the value of foreign products, purchasing or rebuffing said imports, and charged with selling Chinese exports at an appropriate price. Between six and twenty merchant families at any given time made up a *Cohong*. A key function of the *Cohong* was the traditional bond signed between a *Cohong* member and a foreign merchant. This bond stated that the receiving *Cohong* member was responsible for the foreign merchant's behavior and cargo while in China.

The arrival of British warships in 1840 altered Ying Yue's languid life and dress, enriched her purse in ways unforeseeable, and brought her a foreign husband, only, in the end, to take him away once again.

Ying Yue liked business, the exchange of silver for goods like the porcelain she brought from Jingdezhen or tea from Anhui province. Meeting the foreigners, mostly British, forced her to learn English and a smattering of Portuguese. In Shanghai port alone, one of her brothers counted over four hundred junks on a given morning and over one hundred and forty-six-thousand vessels docked per year.

Most of her junks had two parallel raised walls of thick wooden planking. Across the space between them lay bulkheads, secured longitudinally and transversely by large nails, each plank ninety inches in length. After these walls went up, the lower deck was fitted. The sailors on her large junks never lowered the sails. Instead, they changed them based on the direction of the wind. When they cast anchor, they did nothing to the sails, which standing were marvelously effective in catching the wind due to a semi-rigid structure.

She often launched a new ship before its upper works were finished. The pieces of wood in place, parts of the hull near the water line served for the crew to wash and to accomplish their natural necessities. On the sides were the oars, which were as big as the masts and worked by up to fifteen men who rowed standing up. The vessels had four decks, upon which there were cabins and saloons for merchants. Several of these cabins contained locked cupboards, ideal for hiding contraband, easy to use by foreigners and nationals alike.

She did not deal in brothel ships as her agents often took their wives and concubines on board. It often happened that passengers stayed in cabins without others on board realizing it, never seeing them until the vessel had arrived in some port, when the passengers disembarked. The sailors also had their children in such cabins. In some parts of the ship, they grew garden herbs, vegetables, and ginger in wooden tubs.

As each new ship readied, Ying Yue made offerings to *Xuanwu*, the Cantonese Dark Warrior, who was known to have power over the waters of Guangdong province. She went up river to her ancestral temple, Zumiao, at Foshan to make offerings to *Xuanwu*. She was superstitious. If she thought the ship was beautiful, she gave it a poor name like *Chouxiaoya*, Ugly Duckling, so the Dark Warrior would not be jealous and not cause harm to come her new ship.

While there, she attended puppet plays. The hand puppets of the capital of Guangzhou were between three and four feet high with exquisitely carved wooden heads. She collected many of the region's handicrafts for the foreign trade including red sandalwood furniture, rattan chairs, embroidery of handmade silk, ivory carvings from Guangzhou, pottery from Shiwan, fireworks from Dongguan, and ink slabs from Zhaoqing—all of which were famous throughout the country and newly in demand from Europeans. These she brought back to sell at great profit from her warehouses.

She commissioned porcelain from as far north as Jingdezhen, then having it decorated with enamels by artisans contracted in Canton. Canton Famille Rose in the 19th century was typically decorated with alternate panels of figures and birds, flowers and insects, predominantly glazed in pink, green, and yellow overglazes. This "Canton porcelain" was made as "blanks" at Jingdezhen, then carried to Canton where it was painted in styles designed for Westerners at the Thirteen Factories in Xiguan. There, Ying Yue oversaw a large market of armorial porcelain for dining wares, with the design of the coat of arms of the buyer sent out from Europe and to be copied. A British Company, Jardine and Matheson, emerged as the major purchasers of this porcelain, with a William Merrill assigned as procurer.

Most popular for general export were pagoda and blue and white willow patterns, often designed after an old Chinese poem:

Two birds flying high,
A Chinese vessel, sailing by.
A bridge with three men, sometimes four,
A willow tree, hanging o'er.
A Chinese temple, there it stands,
Built upon the river sands.
An apple tree, with apples on,
A crooked fence to end my song.

Ying Yue enjoyed time spent with the artisans, often receiving the honor from a master glazer to lift a brush herself to add the final glaze strokes of deepest cobalt. On her *kakam*, she kept many of the finest of her acquisitions cushioned with silk in a fine chest of camphor wood. She took out a vase for a rose or a plate for her dinner, gaining both tactile and visual pleasure from these art works. Her favorite piece was a small yellow vase she kept for herself, not ceramic, but rather cloisonné, in which she placed a fresh blossom each morning.

Turkish and Arab traders first introduced opium to China in the late sixth or early seventh century. Taken orally to relieve tension and pain, it was used in limited quantities until the seventeenth century. The practice of smoking tobacco had spread from North America to China, and soon smoking opium became popular throughout the country.

Early in the eighteenth century, the Portuguese found they could import opium from India and sell it in China at a considerable profit. It was this trade in opium from India which British merchants also brought to China that changed Lucky's—Ying Yue's-- life. The British saw opium as a potentially valuable export. The East India Company itself neither produced nor shipped opium, but set the horticultural laws in its colony, India, allowing for opium cultivation. It actively facilitated the transport of the drug to company-controlled ports. From Calcutta, the company's Board of Customs, Salt, and Opium concerned itself with quality control by managing the way opium was packaged and shipped. No one cultivated poppies without the company's permission, and the company banned private businesses from refining opium. The company bought all opium in India at a fixed rate and hosted a series of public opium auctions every year from November to March. The difference of the company-set price of raw opium and the sale price of refined opium at auction, minus expenses, was the profit made by the East India Company.

Malwa was an Indian historical doab region of west-central India, occupying a plateau of volcanic upland north of the Vindhya Range. In addition to securing poppies cultivated on lands under its direct control, the company's board issued licenses to the independent princely state of Malwa, where significant quantities of poppies were grown. Agriculture was the main occupation of the people there, who blossomed themselves into the most important producers of opium in the world. The British East India Company established a monopoly on opium cultivation in the Indian province of Bengal where they developed a method of growing poppies cheaply and abundantly.

By 1773, the British became the leading supplier to the Chinese market. By 1787, the East India Company was sending four thousand chests of this contraband to China per year, each chest weighing one hundred and seventy pounds. Soon, estimates varied, between two and ten million Chinese citizens were addicted to opium. Other Western countries joined the trade, including the United States, which dealt in Turkish opium as well, known as *wuxiang* or "black spice." The East India Company monopoly ceased when these American merchants became involved.

Hailed as a titan of trade with a taste for philanthropy, John Jacob Astor, the first American millionaire, made his enormous fortune in part by sneaking opium into China against imperial orders. The resulting riches made him one of the world's most powerful merchants—and helped create the world's first widespread opioid epidemic. Astor sold hundreds of thousands of pounds of opium between 1816 and 1825.

Astor even brought opium to New York, openly selling and advertising it in New York newspapers. Warren Delano, maternal grandfather of President Franklin Delano Roosevelt, made millions engaging in what he called a "fair, honorable and legitimate" opium trade.

The Brits controlled ninety percent of the Chinese opium trade, and Americans handled the remaining ten. Of the Americans, the Perkins had the largest share. They owned at least seven ships and held interest in others. Their ships sailed from Massachusetts' shores to Turkey, where they bought opium; then sailed from Turkey to China, where the drug was sold; and hence, from China to Boston where their ships returned loaded with tea, porcelain, and silk.

Perkins' ships deposited tremendous wealth in Boston. Workers hauled chests of tea, bolts of silk, crates of porcelain and cakes of opium-- which was legal in the U.S.-- off the ships onto giant scales outside Boston's Custom House. The goods were tallied and taxed in basements and warehouses around Faneuil Hall and Quincy Market. Tax revenue from the trade funded Massachusetts police and fire departments, roads, bridges, courthouses, and schools. In fact, opium profits funded many Boston institutions. The Perkins brothers helped found Massachusetts General Hospital, McLean Hospital, and the Boston Athenæum. The names of other opium barons were engraved on university buildings, high schools, and public libraries.

Despite restrictions, silk and porcelain continued to drive trade through their popularity in Europe, with an insatiable demand for Chinese tea in Britain. From the mid-17th century onward, European powers paid around twenty-eight million kilograms of silver to China, principally to purchase Chinese products.

While opium remained the most profitable good to trade with China, merchants began to export other cargoes, such as machine-spun cotton cloth, rattan, ginseng, fur, clocks, and steel tools, although these goods never reached the lucrative level of the narcotics.

Among merchants, there was a robust debate about the morality of selling opium in China, where between two and ten million residents were addicted to the drug. New York merchant, David Olyphant, refused to trade opium, calling it "an evil of the deepest dye."

The partners at Perkins and Co. made fun of Olyphant. "Opium is really a way that we can transfer China's economic power to America's industrial revolution," adding China had a strong economy. "And, we tapped into that."

Earlier, during the American Revolution, the Continental and British armies used opium to treat sick and wounded soldiers. Benjamin Franklin took opium late in life to cope with severe pain from a bladder stone. A doctor gave laudanum, a tincture of opium mixed with alcohol, to Alexander Hamilton after his fatal duel with Aaron Burr.

The hypodermic syringe was introduced to the United States in 1856. It was the Civil War that set off America's own opiate epidemic. The Union Army alone issued nearly ten million opium pills to its soldiers, plus two point eight million ounces of opium powders and tinctures. An unknown number of soldiers returned home addicted, or with war wounds that opium relieved. "Even if a disabled soldier survived the war without becoming addicted, there was a good chance he would later meet up with a hypodermic-wielding physician," one doctor wrote.

By the late 1800s, women made up more than sixty percent of opium addicts. "Uterine and ovarian complications cause more ladies to fall into the opium habit, than all other diseases combined," it was reported.

Opium smoking spread across the United States from the 1870s into the 1910s, with Chinese immigrants operating opium dens in most major cities and Western towns. They attracted both indentured Chinese immigrant workers and white Americans, especially lower-class urban males, often neophyte members of the underworld.

"Almost every town had a Chinese laundry," a white opium-smoker said in 1883, "and nearly every one of these has its layout" – an opium pipe and accessories.

As addiction in China increased, so did importations of opium during that first century of the Qing Dynasty, 1644-1729. It became such a problem that the Yongzheng Emperor prohibited its sale, but that edict failed to hamper the trade. A century later, in 1796, no progress made, the Jiaqing Emperor outlawed importation and cultivation. Despite such decrees, opium trade flourished.

The *Qing* government intended the system to be highly regulated. The "Prevention of Barbarian Ordinances" declared all trade must go through the *Cohong*. They forbade foreign traders to learn Chinese, enter, or trade in any other part of China. Foreigners could only live in one of thirteen factories. They could only work with low level government officials. Only official diplomatic missions could lobby the imperial court.

Social dislocations appeared in the Qing world due to the spread of addiction. Hard-line mentality toward foreigners grew alongside foreign refusal to accept Chinese legal norms, changes in international trade structures, and the ending of Western intellectuals' admiration for China. When the tough prohibitions of 1838 began to take effect, the market diminished and dealers found themselves dangerously oversupplied.

Unforgettable
...Like a song of love that clings to me
...Nat King Cole

William Merrill arrived on the Pearl, or *Zhujiang* river, shipboard with William Jardine, his boss. Jardine, was Scottish, a resident in China from 1820 to 1839, known for his imperiousness and pride. The locals nicknamed him "the iron-headed old rat" after a clubbing he received on the head in a wharf-side brawl when he shrugged off the injury with a dour resilience so common to the Scots. He had only one chair in his Creek Hong office in Canton, and that was his own. He never allowed visitors to sit: he wanted to impress upon them that he, Jardine, was a very busy man.

Ying Yue did not mean to be a pirate. Merrill showed her it was the way the trading worked best, as the British were selling roughly fourteen hundred tons of opium per year to China. Legalization of the opium trade was the subject of ongoing debate within the Chinese administration, where a proposal to legalize the narcotic received repeated rejections. By1838, the government began to confiscate drug shipments and sentence any Chinese drug traffickers to death.

"You like put Ying Yue risk?" she pouted.

William Merrill, on first sighting Chinese merchant junks as he entered Canton harbor, realized that far from being rustic and backward, Chinese naval technology was a model of pioneering design. Going aboard, he observed the watertight compartments in the hull he had read as a youth in Marco Polo's accounts that were in fact an essential step in marine safety. Yet, the first western ship to apply this technique was *Nemesis,* the steam-ship built recently in 1840. He noted the axial rudder, a version evolved from lateral rudders already evident in reliefs from Ancient Egypt, was known in China long before European ships employed it.

Trade restarted on the strict condition that no more opium be shipped into China. Jardine and James Matheson, founders of Jardine Matheson, were British merchants who operated a consignment and shipping business fed by the Pearl River in Canton and Macau. William Merrill enjoyed success in Canton as a commercial agent for these opium merchants from India. He sought aid from local fishermen and merchants to secretly carry the contraband opium upriver. It was highly lucrative to whomever helped him.

He came aboard Ying Yue's junk. He asked for time and tea, interrupting her *qi gong* practice.

"Who you?" she asked, without interrupting her movement. The British often came aboard her junk uninvited as she was a *Cohong*, high up in the order of dealers in foreign trade with thirteen large warehouses of her own. She understood a lot of English and some Portuguese from growing up among traders.

He didn't answer, waiting for her. She had just begun the claw motion of *Dayan Qi Gong:* the Wild Goose. As she turned her head to the right, fluttering her fingers as her arms dipped and rose like a goose preparing to fly, she took a sidelong glance at him.

She had never seen this man before. For the first time, Foo did not bark at a stranger. He sniffed his leggings, and then let out little yipes of joy.

"What's your dog's name?" the stranger asked, leaning down to nuzzle Foo's wrinkled face.

Ying Yue continued her practice, taking a deep, squatting step forward as she replied, "Foo. My dog, Foo."

"Bad name," he said.

"Why you say bad name?" she asked as she stepped back again to sweep the air with her arms.

"The gods will know your dog is guardian and will be jealous. Better name for your dog is Turkey. Then the gods won't cause harm."

"How you know gods?"

"I heard about the one you call Dark Warrior. Maybe you call him *Xuanwu?*"

"Okay, okay," she said, coming to a standstill. "You come here, interrupt my practice, try name my dog. Hrnhhh!" she made a derogatory sound somewhat between a snort and a cough. She looked this stranger up and down before asking, "You superstitious like me?" He laughed at this. She continued, "Turkey? You want call my Foo, *Huo-ji?*"

"Turkey."

"*Huo-ji!*" And just like that, they began to laugh. The newly named *Huo-ji* rolled on his back to let the stranger rub the loose folds of skin on his belly.

"You must be wondering why I am here," Merrill asked.

"No, I not. I not care." Her answer took him by surprise.

"Why not? Do strangers come on your ship every day?"

"As matter fact, yes." He looked so surprised, she began to laugh, an infectious laugh he came to cherish. "I big-wig, I think you say. All merchants come see me. You must be merchant, I think."

"Yes. My name is Merrill," he said, putting out his hand for her to shake.

"Nyah, nyah, nyah," she demurred. "You maybe come my junk, you maybe pet Huo-ji, but you no touch Jiang Ying Yue!" She pulled away, horrified by this affront. No Chinese wanted to be touched by a stranger, whether by a handshake or a pat on the back.

Startled, it was his turn to pull away. "I didn't mean any harm," he apologized, bowing low. "I represent Mr. Jardine."

"Ah, Jardine. Okay. He plenty money. You sit, I make tea."

"What is your name?" he called after her.

"Jiang. Ying Yue."

"What does Jiang mean?"

"River. See? I part this river!" she laughed, returning to set down a slatted bamboo tray. On it were two tiny cups and a pretty, brown clay pot, quite small as well, carved in the shape of a small lotus flower. "Rest name Ying Yue. Mean moon reflect water. Moon river. Foreign people call me Lucky. Easy them remember."

"Alright, then. Lucky it is," he said.

"What your name?"

"Merrill."

"What Merrill mean?"

"My mother's name was Muriel. It came from the Celtic…"

"Stop!" she interrupted. "I not know Celtic."

"Oh, I apologize. The Celts were early settlers in England. Merrill came as a male version of Muriel, my mother. The Celtic word muir means the sea, and gael means bright. Somehow bright sea became a woman's name, Muriel."

"Ah, we both got water in name," she said, thinking of the key elements that made up a person: water, air, fire, wood, earth, metal. "What year you born?" When he told her, she said, "Ah, you rabbit. Gentle, like nice things. I dog. Loyal. Fierce. Good friend."

"Don't dogs chase rabbits?" Merrill teased.

"Nyah, nyah. Chinese dog and rabbit good match." She proceeded to pour hot water from a metal kettle over the clay teapot. The hot water splashed through the bamboo slats of the tray to sit in a pool on its bottom.

"What are you doing?" Merrill asked watching her, baffled.

"Tea very strong. Heat outside." She sat on a cushion, legs bent to either side of her lithe frame in the lotus posture. He squatted awkwardly on his haunches. They waited in silence. She then poured a single tablespoon of dark brown tea into each thumb-sized clay cup. She handed him one with two hands, then took her own, blew on the steaming tea and sipped. He followed suit. The tea was bitter and aromatic, unlike any tea he ever tasted. He thought perhaps it would be oolong or even green tea, but this was entirely different.

"You like?" she asked.

"Yes, yes. It's very good," he answered, drawing his lips tightly in. It was the most bitter, acidic tea he had ever tasted, thankful it came in such a tiny cup. He felt a great need for milk and sugar. Pulling from his coat jacket an official looking envelope, he handed her a letter of introduction. Instead of taking it, she recoiled. "What is wrong?" he asked.

"What wrong?" she hissed, looking at the red lettering on the envelope. "You bring bad news? Why? Why you ask what wrong?"

"I don't have bad news," he responded, perplexed by her sudden recoil.

"Then why you write red ink? Red ink for criminal. I no criminal!" her voice rose in protest. "Red ink mean you kill me?"

He stood, opened the letter, and began to read. "To the Honorable

Jiang Ying Yue, *Cohong* of Lintin Island and Warden of the Thirteen Ware-houses…"

"Who write?" she interrupted him.

"Mr. Jardine."

"Why use red ink?"

"It's decorative."

"No, not decorative. Here, China, red ink for somebody die, dead, for tombstone. No write me red ink."

Merrill was embarrassed and uncertain how to extricate himself, deter-mining to learn Chinese etiquette before returning, if he ever did return, to her junk.

"Do you read English?" he asked. She looked at him defiantly. He thanked her for the tea, and taking his leave, left the unwelcomed letter next to his cup.

He soon learned never to click his fingers to get attention of a waiter or worker, never to whistle at someone, never to put his feet on a desk or a chair. To beckon a Chinese person, he faced his palm downward moving his fingers in a scratching motion, as it was bad form to use the index finger to beckon. The Chinese motioned with an open hand. He learned never to return a used handkerchief to his pocket, as the Chinese considered it vulgar to do so. He learned to suck air in quickly and loudly through his lips and teeth to express distress or surprise at a proposed request. If a Chinese sucked air, Merrill quickly dropped his request, allowing the Chinese to save face. Ying Yue avoided the number four and the color white as they were symbolic of death, especially putting one's parents at risk. Black, as in the West, symbolized tragedy. Perhaps the hardest custom to learn was belching and slurping at a meal. His English upbringing was rigid in forcing such behavior out of his dining repertoire.

Ying Yue introduced him to Chinese food, mostly cooked on a wok on her junk. She employed cooks, but occasionally prepared a meal for him herself. She poured him a glass of *baijiu*, known as Chinese vodka, a white liquor that dominated Chinese wine culture for thousands of years. She introduced him to the stronger *huangjiu* and the rice wines of the southern Chinese.

When he brought her a fine bottle of aged Bergerac from Jardine's storehouse, she said, "Ah, Mister Merrill, now time for you learn something. This grape wine, yes?"

He nodded. "The finest."

"Maybe you not know grape wine start here, China. Four thousand year. China beginning of everything. Grape wine before rice wine, before your mother, father make wine. White rice wine, my *baijiu*, brewed by sixth emperor Xia Dynasty Du Kang two thousand years before your Jesus born."

"Jiang Ying Yue, Lucky," he said quietly, "I hope nonetheless you will enjoy my gift." With that, he set it on a table, collected two bowls, and pulled out his knife. Cutting off the metal wrapper, he pulled out the cork. He set the bottle down without pouring.

"What?" she pouted, folding her arms tightly across her chest, sucking in air through her teeth. "Now you not pour? Not let me taste?"

"Ah, Ying Yue," he teased, "did you not teach me never to present you with a gift directly?"

"Okay, okay," she responded. "Now you pressure! Sneaky, you! Try learn my ways!" He laughed.

The *aijiu* or *shaojiu* she normally drank was a distilled alcoholic beverage, sorghum-based, although some varieties were distilled from *huangjiu* or other rice-based drinks with an alcohol content greater than thirty percent. She kept on hand many varieties, shelved according to fragrance in her warehouse.

"Most these only distill one time," she explained. "Get better flavor and smell than vodka! You try." And, he did.

Next, she gave him Shaoxing Rice Wine, one of the most famous brands of Yellow Liquor. As the name suggested, yellow liquor was a spirit of yellow or brown color, containing less alcohol, fifteen to eighteen percent, with rich nutritional value.

"This one get better with age," she told him. "I keep in warehouse long time."

"You like try White Liquor?" she smiled. "Smell good and very tasty! Mao-t'ai best kind!"

"Enough! Enough for tonight," he begged off. He was feeling the effects of the alcohol and beginning to understand that Ying Yue was far more knowledgeable about many things than he ever imagined.

After he left, she poured a bowl of the Bergerac he brought, drank it slowly, and fell into a peaceful sleep.

He felt safe on her junk, safer than on his clipper ship, as the junk contained several holds to prevent sinkage. It sat flatter on the water and did not rock in the way the clipper ship did where he had to keep a firm hold on his tea cup. Of course, on the junk, the tea cup did not need a saucer, as it was made in the Chinese bowl style. Unlike English tea, her tea required neither milk nor sugar, and he slowly grew used to the taste.

She was lithe, young, graceful. He loved watching her daily practice of *qi gong*, which involved coordinated movement, breath, and awareness for health and meditation, all quite foreign to Merrill. She told him it was about the internal flow of *qi*.

"What *qi*? You like know what *qi*?" she asked in the early days of their time together. He nodded. "*Qi* energy, life. Watch." She took a deep breath, focused her eyes inward, sank a bit into her knees, folded her hands across one another, and whispered, "This first movement. Call Phoenix, bird that die and rise from ash." She rolled her hands toward her lower belly before raising them to roll outward as she twisted to the left. "In *qi gong*, I feel my *qi* flow, then I hold at gate. Then open. Like washing. Like washing dishes but it my body, it my mind, I wash."

When he stepped aboard her junk, he removed his heavy boots. He took to wearing a *ru*. It was a side opening jacket which hung to his knees with ties or "frogs" used as closures. They both relaxed in the loose fitting *yi*, which was any open cross-collar garment worn by both sexes, where the right side wrapped over the left.

As he learned to follow her movements, he stood on a worn red rug and loved the feel of it under his bare feet.

"I love this old thing," he remarked one day.

"Oh, that? It in my family ages. My father say great grandfather got from Morocco trader, Muslim. It call prayer rug."

"Muslims say you mustn't let a prayer rug get dirty," he scolded her. "Dirt defiles it."

"Ha! Lucky I not Muslim, then!" she laughed. She trod upon it many times a day, and it had grown ragged from misuse.

He loved the unique smell that came from the sesame oil used to cook river crabs, frogs, and fish for the crew's lunch or to stir fry noodles and vegetables. Ying Yue introduced him to Chinese food, mostly cooked on her wok and characterized using a variety of fresh ingredients, minimal seasoning, and quick cooking. She kept ducks aboard, allowing them to waddle on the deck, their wings clipped, feeding on discarded vegetable peelings and day-old rice. Roast duck was a dish she was very fond of in addition to the soups she made from a variety of fresh ingredients.

At sea, he had grown tired of the boiled meats and hardtack. Living in a coastal province, her family was particularly fond of seafood. Especially in winter, she served tench in a fish salad, raw. It was known as the "big-headed fish." Merrill was not a fish-eater but he learned from her. Only there in the south did the people eat food raw, enjoying delicacies such as newborn rats, monkey's brain, and fried snake. Chinese in other provinces regarded such food as revolting, and Merrill concurred, never trying any of these specialties despite her entreaties.

"Today I eat baby rat. I know you no like. I make you *congee*." He accepted the bowl of gruel made of rice or millet thankfully and turned away, so as not to see her consume her raw lunch.

Merrill sang, especially when they were sailing upriver with the wind in his face, and he could pitch his voice at full volume. He had a deep baritone and often rolled a sheet of paper into a megaphone raised to his lips to project his voice into the air like an actor in a Greek theatre. His favorite songs were from English art song composers like William Shield, famous for Robert Burns' song "Auld Lang Syne." Singing at the top of his lungs beneath the foremost red sail, Merrill belted out,

>"Should auld acquaintance be forgot,
>And never brought to mind?
>Should auld acquaintance be forgot,
>And auld lang syne?
>…For auld lang syne, my jo,
>For auld lang syne,
>We'll take a cup o' kindness yet,
>For auld lang syne."

The crew laughed and joined with what words they could as they sailed up river. Coming back, on sighting Lintin Island and her warehouses, Merrill delighted Ying Yue with his rendition of Sir Henry Bishop's "Home Sweet Home," which he had heard in London before his journey to China.

>"'Mid pleasures and palaces
>Though I may roam
>Be it ever so humble
>There's no place like home…
>To thee, I'll return…"

She played a *pipa*, a lute of five strings of twisted silk in the *wen* style, which was lyrical and slow in tempo. She favored its soft dynamic and subtle colour. She played it most often on calm nights when they could lie on the deck and watch the moon or sight the constellations. Its melancholy sound was soothing to their souls.

Her lover was English, new to the Orient, discreet in his visits, careful yet deeply confident in lovemaking. Atop, he grasped her braid tautly at the base of her neck like a lion steadying a lioness in heat, pulling her head back, forcing her to arch both up and away from him as though already orgasmic, which certainly brought her quickly enough to such a state.

She thrilled to the whisper of his breath on her neck, to the soft words of encouragement he almost growled. With him, it was all so simple. His fingers brushing first her shoulders, then before she realized it, her nipples, and then her belly and pubis. She lost interest in who might be watching, who might be present as time halted with her in his thrall, netted for pleasure, his and hers, taken by lust and longing to belong together, merged.

She was never one for rules or mores. She was alive and ready, always on the edge, the fringe, but diving, plunging into the next moment as though an Olympian hopeful, stepping confidently on the plank to do a triple whatever splash-less, quiet entry, monster dive. She tasted sweet and smelled feline. There was a deeper flavor beneath the sweetness, the taste of meat: she offered something chewy, something that lingered, that took a while to digest, a richness.

What had he sought and found in her? Quiet. Resplendence. Joy. She opened herself, her womb, allowing him entry to be reborn. What more could any man desire? She did not attempt to remake him, change him. She celebrated him exactly as she found him, never pointing out a flaw, and made him feel like a god capable of any achievement.

Was that not love?

Merrill ordered carved for her a tiny pendant in lavender jade in the shape of her junk, with its trapezoidal ribbed sails and crescent shaped hull. The pendant slung on a short and fine gold chain so that it cradled in the notch between her clavicles, below her melodious vocal cords, her voice that so reminded him of the song of the laughing thrush and the tinkle of the glass wind chimes suspended near the entry to the teak cabin. When she moved, he hoped, the pendant would swing free of the notch as though gently rocking on the waves.

He presented his gift with both hands. She refused it. It wasn't that she didn't want it. It was only polite to refuse a gift on first presentation.

He offered it again, saying,

"Jiang Ying Yue, beautiful and precious Jiang Ying Yue, please accept this humble token of my respect for you."

She took the small box and placed it casually on the table behind her.

"Aren't you going to open it?" he asked.

"Maybe later."

"Why not now?"

"So, Mister Merrill, this some worthless gift? If worthless, I open."

"I assure you, Jiang Ying Yue, it is of great value."

"Then you go. I embarrass. Maybe I open later. We see."

He left, confused. He related the incident to Jardine who had been in China much longer.

"Gifts of great value can only be given when a relationship is of equally deep value," Jardine explained in his cryptic manner.

She loved it, and sent a servant to summon Merrill back. They were married, a few months before Mr. Jardine's scheduled departure from Canton.

A respectable old woman from the merchant class helped Ying Yue prepare, tying her hair with colorful cotton threads. She wore a red silk skirt, a *qun*, because red symbolized happiness as well as life-sustaining blood. She wore ropes of golden pearls, as she believed they brought prosperity and luck, not to mention fertility.

Before the procession to the East India Company where the wedding was to take place, Ying Yue cried with the old woman who pretended to act as her mother, as her real mother was long dead, to symbolize the bride's reluctance to leave home. Ying Yue was supposed to be led or carried by an elder brother to the sedan. Her brothers refused. Her father refused. They were furious that she dared to marry a foreigner. As she had no brothers to help, she had no brothers anymore at all, as they disavowed her, two workers from the marina carried her from her junk in the wedding procession, which consisted of a traditional band, the bride's sedan, the maids of honor's sedans of which there were none, and her bride's dowry which was but a *pao*, the robe worn only by men, for her groom and a pair of scissors, a ruler, tea, and vases. A special cart pulled by a water buffalo held willow patterned vases along with the scissors, ruler, and tea. What this odd dowry represented was that scissors were like two butterflies never separating, the ruler measured the acres of fields they might amass, and the vases were for peace and wealth.

Merrill did not know how to give Ying Yue a ring. He remembered how she had responded to the jade pendant. This ring was his most important gift. Should he just slip the ring on her finger without saying a word? Or, put it on after she fell asleep on their wedding night, allowing her to discover it in the morning?

The gimmel ring came to him from a far distant relative in England. It had interlocking bands, wonderfully symbolic in that each band was free yet could meld with the other to create the whole. With early gimmel rings, the wedding couple each wore one of the bands prior to the wedding day. Then, they joined on the bride's venal finger to symbolize the union of two people as one. Many gimmel rings housed beautifully cut stones and ornately carved features highlighted with colorful enamels. Common symbols in gimmel rings were the fede hands, forget-me-not flowers, and red hearts.

Merrill thought this ring suited Ying Yue perfectly as its center piece was a pearl, like her moon, held by two golden hands. Inside each interlocking band was an engraving, one of a newborn, and the other, a skeleton, and when put together symbolizing a love reborn. He hoped she recognized that the pearl was old and of great value and not in any kind of competition with her own pearl business.

The entire foreign community entertained them at a dinner in the dining room of the East India Company's Factory. She made certain according to Chinese custom that the wedding ceremony was in the evening, considered to be a time of fortune. She taught him they first bowed to Heaven and Earth. Their second bow was to their ancestors, both Cantonese and British. The third bow was to their parents, who were not present, and the fourth to each other.

About eighty persons from many lands: India, England, America, Holland, Sweden, France, and Portugal, were present, and they did not separate until several hours after midnight. The wedding was an event frequently referred to for years afterwards amongst the residents, as it was almost unprecedented for a Westerner to marry a Chinese.

The gathering began with the traditional Chinese tea ceremony. Tea was an important item in any bride's dowry.

Then, in front of the party, they joined hair. Merrill had never heard of such a thing.

"In Ying Yue culture," she explained, "hair represent self. At wedding, bride and groom cut piece hair, tie together in knot. Okay? Put in silk bag. Safekeeping." She held aloft the dowry scissors and, reaching from behind, snipped a lock of Merrill's white hair. She quickly snipped an equal length of her own black hair and wove them into a braid.

Mystified, he soon took delight in this small ritual.

"Tying knot," she laughed, "mean you and Ying Yue one flesh, one blood."

Friends and workers, even Mr. Jardine, accompanied the bride and the groom into the bridal chamber, where they played a lot of tricks and teased the newlyweds. Then they shared drinks: she offered rice wine, he followed, pouring champagne for all and lifting his glass to hers. Their life was happy in China, she thought, and rich from the wealth of their secret trade.

But, when Merrill slipped the gimmel ring into her champagne, she dropped the glass to the floor, where it shattered, spattering the guests, and causing the discomfiture of all.

"What I tell you?" she cried. "No give me present! Make me lose face!" she imperiously shouted.

"Go! Out! Now!" she yelled, stomping her foot in its elaborately embroidered slipper. She turned her back to face the wall.

"Ying Yue, it is our wedding night. I cannot go!" he pled.

"You go, I stay!" as to her it was no laughing matter.

Her maid bent to pick up the broken glass; another servant ran in with a rag. The guests filed out, eyes downcast, the merry mood of the wedding broken like the glass. Merrill picked up the rings from the floor, and placed the two parts on the duvet. He did this quietly and left without saying another word.

When everyone was gone and the mess removed, Ying Yue picked up the ring from the bed to examine it. The pearl was opalescent and smooth, the golden hands clasping it dainty and feminine. An infant was carved inside one band, a skeleton in the other.

"Ah, Merrill!" she sighed. "You getting Chinese. This ring like Phoenix, new life rising from ash." She slipped one and then the other band on her finger where the ring fit perfectly. She understood the pearl represented the journey of the soul or spirit along the path to perfection. She traded in pearls and lived on the Pearl river, after all. She ran to the door to summon her maid.

"Go, go, bring Mister Merrill. Quick!"

They honeymooned in Guangdong where a wealth of scenic areas abounded should they choose to roust themselves from their mats to explore. It was a time away from trade and greed; a time to mirror themselves reflecting harmony as all honeymoons were meant to allow.

There was the lake near Dinghu Mountain at Zhaoqing, stunning with its deep and serene gorges, cold and clean waters for bathing. Nearby stood the Black Dragon Playing Pearls, Dragon Mother Borrowing a Vessel, and Heavenly Lake. Managing to sightsee, they climbed Mount Danxia with its karst penal rocks at Renhua. With a hired guide, they visited the Hundred Buddha Cave, Green Trees Surrounded by Clouds, Flying Waterfalls of the Dragon Pond, and Double Rainbows. Yunxi-Laoding had Water Curtain Cave, Dragon Hidden in the Ancient Pond, White Clouds Embracing Ancient Trees. Known as the "green gem on the Tropic of Cancer, the mountain's peaks rose above ancient towering trees and flying waterfalls.

It was a land where fresh breezes filled their lungs, various birds sang new songs, and flowers colored the landscape.

When they returned, fall slid into winter, and nights grew cold on the river. She gave him a gift, the first ever. It was a solitary gold pearl held by the mouth of a jade dragon. "You my protector, Merrill. You my good luck dragon."

Pirate Blues

"Merrill, Merrill!" she cried, running from her warehouse to the junk where he awaited her. "Imperial Commissioner Lin Tse-hsu destroy twenty thousand case opium!"

"What? Jardine just brought it on this morning's ship."

"Imperial Commissioner send warrant! He arrest your friend, Lancelot Dent!" Dent and Company held thirteen clipper ships. "Imperial Commissioner took all opium and shoo-shoo Dent, send Dent away."

Jardine, outraged by this huge loss, exclaimed, "I'll petition Parliament to declare war on the Chinese." After all, Jardine had nineteen intercontinental clipper ships in addition to hundreds of small ships, lorchas, and small craft for coastal and upriver smuggling he didn't want commandeered by the Chinese, which he now saw as a real possibility.

In fact, Lin Tse-hsu seized over twenty-thousand chests weighing thirteen hundred tons of opium without any compensation to the foreign merchants.

He also wrote Queen Victoria to demand a halt to the British trade in opium. Chinese Emperors had passed many decrees making the opium trade illegal but to little effect in 1729, 1799, 1814, and 1831. Smuggling had continued for over a century, as the British paid smugglers well.

The Daoguang Emperor of China wrote: "Opium has a harm. Opium is a poison, undermining our good customs and morality. I prohibit its use many times. Now the commoner, Yang, dares to bring it into the Forbidden City. Indeed, he flouts the law! The purchasers, eaters, and consumers of opium have become numerous. Deceitful merchants buy and sell it to gain profit. The customs house at the Chung-wen Gate was originally set up to supervise the collection of imports. If we confine our search for opium to the seaports, we fear the search will not be thorough. We should also order the general commandant of the police and police-censors to prohibit opium and to search for it at all five gates to our cities."

Trade and politics united when a deputy of the British crown assumed a newly created post of superintendent of foreign trade. The British superintendent had authority in China to directly call on the aid of British armed Forces and the Royal Navy in time of any serious trouble. If the Chinese crossed the superintendent, they insulted the British nation rather than simply finding fault with a business transaction.

Looking for a way to effectively police foreign trade and purge corruption, Lin and his advisers decided to reform the existing bond system. Under this system, a foreign captain and the *Cohong* merchant who had purchased the goods from his ship swore that the vessel carried no illegal goods. Infuriated upon examining the records of the port, Lin found that in the twenty most recent years China declared opium illegal, no one reported a single infraction.

Lin summoned Ying Yue and her family and all the other *Cohong*. He proclaimed, "All foreign merchants must sign a bond promising not to deal in opium under penalty of death. Make all merchants pay customs fees and measurement duties. Merchants must provide Chinese with gifts.

They must hire Chinese to navigate their ships on our waters."

The new British superintendent opposed signing the bond. "It violates the principle of free trade."

The merchants who did not trade in opium such as Olyphant & Co. signed. Trade in regular goods continued unabated. But, the scarcity of opium caused by the seizure of the foreign warehouses caused a black market to flourish. Some newly arrived merchant ships learned of the ban on opium before they entered the Pearl River estuary, and so they unloaded their cargoes at Lintin Island, *Nei Lingding*, the merchants' outer anchorage, where Ying Yue's family held sway.

Some of the *Cohong* trading houses and smugglers, who were able to evade commissioner Lin's efforts, smuggled more opium into China. Superintendent Elliot was aware of the smugglers' activities on Lintin and was under orders to stop them. Fearing any action by the Royal Navy might spark a war, he withheld his ships.

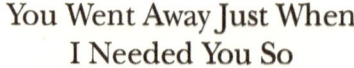

You Went Away Just When
I Needed You So

A cough developed in Merrill's chest from the damp and did not leave, despite the herbal teas she brewed for him, despite the warmth of her silk duvets, and despite her tiny body curled into his.

"I think it *lao*," she said, "that make you cough."

"*Lao?*" he asked.

"I think maybe you call consumption."

"Ah, consumption. Yes," he said. "Many people in England have that, especially the poor. The sailors on the ship coughed day and night. We had to throw some of the poor chaps who didn't make it overboard. We worried about contagion."

His joints ached, he felt listless, hardly able to get through his work at the warehouse each day. He feared falling victim to the white plague. As his nails began to fatten, looking like drumsticks, he ran a low-grade fever and suffered night sweats. He tired easily though he still rousted himself to work. She saw blood on his pillow.

"*Ku bo he,*" she told him one morning, putting a new tea in his cup. "Use for lung and spleen. It clear heat and phlegm; it move *qi*, it calm shake, fever, headache, red eye, coughing." He turned his head away.

"You drink my tea," she commanded, "and maybe you not be so irritable, maybe you feel like eat again."

"In England, Jardine says there's a cure," he told her.

"What kind cure?"

"An easy but certain cure he says is to mix two ounces of juice of horehound with a pint of milk sweetened with honey."

"You drink my *ku bo he*," she retorted, not knowing what horehound was.

"Listen," he said. "Jardine gave me an article. A physician of our London College, John Gerard, writes: syrup made of the green fresh leaves of the white horehound and sugar is a most singular remedy against the cough and wheezing of the lungs . . . and doth wonderfully and above credit ease such as have been long sick of any consumption of the lungs."

One night before drinking an infusion of *ku bo he,* he began mumbling. "Consumption, oh, consumption: the white death, the great white plague, the robber of youth, the king's evil…" he droned before falling asleep.

Jardine, readying to set sail for London, commanded Merrill return with him. "We'll find you a cure there for your lungs," Jardine assured him. "And, when you are well, I want you to accompany me to Parliament where we'll discuss the trade in China."

While his marriage survived in the East where English mores were not so rigidly upheld, Merrill knew Ying Yue would be a definite liability in London, looked upon as a servant or worse, as his whore. As a mixed couple, he feared being ostracized from all social privilege.

"Ying Yue," he said, in an effort to mitigate the pain of leaving her, "if I stay in China, I risk being caught for trafficking."

"You get killed, yes," she agreed. "Me, too. What think happen me, your Ying Yue?"

"No harm will come to you," he said. "You are *Cohong*."

"But, I like go," she stated.

He had learned by then that Chinese found "no" difficult to say. They might say "maybe" or "we'll see" to save face, but never "no." So, when she begged to go with him to London, he gently responded, "We'll see."

She staged temper tantrums. She told him she was pregnant, which may or may not have been true. She feigned urgency, demanding to go with him.

He stared into her eyes a long while. Then he said, "If this tuberculosis doesn't kill me before the ship sails, I must return to England for this cure."

She worried endlessly about his departure, whether from their marital bed, their Chinese river world by clipper ship, from life by consumption or perhaps by her own hand, as anger led her to begin imagining how she would kill him if he left her.

She wanted to kill him rather than let him go, a letting-go which she knew would kill her: she would die of a broken heart. She no longer had family; her father and brothers would not take her back.

She had access to herbal poisons and could feign dosing Merrill with a "remedy" in a pretense of finding the desired horehound. She could trip him at the dock and let him drown, as he, like many Englishmen, did not know how to swim. She could smother him with her neck pillow when he'd fallen asleep after making love to her for what would prove to be the last time.

Merrill left, and she slit her wrists with the sharp edge of the pendant's jade sail.

He left, and she stabbed her belly, killing their child.

He left, and she threw his pendant into the river.

He left, and she wept endlessly.

He left, and she set fire to their junk.

Or, did she?

What she did do was tear the jade pendant from her throat and press it into his hand. Looking deeply into his eyes, she demanded, "Hold jade as if it me."

And so, while he didn't openly refuse to take her on the voyage, when he finally did leave, her jade in a buttoned pocket, it was with Jardine, whose mission was to press Foreign Secretary, Lord Palmerston, for a forceful response to the Chinese. William Merrill left her behind, tied hair and all, to survive as a pirate or not, as only time and war would tell.

Her fantasies like her anger faded as she watched his ship sail from Canton. She entertained herself by practicing *qi gong* in the day and playing her *pipa* on most nights spent alone aboard the junk under the faint, ivory light of the moon, playing pieces describing love or sorrow, letting the notes glide out on the wind. She plucked the strings with a deliberateness; as she needed the music to drown the remembered sound of his breathing in her ears, the sound of his whispered endearments, the sound of his heart beating next to hers.

Sometimes, shadows flickered at the edge of her vision, then were gone. She felt severed in half, cut mid-torso. Did he know he had killed her?

She fell ill. A strange flu and ennui consumed her. She could not eat and if she tried, she vomited violently. She could not roust herself from her mat, lying for hours in semi-consciousness. Her crew asked if there was word of Merrill from every incoming vessel. And, week after tortured week, no letter came from him. She grew increasingly listless; her belly bloated with gases. There was no foreign trade to attend, and so she drifted alone in unhappiness on the swells of the river.

She wondered whether Merrill still lived and, if so, if he flourished in his resumed life in London. Or, whether he had succumbed to the consumption that so busily devoured his lungs in Canton. Perhaps, she thought, he never reached London. Perhaps he died aboard ship and was cast overboard to return to her on the tide as a seal or dolphin. No letter ever reached her, if he had written any, whether in red ink or in black.

She gave birth to a healthy boy with a head of wavy black hair, the black her color, the waves like Merrill's. The sight of this baby, this new child assaulted her senses. She bled. She was bleeding, Blood was everywhere. She felt faint. The room was dark, so dark. The child was silent, so silent.

"You eat!" ordered the wife of one of her crew, waking Ying Yue from her slumber. "Get strong fast! Soup bring out old blood," the woman assured her as she spoon-fed a simple boiled soup of pig's feet, Chinese black vinegar, ginger, coconut sugar, and salted duck eggs. "No eat or drink cold. Eat hot! Cold not good."

Months later it seemed, Ying Yue lay abed, the opening shot of a cannon barely rousing her. British cannon balls flew across the Pearl, demolishing Chinese junks, some of hers among them. Her brothers, whom she hadn't seen in months or was it years, raced below deck to lift her from her bed and carry her to relative safety behind their furthermost warehouse. They settled her, then raced back to the dock.

The first opium war was underway. Another of what were to be hundreds of cannon balls struck. She didn't learn until much later that her father and her brothers were blown to bits along with many others on the island. All communication disbanded while the fighting went on, quashing any lingering question of Merrill's fate. She did not worry when she did not hear from her family as they were estranged anyway, at least they were until her brothers carried her to safety. She felt like an exile, a refugee from the violence and terror surrounding her.

She dreamt. She sailed on her small *kakam* on a red sea, the sea and sky co-joined in color, bleeding crimson, lit by orange cannon fire. And, then there was silence. She was alone. She was not sailing. She was drifting alone in that silence on that red sea in a perpetual sunset, drifting nowhere, drifting toward oblivion.

A son, her son also drifted, carelessly through her mind like a gentle lemon mist, refreshing and beguiling. He was so beautiful. A special creature like a unicorn. She loved his almost smile, that *Mona Lisa* look. She was never quite certain it was a smile, but she called it such anyway.

When the confinement ended along with the fighting and her health returned, Ying Yue learned of her family's death. The crew member's wife brought the news.

"Where son? Where my son?" Ying Yue asked.

"What baby?" the crewmember's wife shrugged. "Baby no smile. That gas."

"You fed soup after baby came! 'Stop blood,' you said."

"You sick, very, very sick. I feed soup. You better."

There was no son? There was no baby? She did not see a baby anywhere.

Ambivalence ruled. Had six months really gone by? Had her baby died? Had she not seen Merrill for those six months? O where had time gone? Had the tide of her, of herself, washed out, leaving a bare-bottomed bay of flopping memories, wet and salted with tears? Had she not been able to save her son? Had her baby weakened? To not know was torture, not to be able to save her son was torture. No one knew what it was to have someone so dear, so precious, so hoped for, lost. Was it her fate to have her heart while it still beat torn from her body?

"There is good reason son and sun are pronounced the same," she thought. "Because, sons, my son, are suns shining brightly, lighting life." And, she had lost her son, her sun, her light, her warmth, her delight.

"Ma," he said when he came to her one day, many years later when he was grown and she was living in Kunming before Sultan Du died in that next life, clasping her hands in his as they sat for a meal, "Ma! You don't get it, do you? You just don't get it."

"Get what?" she asked, completely puzzled.

"Nothing. Nothing. Never mind." And, never mind was how he left. He left. Yes, she remembered he left. He got up and left without eating. He left, didn't he? Her son? Well, in any case, he wasn't there. And, maybe, just maybe, he never was. She didn't know for sure.

Her warehouses on Lintin Island went miraculously unscathed. And, Ying Yue finally became the pirate Merrill taught her to be. Her role as surviving *Cohong* strengthened as did her illicit trade in opium, making her very, very rich. After the death of her father and brothers, and so many others, she became the most powerful *Cohong* in Canton. She had wealth, control, and prestige. Best, she had knowledge and experience. She could deal with the smuggling and the foreigners.

Ying Yue converted her large junks into floating warehouses, anchored off the Chinese coast at the mouth of the Pearl River in case the Chinese authorities moved forcefully against the opium trade again, as the ships of the Chinese navy had difficulty operating in open water. Inbound opium ships unloaded a portion of their cargo onto her floating warehouses, where Chinese opium dealers purchased it. By implementing such a system of smuggling, foreign merchants avoided inspection by Chinese officials and prevented retaliation against the trade in legal goods.

The First Opium War, fought over this illegal trade, financial reparations, and diplomatic status, began in 1839. Ying Yue learned that it was Jardine who persuaded Parliament to fight the Chinese. The war that resulted in her family's death was that old man's doing in addition to taking her Merrill away. She hated Jardine. She wanted revenge, but the best revenge she found was wealth and property, and she amassed both. She survived that first and then the second Opium War.

The East India Company sent the opium to warehouses in the free trade region of Canton. She, the newly minted pirate, took the opium up the Pearl River farther into China. She continued to work hard, never once trying the opium she trafficked. She did not want to lose herself in dreams, even though dreams were all she knew.

Thirty to forty percent of Chinese soldiers at the time of the First Opium War carried matchlock muskets. Though the British fought with around nineteen thousand troops and the Chinese with two hundred twenty thousand, the British only lost sixty-nine men while the Chinese lost almost twenty-thousand. The British warships like the *Nemesis* cannoned the Chinese junks and soldiers, killing thousands and taking Hong Kong as well as the ports of Shanghai, Canton, Ningpo, Fuchow and Amoy as part of a subsequent peace treaty.

As a respected matriarch, was she a matriarch? Ying Yue took her fortunes to Hong Kong. What changed when she moved to Hong Kong was that she learned to take pleasure in luxury instead of in love. She invested in property, feeling secure under British rule, and hoping that Merrill would come back to her, if not as a seal or dolphin, perhaps as a magistrate.

Jardine remained very much active in business and politics. He built a townhouse at 6 Upper Belgrave Street, then a new upscale, residential district in London near Buckingham Palace. He bought Lanrick Castle in Scotland, and became a partner in the merchant banking firm of Magniac, Smith & Co., later renamed Magniac, Jardine & Co., the forerunner of the firm Matheson & Co. Jardine even got himself elected to the House of Commons.

Prior to the 1868 Pharmacy Act, which restricted the sale of opium to pharmacists, opium was widely available in England. Its uses were manifold, from toothaches and bruises to cough and diarrhea. The working class typically purchased opium at the grocer and took it as a stimulant prior to going to work. Mothers found laudanum, a form of opium, useful for quieting babies.

Then, in 1874, the Society for the Suppression of the Opium Trade campaigned against Britain's involvement in the opium trade with China.

"My, my," Ying Yue thought, sitting in the cool of her veranda high above Hong Kong harbor, "how the world changes." Suppression of the trade did not matter to her any longer, for she had invested her money in other venues: her three "P" s of Prosperity: Property, Porcelain, and Pearls.

BLIP SIX

A Ray of Sun Burning Through
the Darkest Night

Ying Yue, yes, Lucky found herself once again Ying Yue, sailed her junk up the Pearl to consult the Dark Warrior at her ancestral temple, Zumiao. Her foo dog, Huo-ji, had aged but still traveled everywhere with her. The Dark Warrior indicated she should not return to Hong Kong, but rather continue northwest to the source of the Pearl. There, he said, she would find happiness.

"Find Quan Yin, the goddess of compassion, and you will know yourself," the Dark Warrior prophesied.

She voyaged for several weeks far up the Pearl. On the way, she heard talk of unrest to the West. A rebel named Du was leading followers of Islam—Muslims—against the emperor. Although Du was the son of a Han Chinese, he had publicly converted to Islam. This Du led both Hui Muslims and Han Chinese in a rebellion against the Imperial Qing government, declaring themselves to be a separate political entity from China.

Du's rebels captured the ancient, holy city of Dali on the shores of Erhai Lake, the very place where Ying Yue was heading. It became the base for the rebel operations. Du proclaimed it the "Islamic Kingdom of Yunnan."

A true leader and hero, foreigners called him Sultan, establishing Muslim supremacy in Yunnan.

Dali was a beautiful place, sacred as well with its Buddhist Chong Shen Monastery. Beyond the walls of the old city sprawled traditional homes and towers from the Bai ethnic minority. Three Pagodas rose pencil-like into the sky in ten layers and within each layer stood Buddha statues sculpted from white marble. Umbrella-like roofs with copper gourds and copper bells capped these white towers. The clear waters of the lake reflected the pagodas making Dali town look like a charming painting. Fields of emerald grasses flanked the snow-capped Cangshan Mountain, itself surrounded by cloud and mist to the west of the Three Pagodas, where the ripples of the lake pushed against its eastern shore.

There Muslim Hui men wore white prayer caps with traditional Chinese clothing including the Chinese suit and a robe called a *changshan*. The rule that Muslim men could not wear silk was ignored in China, because in China, silk clothings were unisex, while in the Arab world, silk was a feminine fabric.

On the ear-shaped Erhai, known as the pearl on the plateau, sat tiny Putuo Island. And, on Putuo sat a Buddhist temple. And, on the second floor sat Avalokiteshvara, known as Quan Yin. Ying Yue came upon the island in early morning while a mist lay over the lake, shrouding the green island in mystery. She thought the island rose like a seal from the water and immediately wondered if Merrill was returning to her as she imagined he would, as a seal.

When Du stepped onto her junk, she recognized him though she had never seen her husband incarnated as Chinese before. There was the usual shock of white, wavy hair, unusual for a Chinese, curling out from the confines of an elaborately embroidered cap, the eyes of gold-flecked hazel she knew so well, the thick, leonine hand like a paw, its fingers firmly grasping his sword hilt. She was surprised, as it usually took a century or two before they reunited.

"Ah," she gasped, "you've come back so quickly!"

He thought the junk carried an emissary of his adversary, the Qing emperor, with whom he was to meet on Putuo Island. After a preliminary search, he found no such adversary. What he did find was Huo-ji, sleeping on a frayed Moroccan prayer rug. Du recognized both the dog and the rug immediately. How often had he practiced *qi gong* on it barefoot on the junk on the Pearl tied up at Lintin Island when he was Merrill? So, at the very moment Ying Yue unwittingly sailed back into his life, Du also stepped into hers.

He was not a seal, of course, the seal she imagined. Merrill came back as Du, the "Sultan of Dali," leader in the Sultanate's civil and military bureaucracy. He and his men wore cotton robes to Friday prayer, *jumu'ah*, and he mandated the use of the Arabic language in his regime. He even banned pork, a staple in China, from the people's diet.

With him, Lucky's dormant knowledge of Islam reawoke as memories of her time as Hiza in Fez returned, though she had lived that life almost five hundred years earlier. As Ying Yue, she resumed prayers five times each day on the worn prayer rug on her junk. Du prayed at a mosque he had built atop a Buddhist site he razed in the rebellion. The resurgence of faith bathed her in a moral universe long-abandoned in her previous lives, whether English or Chinese. The ritual of daily prayer made her mindful of each step she took in this life. She hoped on her death to be worthy to enter the garden Muslims call *Jannah*. And so, she left behind much of her life: piracy, haughtiness, and greed. But, the single vice she failed to leave behind was lust.

"You help me extend my life," Du told her, his eyes shining.

"How?" she asked.

"Many ancient Taoist texts I study call the act of sex 'the battle of stealing and strengthening.' Man's life extends through the absorption of the woman's vital *qi* and *jing*. My father taught me that *qi* is part of everything in existence."

"I know. Don't you remember I practice *qi gong?*" she asked him.

"*Qi* is related to another energetic substance, a fluid, contained in the human body known as *jing*. When all *qi* and all *jing* are spent making love, my father cautioned, your body will die. Semen, he believed, contained the most *jing*. 'Do not ejaculate!' My father warned. 'Must conserve life essence.'"

Du told her he believed loss of ejaculatory fluids resulted in premature aging, disease, and general fatigue. Retention of the semen was one of his foundational tenets.

She oft awoke to the weight of him above her. She knew it was he by the silvered glint of hair captured between her lids partially opened. As she closed her eyes, sinking back into the reverie of sleep, she saw behind the black curtain of her lids, a horizon suffused with color. It was not the moon which blinded her, but rather a setting sun emblazoned by reddened flames. It felt to her as though she, too, was suffused by its colors, its yellow tongued rays licking the canvas of her waking dream.

But, it was he. It was his tongue and his light that roused her, pressing her eyes shut not only by the vision but also by the pleasure. He caressed her eyes with his lips, lips slightly opened, whispering as though to gild the lashes of her rapture with edges of gold. As the pressure of his touch ebbed, she opened her eyes, only to close them in the ecstatic onrush penetrating the wetlands of her dream. The crimson of his ardor warmed her, heating her loins, melting her body into a pool pulsating like the liquid in the cratered landscape of her volcanic isle, heated beyond the boiling point, forcing its steam to rise. And so, he fountained love upon the surface of her sleep, the colors of her inner sun vaporizing into the dawn of an ancient moon.

They came often. Each coming propelled them further into the spaciousness of their love, broadening their horizons, solidifying their union. Yet, in this union, their bodies were not important. They had a map and a destination, they simply needed a vehicle to get them there…whether a horse, a sleigh, a palanquin, a camel, a plane, a boat, a magic carpet…so, being carnal creatures, the vehicle they used was their bodies. They were the carriages, unimportant in and of themselves, taking them on the journey to the place of union of harmony and of soul.

She longed for the feeling of his touch, hot and wet in open pursuit of happiness. That first touch, that entry thrilled her, excited her beyond her initial longing, heated her loins and heart, raising her temperature up and up into an ever expanding universe of joy, allowing her mind to set aside worries and woes, and, upon full and deep entry, to launch her body as a rocket loosened from its mooring to shoot her in a high-reaching propulsion to the moon and stars and, if lucky, allow her to orbit like a probe entering far galaxies of pleasure for light-years to come.

How they loved. How they fulfilled and complimented each other's rarely contemplated yet evident desires. He licked the salt from orifices, kissed those same openings, whether of an ear or an armpit or a navel or a place below. He loved her saltiness and she, his. She licked the salt from his lips and stubble, his navel, his groin. She ran her tongue from his wrist to his clavicle and down, down his ribs to his hips, and from there, oh, a stop, and what a lengthy stop to suck and drink, only to move lower to run her tongue down the inside of his left thigh to his knee, circle round it, down to his tibia and ankle, landing at last on his toes, to enclose his big toe in her mouth as though it were his member and to linger there, kissing and caressing it, hugging it in the warmth of her mouth, before releasing it, catching her breath, as she moved to the right toe, repeating her motions as she moved up that leg, tenderly, so tenderly, until she reached his fully erect and gyrating manhood, and after taking it quietly into her mouth to swallow it, yes swallow it, drawing it deep into her throat, she let go and pulled herself upright to sit atop his tower of love to begin another type of ascent, this one together.

Du ingeniously employed his sexual methods in his military maneuvers. Instead of storming the gates, the battles he waged were often a series of feints designed to slowly sap his enemy's resistance.

If no fighting was going on, Ying Yue enjoyed pillow life with Du far more. A pleasing concept he employed at times of peace was "the joining of the essences." He said their lovemaking created *jing*, and he could transform some of this jing into *qi* replenishing his own lifeforce. By having as much sex as possible, he had the opportunity to transform more *jing*, and he imagined he experienced many health benefits.

Yang referred to the male sex, whereas yin referred to the female. Man and woman were the equivalent of heaven and earth, but became disconnected. Therefore, while heaven and earth were eternal, man and woman suffered a premature death.

Every interaction between Yin and Yang had significance. Because of this significance, he taught her that every position and action in lovemaking was important. They studied Taoist texts by candle light learning many special positions that served to cure or prevent illness.

He wanted Ying Yue to be stimulated and pleased from coupling. He believed one of the reasons women possessed strength was that they walked away undiminished from the act of sex. They brought forth life and did not have to worry about ejaculation or a refractory period of rest.

During times of the rebellion, when he had to direct and fight in the battles, Du pulled out immediately before orgasm. Or, he placed Ying Yue's thumb on his perineum, applying pressure to allow him to retain his sperm. This practice caused him to have a retrograde ejaculation, in which he believed his *jing* traveled up into his head to nourish his brain.

Ying Yue possessed a dynamic life force, and it kept Du enthralled with her. She was playful, kittenish, liking to lick him and growing feline when he licked her. When his licks became faster and more staccato, she emitted fierce cries, pushing him away only to press his tongue back into her, deeper this time. If he added his fingers to his tongue, she moaned, and if he added a finger or two in her nether orifice, her impassioned grunts sounded far beyond their quarters.

Du rolled her onto her stomach, mounted her, and bit the nape of her neck without drawing blood as he became the lion himself, dominating her with his teeth and his thrusts. Coming, she mewled, and he thrust harder and longer, and she mewled again, and again. Her explosions of *jing* ran down the front of her pinioned legs, wetting the sheets, and he roared with satisfaction.

Du read the Qu'ran aloud to Ying Yue after morning prayer. In the evenings, she played her *pipa*, the same stringed lute she used to soothe Merrill on many of their nights on the Pearl. Du ruled from 1856 to the end of 1872. His Sultanate, fashioned after those of' the Middle East, reached the highwater of its power and glory in 1860; the eight years from 1860 to 1868 marking its heyday.

When their world was at peace, she and Sultan rode by horseback to high Mt. Cangshan with its nineteen snow-crested peaks, located to the west of the lake. Eighteen streams flowed eastward from the peaks to fill the lake. She kept her junk, and together they sailed on Erhai's clear, green water. At night, they admired what they imagined was a rabbit pounding an elixir of life for the moon goddess, *Chang'e*, in the albino moon reflected on the calm surface of the lake.

Sultan said, "Ying Yue, people here believe the snow on the mountains and the bright moon above the lake symbolize lovers' vows."

"Ah, so what is your vow to me?" she asked.

"My life," he replied. "My love as white and pure as that light. I am but the snow reflecting the light of your moon in the darkness all around us."

And, so it was.

"Ying Yue," Du said, "We are going to find Shuxing'a."

"Is he here in city?" she asked. Shuxing'a was the Manchu who started a massacre of Muslims.

"We believe so. He hates all Muslims after he was nearly killed by some."

"What happened?" she asked.

"He behaved outrageously toward us for a long, long time. A mob got hold of him. They stripped Shuxing'a naked and nearly lynched him from a gingko tree. They weren't Hui Muslims, like us. They belonged to another ethnicity. But, Shuxing'a blamed all Muslims for the incident."

"Did he hurt anyone?"

"Hurt? Oh yes. Before you came, he killed over three thousand Muslims. And, in further retaliation, Shuxing'a ordered many Muslim rebels to be slowly sliced to death."

"Ahhh," she gasped, horrified. She had seen the British style of warfare with cannons and guns, but she had never witnessed Manchu cruelty.

"Do you blame Han Chinese for massacres of Hui Muslims?" she asked.

"No. I blame the tension squarely on the Manchu. The Manchu are foreign to China and alienate the Chinese and other minorities like us. I am going to call for their complete expulsion." And, he did. Du hung banners around the city that said "Deprive the Manchu Qing of their Mandate to Rule."

"Our army has three tasks," he declared. "Drive out the Manchus, unite with the Chinese, and eliminate traitors." He and his followers determined to destroy the Manchu government and the Qing court. The Hui of Yunnan rose against oppression. They rose against the tyranny and extortion universally practiced by the official Mandarin class which hounded minorities, provoked riots, and destroyed mosques.

Du came running one day, yelling, "Ying Yue! The rebellion has started!"

"How?"

"The laborers of the silver mines of Lin'an village in Yunnan! They rose against the Qing. The Chinese Governor of Yunnan has sent an urgent appeal to the central government in Beijing."

Problems erupted all over the sprawling empire, crippling the Imperial government. After the Manchu massacred even more Hui, the rebellion gained momentum in earnest. Du used anti-Manchu rhetoric against the Qing, calling for Han, fed up after two hundred years of cruel rule, to join his rebellion. Ying Yue was surprised to see that his forces were not only made up of Muslims but also included Han Chinese, Li, Bai, and Hani. They chanted Du's revolutionary slogans: "Have Peace with Han, Down with Qing Court, Unite Hui and Han as One, Erect Flag of Rebellion, Get Rid of Manchu Barbarians, Resurrect China, Cut Away Corruption,

Save People from Water and Fire!"

During the revolt, men from provinces which were not in open rebellion, like Sichuan and Zhejiang, served as negotiators between rebel Hui and the Qing government. The revolt was not religious in nature, since Muslim Shan, Kakhyen, and other non-Muslim hill tribes joined. Du invited the fellow Hui Muslim leader Ma Rulong to join him. Together, they repulsed the desultory attacks of the imperial troops. Du wrested one important city after another from the hands of the Mandarins. If a Chinese town or village resisted, he pillaged it and massacred the male population. If they yielded, Du spared them.

After the Hui took or destroyed forty towns and one hundred villages, Du, as Sultan, went with Ying Yue on a pilgrimage to Mecca. They visited Rangoon, via the Kengtung route, and from there to Calcutta where he had a chance to see the power of the British colonists. He created governorships of the sultanate in a few important cities, such as Momein, not far from the Burmese border.

Kunming city rapidly grew to become the major market and transport centre for the region. But, years earlier, an earthquake displaced many there. On multiple occasions, Du's rebel forces attacked and sacked Kunming city. Du's comrade, Ma Rulong, besieged it as well. But, bribed with a military post, Ma quit the siege and defected to the central government forces. The Sunni Muslims under Ma readily defected, while the Sufi Muslims did not.

Most of Du's followers remained loyal. They killed the Governor-General and wrested control of the city again from Ma Rulong and the Qing. Ma Rulong had only pretended to surrender in order to gain access to the city of Kunming. Ma left, taking many of Du's loyalist Muslim forces with him, thereby helping the Qing. Ma's betrayal might have had to do with the varying sects of Islam practiced among the rebels.

The rebels waited to hand the city over to Du. However, before Du's forces arrived, the traitor, Ma Rulong—with the assistance of a rising Qing military officer, Cen Yuying—raced back to Kunming. Like a match of ping pong, the city was volleyed back and forth. And, in the final battle, the rebels lost Kunming yet again.

Du's power declined as the Chinese Imperial government reinvigorated itself. The Chinese, though suffering the loss of more than twenty-thousand lives, soon directed a campaign to annihilate Du's obdurate Hui Muslims. By degrees, the Imperial government tightened the cordon around the Sultanate. Town after town fell under well-organized attacks from imperial troops. Dali itself was besieged. Du found himself caged in by the walls of his own capital. He realized that only British military intervention could save his Sultanate.

The British authorities in India and British Burma sent a mission led by Major Sladen to Momien that spring and summer for seven weeks. The main purpose of the mission was to revive the Ambassador Route and resuscitate border trade, which had almost ceased, mainly because of the Yunnan rebellion. A British officer testified later that the Muslims did not rebel for religious reasons, and that the Chinese were tolerant of different religions and were unlikely to have caused the revolt by interfering with the practicing of Islam.

Taking advantage of the friendly relations resulting from Sladen's visit, Sultan, in his fight for the survival of his Yunnan Kingdom, turned to the British for vitally needed military assistance. Ying Yue knew British traders well as Britain was the only western power with whom the Sultanate was on friendly terms. Desperately looking for outside help, he sent his beloved Ying Yue with a personal letter to beg the British for military assistance. British Burma accorded Ying Yue and her mission courtesy and hospitality. However, the British refused Du's request to intervene militarily in Yunnan against Peking.

Ying Yue returned to Dali, her mission a failure, at the very time the Imperial government waged an all-out war against the Sultanate, this time with the help of French artillery experts. Their modern equipment, trained personnel and numerical superiority were no match for the ill-equipped Sultanate. Thus, in less than two decades of its rise, the power of the Muslims in Yunnan fell.

But, Sultan Du refused to surrender. Seeing no escape and no mercy from the relentless Imperial foes, Du wanted to take his own life. But, he was captured before he could do so. He drank opium, but before it took full effect, his enemies dragged him into the courtyard. Ying Yue closely followed, only to be blinded by a sudden glint of silver slicing through the air and a spray of red wetting her clothes. Huo-ji, old as the dog was, ran frantically barking around his master, who toppled to the ground, beheaded, blood pulsing on the ground where his body fell. In a second swift motion, the executioner brought his sword through the air a second time, cutting the loyal dog in half. Ying Yue witnessed in horror the double misfortunes of her lover and her dog. Her beloved Sultan's body writhed without its head, and Huo-ji lay split in two bloody parts.

The prize the enemies sought was Du's head, which the executioner whisked away and dispatched preserved in honey to the Imperial Court in Peking, as a trophy and testament to the decisive nature of the Imperial Chinese victory over the rebels of Yunnan.

Alone when the soldiers left, Ying Yue gathered Du's body in her arms. Then, laying it back down, she bathed it with warm water as was the custom on the dirt where it lay. She ripped three sheets of white cotton and wrapped him in them as a shroud. Quietly, she said *salah*. She had this headless body secretly carried to a cave near Xiadui outside of Dali by his followers where she hoped it would not be desecrated. She made sure the body lay on its right side and faced the direction of Mecca. She grabbed three fistfuls of dirt, placing one where his head should have rested, one where his chin should have been, and the third under his shoulder. She wrapped Huo-ji in a white shroud as well and placed him nearby in a shallow depression. Then, she carefully watered each of her beloveds' graves.

His followers performed the *janazah* before finally sealing the tomb, reciting, "We created you from it, and return you into it, and from it we will raise you a second time."

Sunni Islam demanded her expression of grief to remain dignified, prohibiting loud wailing, shrieking, beating her chest or cheeks, tearing her hair or clothes. She was angry, deeply angry. But, it was anguish that crushed her heart. The Dark Warrior had told her to find Quan Yin. She had. But, what had the goddess of compassion done to help her? Where was the Dark Warrior's promise of happiness?

Manchu troops massacred the rebels, killed thousands of civilians, and sent severed ears along with the heads of their victims to Peking. Even so, scattered remnants of the Yunnan troops continued to resist. Persecutions began. When Imperial troops besieged and stormed Momien, the resistance broke completely. Du's troops saw their governor captured and executed. The Imperial mandarins hunted down all adherents to the Yunnan cause.

Thus, within two decades of its rise, the power of the Muslims in Yunnan fell. The bloody rebellion caused the deaths of up to a million people. For a period of perhaps ten to fifteen years following the collapse of the Yunnan Muslim Rebellion, the victorious Qing widely discriminated against the province's Hui minority, especially in the western frontier districts contiguous with Burma. During these years, as the refugees settled across the frontier within Burma, the Hui gradually established themselves in their traditional callings – as merchants, caravaneers, miners, restaurateurs, smugglers, or mercenaries. Those Muslims who fled with their families across the Burmese border took refuge in the Wa State, where they set up an exclusively Hui Muslim town they called Panglong.

But, Ying Yue was not among them. Ying Yue did not stay to observe a three-day mourning period after Du's burial. Instead, she ran. She fled west, crossing Burma, India, the Bosphorus, then across Greece and Italy to France, choosing to mourn Du once she was safely far away, rather than risking her own life in China as the fallen hero-now-traitor's widow. She knew she had a life to live elsewhere.

BLIP SEVEN

Blinded by Love

Once, she was born in Delphi on the steep southern slope of Mount Parnassus where one of the priests impregnated her mother, a sybil, the Pythia at the oracle of Apollo. The Pythia normally sat on a tripod above a crack in the earth where vapors rose around her as she was brandished with bay leaves by the priests. Her prophecies were believed to come from divine inspiration; her frenzied utterances rushing from lips through which the people believed the gods spoke. Often, a Pythia was a woman of prodigious old age, well-educated and well-read, even married. But, the girl's mother was young, taken from her parents by the priests as a child and kept at the temple of Apollo at Delphi, where they said Tiresias, the blind prophet of the god, transformed into a woman, a transformation that lasted for seven years. There, the priests translated the young Pythia's uttered nonsense into Greek hexameters and dispensed it as prophecy.

The priest raped the young Pythia, held captive underground, away from any watchful eyes or awaiting ears. In a dazed state of euphoria from days inhaling smoke and herbs, the Pythia could not recall the identity of the priest.

Dishonored when she gave birth and banished from Delphi to the low, farmland of Amfissa, the fallen Pythia raised her child alone in an olive grove where she eked out a living and found shelter in a sheep shed.

She named the child Tyche, which meant good luck, which the mother knew her daughter would need. The disgraced Pythia taught the girl to read, told her tales of old, and trained her in the art of making the clay *amphora* needed to store olives and the jugs called *oinochoe* to hold oil. The girl grew strong and agile, climbing the sides of Mount Parnassus gathering faggots each day to tie on a donkey's back for the return by dusk to the shed for cooking and warmth. In the orchards, she shook the olive trees vigorously, forcing them to drop their fruits. She crawled over the orchard floor on her knees, stained and scraped, gathering the fallen olives into baskets. She loved the olive trees and groves. In the winter, before the trees yielded the fruit and oil she pressed, she shaped many pots and fired them with the dried dung from a neighbor's cattle. The olives became symbols of peace and friendship.

Her only real friend was the guardian of the Pythia's flocks, a large dog, a muscular beast, Molossus. Though fiercely aggressive, the dog wore a spiked collar to protect itself from the attacks of wolves and would do anything for the girl. They slept side by side, and particularly so if they stayed in the fields at night where the danger of wolves was real.

The Pythia gave the girl-- along with a donkey-- to an olive oil trader. From Athens, he was a regular at their table each season when he came to collect their barrels for the market. Year after year, he had carefully watched Tyche grow until she reached adolescence. She rode off with him on his cart one autumn day just after her fourteenth birthday. The cart rolled slowly down the dirt road, then turned up the mountain, lurching to one side or the other as it hit a stone or two or more, the faithful Molossus running behind, barking. Abandoned at the shed and despite the Pythia's attempt to hold him fast, Molossus rebelled against restraint.

"Please! Stop the cart!" Tyche begged the trader. With his help, she gained the mighty dog a perch atop the barrels, He grappled there for stability but remained quiet during the rest of the tiresome, sixty, dusty miles to Athens, a journey that took them several days.

Tyche spent her first nights as a bride at *lesche*, which were public stops along the way. But, near Thebes they found an inn which held a bed better than any she had ever known. It was not easy to rest with the oil trader next to her instead of Molossus.

Once settled in Athens, as a wife, she found herself confined to the house.

"Why can I not go out?" she begged her husband. "I always ran free at home. I went to the orchard and the mountain every day!"

"It's not allowed in the city," he explained. "Good women are never outside the home."

She longed for the outdoors, for the country, for books, for her pottery, for friends, for her mother. Her only true companion was Molossus, who longed almost for the very same things. He paced the inner courtyard hour after hour, lifting his muzzle to sniff the sky above and gaze at the passing clouds not confined to four dull walls as he now was. Dread loneliness would have possessed them had they not had each other. She told and retold Molossus the stories she'd learned from the Pythia and some she invented herself as they endured far too many uneventful afternoons.

Her husband acquired a slave girl, known as a *metic*, as his business grew, who shopped the markets for food and fabric. Slaves were the only females free to walk in public. The slave girl spoke only broken Greek and was hardly a suitable companion for Tyche. Merchants brought necessities the *metic* could not obtain for Tyche to purvey at home as was the custom.

The oil merchant was known throughout Athens and its surrounds by the excellence of the olives and oil he sold. Throubes black olives he took in baskets for the market and did not press as eating them fresh from the tree was best. Plum olives harvested in November were large, and he recommended they be fermented or baked. Nafplion green olives grew in the valley of Argos in the Eastern Peloponnese peninsula, a fifty-mile cart ride and several days away. Kalamata red olives were picked once fully ripened in December. The trader traveled by cart to collect large wooden barrels filled with the fruits at various and far flung parts of the country, which meant he was away a lot, leaving his young wife bored and anxious.

Several barrels of the tiny green and black olives he had bought from her mother back in Amfissa stood in the courtyard of his Athens house. Most of these he took one day, along with several barrels of prized oil, to the port of Piraeus to ship to clients in Thrace far to the north.

"We'll be rich from this shipment," he told Tyche with great enthusiasm. "We'll celebrate on my return. Have the *metic* help with household chores and prepare some *fassolatha* for my return." With those words, he departed Athens on his cart pulled by both his donkey and hers.

Quite unexpectedly, he failed to return from Piraeus. Days passed with no word from him. Tyche sent the slave girl to the port to make inquiries. The walk to Piraeus took the girl two days whilst a white sheeted sky closed out the sun, preventing the days from waking properly. It imposed a shrouded humidity across the bed of that world. The days didn't pour rain; instead, they absorbed moisture, allowing it to ooze like a sponge squeezed now and again by the hand of a god. The flocks of pigeons that rose and fell with the drizzle were only slightly grayer than the sea and stony shore.

Once there, at a nearby *taverna*, the slave learned that there had been a dispute a week or so before. She found her master's cart close to the dock where it stood empty, but the donkeys were nowhere to be seen. In the *taverna*, the men sat on small wooden stools. They told the *metic* that authorities held the cart. A local merchant had taken the donkeys and was surely returning with them to the trader's widow the next time he traveled to Athens.

"But, I do not understand what happened to the trader," the slave said, puzzled.

One of the men who was cleaning his teeth with the long fingernail he grew on his baby finger said he witnessed the calamity.

"After the trader stowed his barrels of oil in the hold of the ship, the owner of the large trireme demanded money. He yelled 'Pay me, pay me!' so loudly we all stopped to listen. The cheat was going to take the trader's cargo! We saw the trader show a bill of lading: proof of his prior payment for transport. But, their argument escalated."

"What happened?" the metic asked.

The witness continued, "The trader charged past the owner and ran up the gang plank. 'I'll take my barrels back!' he shouted. But, dozens of oarsmen began boarding at that moment."

This trireme like many others had been decommissioned at the end of the Battle of Salamis. It was currently used for trade. It housed over one hundred and seventy oarsmen on its three levels, most of the men slaves, to power it across the sea.

"The slaves," the man went on, "accidentally knocked the trader off balance from behind. I saw his head strike the side of the plank. And, he fell into the water. A sudden swell lifted the ship, shoving it sideways into the dock. It crushed the trader. No one could withstand being struck by the ship's iron clad sides. I could even hear his ribs and skull crack."

The metic was clearly shocked.

"Everyone in the crowd heard a gurgle," the man added. "The man's lungs sucked in the dirty sea. We gasped in unison as we saw him sink. After a moment of silence, his body floated to the surface; his blood blending into the already maroon water."

"Did no one help the poor man?" the horrified *metic* asked.

"We did. We fished him out of the water, but he was already gone. The owner must have been scared. He ordered the ship's captain to unmoor and set sail. By the time an alarm sounded and authorities arrived, the ship had reached the mouth of the bay moving fast. I saw its striped sails fill with wind."

The slave girl retrieved the two donkeys herself. She returned to Athens a few days later and related the news to Tyche, suddenly a widow. Though relieved of her marital duty, she became very much afraid, left on her own in a city she was not allowed to explore, without any male protection, except what Molossus, the slave girl, and two donkeys might offer.

Her husband had not been a mean or forceful man, always behaving kindly to her, partly because she was still a child and because he loved her. She did not become pregnant in their time together, because he never penetrated her. Not that he didn't try. Oh, he tried many, many times, but she was tight, so tight. He sported a short and pudgy erection that couldn't take him very far anyway. His age did not help him either. He satisfied his desire for her by rolling her onto her stomach and placing his member between the cleave of her buttocks. There he rocked a bit and usually came in a quick grunt of splunge.

She met Vassilios quite by accident. The slave girl was emptying the chamber pots by throwing the contents from the second-floor balcony of the house into the rutted center of the street, which acted as an open-air city sewer. She failed to look down as she did so, and at that moment, Vassilios was passing by. He walked with an elegant grace, dressed in an expensive *chiton,* a tunic type of garment, which he could easily afford on his lavish salary from the Attic state where he was employed as an actor. Though he was celebrated throughout the city as its finest thespian, few recognized him, for when he performed in the Festivals of Dionysos, he wore a large linen mask over his face.

When the excreta poured over his head and shoulders, he let out a yell most of Athens could hear. Startled, the slave girl leaned over the balcony and let out a scream herself. The young widow opened the door to look. Without a second thought, she pulled on the edge of Vassilios' *chiton* and led him to the back of her courtyard. Strangely, she noticed that Molossus did not bark, did not sniff the stranger, but rather lay quietly on the tiles to watch the bath and listen with his ears up. There without a word, she sat Vassilios on the stone floor and repeatedly poured a *hydria* filled with water over him until nothing foul remained, and the stench disappeared. He, too, was wordless. The slave girl brought a towel.

"Get one of my husband's *chitons*," the widow ordered. She left the room while Vassilios changed.

"Bring a brush, some olive oil, scrub his sandals..."

"No need," he interrupted her. "You have been very kind. I must go as I am sure your husband will not want to find me here."

"My husband won't find you," Tyche said matter of factly. "He is dead."

Instead of dismay lighting Vassilios' hazel eyes with sympathy when he heard of her loss, they lit with interest. He sat back down and waited for his sandals to be cleaned. Molossus cocked his head. Wet, the sandals were not wearable. Vassilios could have taken them and walked barefoot through the streets as was the custom of many citizens, as Greeks were not particularly fond of shoes, usually eschewing them, especially at home. It was common for a Greek to go barefoot for his entire life. But, on special occasions or on matters of business, Greeks wore leather sandals or boots with their tunics.

"I am sorry to delay you," Tyche apologized.

"I was on my way to read a new play," he bragged, "*Antigone* by Sopho-cles. If I choose, I could play any of three leading roles, King Kreon, Ismene, or the title character, Antigone."

"You're an actor?" she marveled. "I've only heard of theatre. I've never been. What is it like?"

"It is a place for ideas. I like Sophocles' work very much," he said smiling.

"Why?" she asked.

"He explores how life and how events transpire. He pits right against right. He wants the audience to choose sides."

"But, wait! I don't understand," she interrupted.

"The side they choose depends on their own codes of ethics. A man who is truthful will choose the side of truth. A liar will not. Sophocles' characters make mistakes in what they see as right or wrong, and tragedy results."

"I still do not understand."

"When, in fact, it is all too late after making wrong choices, only then do his characters recognize truth," Vassilios told her. "I like that I get to play a hero, usually someone with exceptional abilities, but whose over-confidence and pride ensure his downfall."

"I hope this new play suits you," she smiled. "But, I am confused. The name Antigone is a woman's name. How can you play a woman?"

He began to laugh. "In the theatre, actors wear masks. It is a place for men and ideas. Only men can act. Only men can be in the audience." Tyche turned away, dismayed once again at her own misfortune to be born a woman.

Reading the play was on Vassilios' mind when the excrement rained down on him. Now, cleaned and dry, instead of hurrying off, he chose to linger.

"Might I wait here while my clothes dry?" he asked. "Then, I could leave your husband's clothes with you?"

"My husband has no need of clothes where he is."

Tyche turned to look at him. He had looked too young to be adorned by William or Ibn's or Merrill's shock of wavy white hair. But, now she could see he was older than she first thought. And, his eyes, he had those eyes, hazel, flecked with gold. In the silence, she looked more deeply into them.

"Ah," she took in her breath. "I think I have met you before."

And, so, it began, again.

"Your name?" she asked.

"Vassilios," he answered.

"The king," she said.

"Yes. So, they say. Your name?" he smiled.

"Tyche," she replied.

"Luck?" he asked, not having heard a woman so named.

"Yes. My mother was the Pythia at Delphi. Even though she fell into misfortune at the oracle, she wanted me to have good luck."

"Lady Luck, then!" he said, bowing.

Lucky knew William, the man she married centuries later in England, meant Vassilios in Greek. As Tyche, she learned this Vassilios was the reigning king of the Dionysian Festivals and Sophocles' most treasured actor.

She ordered the slave girl to bring a bowl of the *fassolatha* she had prepared that morning. She used very simple ingredients: olive oil, vegetables, and bay leaf to perfume the rich, white beans she had first cooked in water. It was cheap and got them through the cold and penurious winter months, which they ate while her husband was away. She now offered it to this new man, freshly bathed, sitting on a wooden stool in the main room of her house.

He delayed his appointment with Sophocles. He showed her the constellations that night and taught her their names. He told her about the theatre and his life as an actor. He taught her the ways of love a woman should know as he recited the poems of Homer, his voice blending with the words to bring her soul to the same point of ecstasy his body was taking hers, their private odyssey racing through the islands of love, those of mind, body, and spirit. For her, the taste of coming home was in his fluids and from him, she learned the smell of love.

Sophocles let Vassilios read the new play, who knew at first reading that taking the role of Antigone would cement his fame. In the tragedy, Antigone paid the ultimate price for burying her brother Polynices against the wishes of her uncle, King Kreon of Thebes. On the political right, the king wanted his nephew, whom he considered to be a traitor, denied burial rites. Antigone asserted her moral right as a sister to lay her brother to rest according to custom. Antigone acted on her own moral responsibility when her uncle relied on political expediency, refusing to bury his nephew.

Burial rites and religious observation were the only areas of public life in which women like Tyche could participate freely. She visited the oil trader's grave with offerings. She ordered the metic to bring her red clay. In the courtyard, she pinched pots into pitchers and vessels as she had learned to do as a child in Amfissa. Religious activities, including mourning at funerals and involvement in female cult activities formed an indispensable part of her life. Laws designated mourners had to be cousins of, or more closely related to, the deceased, but the oil trader had no family other than her. She made clay objects for his tomb like the slender *lekythos* vases she covered in a white slip carved with red female figures. As she became more proficient, she sent her pots to the market with the slave girl to sell.

As Vassilios began rehearsals, he continued to see the young widow.

"You, like all women here, Tyche, are barred from politics," Vassilios told her. "And, you cannot represent yourself in court. If you allow, I'll help you."

For her benefit, he sold the slave girl along with both donkeys and the cart. These sales allowed the young widow a window of financial freedom before she dealt with the legal matters surrounding any inheritance she might receive from her husband's business holdings.

Vassilios owned a house in an area called Thissio near both the temple of Hephaestus and the theatre of Dionysos Eleuthereus, where he performed. Thissio had a small wooded park and some less frenetic streets offering numerous quiet places to eat. He often climbed forested Filopappou Hill for exercise and to keep his lungs in shape, well worth climbing for its panoramas of the city with the acropolis and its magnificent statuary below.

As required, she visited the trader's grave three, nine, thirty days, and a year after his funeral, each time bringing several clay pots or sculptures with her. Several months later, finding they were inseparable, Vassilios moved Tyche into his home to co-habit with him. On their long walks, she and Vassilios visited many graves, remarking on the beauty of the carved stones, where the creators of funerary art were often *metics*. The year after her husband died and she felt secure in her new life with Vassilios, Tyche had taken up pottery as she wanted to create her own grave stelai for the oil trader's grave.

"Tyche, this is wonderful, "Vassilios remarked. "I can see you carrying offerings to his grave on this vase." He turned it round to see the scene painted on the vase.

"I like using the red earth clay. It absorbs and shows off the black and white slip I paint over it." In addition to the *kerameikos* and the white *lekythoi*, she made figurines and vases.

"We must sell these," Vassilios told her. "Your drawings are exquisite. The wealthy pay a lot for painted *amphorae*." She readily agreed. "I can arrange for their sale," he told her.

"So, I must give my power to you?" Tyche asked testily, but she did not receive more than a smile from Vassilios.

He found a tradesman who sold them for her at the marketplace, unaware a woman made them, for it was not possible for a woman to conduct economic transactions worth more than a nominal amount. Her clay work became an invaluable part of their income over the summer and fall when the theatre was dormant. The freedom she felt masquerading as a man was as liberating as her rights as a woman were limiting.

They did not marry as Tyche did not want the restricted life of an Athenian wife again.

Vassilios taught her how to enjoy life in male dominated Athenian society. She and Vassilios often went out together looking quite like a common homosexual pair; she relishing the freedom this disguise gave her. She took up wearing the *chlamys*, the short cloak worn by young Greek males. And, on hot Athenian afternoons, she wore a *petasos*, a wide-brimmed man's hat, letting its long string dangle down her back. In colder weather, she wore a cloak over her tunic for warmth. The *himation* was wool, fashioned from a rectangular piece of cloth that she draped over her shoulders. It served a dual purpose as it came in handy for soldiers away from home as a warm blanket on cold winter nights

The freedom she gained by her disguise lay at the root of the Greeks' love of Dionysos. Although Dionysos was the god of wine, it was the wine's transformational power that most characterized him as the god of change-ability: grapes became wine, sober became drunk, human became animal, order became chaos, female became male. A drama festival in honour of Dionysos was the Lenaia. The name, Lenaia, probably came from *lenos*, wine-press, or from *lenai*, another name for the Maenads, who were the crazed female worshippers of the god.

Tyche kept her *peplos* locked in a trunk at home as it was women's wear. They were simple to fold as they were simply large, rectangular pieces of fabric. Made from a heavier wool material, they could be draped and fastened with buttons, pins, or brooches in different ways to reflect different styles. A *peplos* was a full-length garment, because a proper Greek woman revealed nothing. She hid the *epiblema*, women's shawls, as well. Her gold silk hair-nets she placed on top of the clothing. The *ampyx* she had worn, a thin sheet of gold wrapping her forehead, she carefully stowed away along with her many-colored fillets she had once worn for her long hair.

She cropped her hair in the same short style as Vassilios wore, parted in the middle with a tiny fringe of bangs. They abandoned the popular knotting of longer hair at the base of the skull, preferring to keep their hair short. Old men tied their hair in these knots with golden grasshoppers called *krobuloi,* as by keeping their hair long they sought the look of eternal youth. Vassilios often wore a narrow *stephanos* of leaves around his head. They wore the same *chiton*s, hers smaller of course, and generally walked barefoot through the streets and *plaka.*

She and Vassilios kept their locks a natural black, not wanting to attract unwanted attention to themselves when in public. They took care, brushing each other's cropped heads every morning before anointing them with perfumed oils. There were women who dyed their hair blonde by using saffron, as though ashamed of their country, sorry that they were not born in Germany or in Gaul. In fact, blonde hair, *xanthi kome*, had become the most prized color.

Vassilios kept up with his male associates: actors, drinking companions, hunting friends, and family. When, as he slowly introduced Tyche to them, many marveled at the actor's good luck in finding such a soft-cheeked, handsome youth as a playmate. The celebrated thespian strode through the streets with his youthful lover who held, on a chain by his side, the muscular Molossus, adorned with a spiked collar around his thick neck. They made a striking threesome.

One or two men tried to lure her away on the sly, but she paid them no mind, saying resolutely,

"Leave me. I am pledged to Vassilios and his care." Then smiling, she added, "Do you wish me to tell him of your interest?" Some wondered how Vassilios' young man stayed downy cheeked year after year, but none dared ask.

Tyche liked sitting at a *taverna*, perhaps sampling the grape leaf *dolmades* stuffed with pine nuts. Or, if it was late in the afternoon, drinking mint tea and savoring a *baklava* called *gastrin*, delicious in its nuts and *phyllo* dough, layered thin as the cirrus clouds that blew overhead. At night, they watched the stars while sipping *ouzo*, allowing its licorice flavor to coat their tongues and whet their appetites with its anise base, perhaps trying various marinated black and green *Kalamata* olives, or the tiny green Cretan *elitses* or *koroneiki* before ordering their meal.

Vassilios played the syrinx, a flute whose sweet notes she thought sounded like birdsong from her beloved olive orchard in Amfissa. She delighted in his playing. Instruments were simple and most imported from other cultures. The crudity of most stood in stark contrast to the refinement in the city's architecture and sculpture. Lyres were commonplace, as musicians used them to honor the gods. Some played reed instruments called *aulos*.

In autumn, Vassilios ordered a bowl of *halkidiki*, playfully called donkey olives due to their large size. These light green beauties grew exclusively near Mount Athos and were a seasonal delight. Of all olives, the green Amfissa from her childhood suited her palate best, but which she rarely ate as they made her long for news of her mother, whom she never saw again.

Her favorite entrée was lamb, whether as a dripping and succulent *souvflakia*, kebabs, or roast. The marketplace sold goats, pigs, lamb, sheep, and donkeys, but they were costly, although sausages were common fare for both for the poor and the rich. She and Vassilios ate meat rarely, usually after the festival was over, and Vassilios had received his pay. The wealthy reserved meat, except pork, for themselves.

Vassilios' voice was naturally rich and deep, but his popularity was partly due to his ability to play many roles and to transform his voice with such variety like the cry of a raven differs from the trilling of a cardinal, the laugh of the thrush differs from the crow of the rooster, or the melody of the meadowlark differs from the screech of the seagull. His voice boomed through the open, megaphone-like mouth of his linen masks as he enunciated slowly and precisely, so that the playwright's words reached the ears of the thousands seated in the ampitheatre. His stature increased when he donned his high-soled, leather boots called *cothurnus* for the performances. If he was playing a male, he laced his boots; if he took a female role, the laces were loose.

Vassilios took her to the huge theatre on a day of no rehearsals when they were certain to be undisturbed.

"The size of this theatre in the open air demands unusual powers," he told her. Tyche stood open-mouthed in awe, never having seen such a vast arena.

"My voice must be exceptionally clear and powerful to be heard by the vast multitude of spectators, and for grand gestures to be seen, my body must be fit. At first, they called me 'hypokrites' which means 'one who answers.' Do you know, Tyche," he asked, "that an actor named Thespis, won the first Dionysian festival? He was so influential we actors are now known as thespians. Thespis was the first speaker of individual lines in the dithyramb."

"What is that?" she wondered.

"Dithyramb is verse. Decades ago, it was a religious ceremony. Fifty men dressed in goat skins pretending to be satyrs chanted a choral song to the god Dionysos. And, Tyche, guess what? They sported protruding phalluses."

Tyche guffawed. "No!"

"Yes," Vassilios laughed. "Their 'goat song' was made of the words *tragos* and *ode* which combined to become tragedy. They sang dithyrambs as improvisations until the poet, Arion of Mehtymna, wrote formal lyrics." He fell silent.

"Tell me more," she begged.

"With Thespis, actors began to perform dramatic episodes while the chorus commented to the audience. In the early drama," he explained, "the chorus played the principal part. The main function of the actor was to reply to the chorus. Then, the poets began to write their plays to exhibit the capacities of the actors. Some scenes have been written for me to perform that have no connection to the plot."

"Why?" Tyche asked.

"They were introduced for the sole purpose of enabling me to display my talents."

"Oh, lucky you!" she said, laughing.

"Under the new state system, each tragedy is to be performed by a different actor, allowing all the competing poets to enjoy in turn the services of all us actors." It was, after all, the state which paid Vassilios. "We formed a union, the first of its kind, I believe, to protect our rights as performers. Listen to this," he went on, "I do not have to serve in the military and can travel through enemy territories without hindrance if I am performing.

Now you know everything about the theatre."

"No, I don't. And, I won't know until I see a performance for myself," she cried.

"Females, except for slaves and prostitutes," he cautioned, "are forbidden to attend the festival."

She looked so crestfallen, he wanted to cheer her. "You'll go as a man."

Tyche ran to the *orchestra,* a large round area, in front of the stage. She began yelling, then singing, bits and pieces of any *dithyramb* she knew, gesticulating wildly with her arms and standing on tiptoe.

Vassilios laughed seeing her joy.

"This is where the chorus performs," he told her. "That," he said, pointing to a long, shallow area, "is the *proskenion* which we use as the stage. Behind it, see? Is the *skene.*" It was a walled area with three doors at the back of the *proskenion.* She saw panels painted with scenery and behind which perhaps actors hid.

"This whole area was rebuilt after the Persians destroyed Athens," he told her, happy to share the history of his theatre world. "The town of Agios Prokopios and acropolis are new. Here theatre was born, and we Athenians take pride in it. The centre-piece of the annual Dionysia includes five days of dramatic performances in this beautiful theatre."

"Once a year?" she questioned. "I thought it took place once in winter and once in spring. It does, doesn't it?" she asked.

"Yes, you are right. Those performances now are the competitions! Three playwrights submit tragedies, plus a satyr play."

"I don't understand," she interrupted. "What is a satyr play ?"

Vassilios understood her ignorance. "The satyr is a comic approach to the mythological subject matter of tragedy. It is a comic version of a mythological subject. You see, tragedy and comedy are separate genres. No serious play can merge the two. So, the satyr play fills a spot as a rather satisfying and raunchy burlesque."

How she wanted to see these plays, impatient for the time to come.

Her envy was roused along with her curiosity, for she wanted to stand on the dirt floor of the rounded orchestra herself and act.

"Before the Battle of Salamis," Tyche told Vassilios, "one of my mother's old friends, the priestess of Athena, encouraged the evacuation of Athens. She told the Athenians that the snake living here on the Acropolis and sacred to Athena, had already left, so they should go, too."

'Yes, I know the priestess often uses her influence to support political positions."

"Have you ever gone to the festival for Athena?" she asked him.

"You mean the Lesser Panathenaea,? Yes, it is held annually. It's open to both sexes. Would you like to go?"

"Yes," she answered. Yet, Tyche was torn between a sensitivity of duty to her deceased husband and a fear of discovery as a woman. She felt safest maintaining her male disguise. "But, I'll not go as a woman. I'll go as a man."

The Panathenaea was Athens' religious festival, its procession sculpted in memoriam for all to see on the Parthenon Frieze. The prize at the Panathenaea was a large clay *amphora* decorated with Athena on one side and a sport on the other. Tyche hoped one of her pots would be chosen as the prize one day. The women's cult of Athena Polias reinforced morality and maintained societal structure. A few weeks later, Vassilios and Tyche followed the procession of sacrificial animals, which was the most religiously-significant part of the festival. The women, except Tyche, stayed for three days on Demeter's hilltop sanctuary, conducting rites and celebrations. They kept the specific rituals of the Thesmophoria secret.

"Do you know what goes on there, Tyche?" Vassilios asked.

"My mother told me pigs are sacrificed and buried as offerings to the goddess. She said women's festivals are rites of passage in which girls become adult women. See, the girl leading the procession is carrying an incense burner, and those behind her are carrying the jugs for libations."

They watched young *kanephoroi* carrying sacred baskets.

"I was too young to participate when I lived in Amfissa. But, my mother told me that before marriage, girls make dedications to Artemis, such as a favored toy or a lock of hair. Girls sacrifice to Gaia and Uranus, the Erinyes and Moirai, and to their ancestors as well. The noble girls must be virgins."

"Oh?" he asked.

"To question her good name would prevent her selection. It is customary for a bride to bathe before her wedding, washing in waters held in *loutrophoroi*, the jars dedicated to nymphs."

"Ah," Vassilios said, "even the most respectable Athenian women can come to these festivals, sacrifices, and funerals."

Tyche ceased participating in any civic gatherings of women.

She participated instead in an all-male drinking symposium with Vassilios. She made many of the pottery pieces used for the event. There were the *krater*, large open bowls for mixing water and wine. Then there were the *kylix*, stemmed cups for drinking. She made red figure *hydria*, the jugs decorated with scenes from the Trojan War or stories of the gods. She created the art and enjoyed the event with her lover, because no one suspected the clay artist was a woman.

Vassilios practiced his lines at their hillside home. Tyche learned his parts as well as he. Memorization helped her learn to read, a skill she had forgotten as a wife forbidden to read. The trader had no books in any case. She wore her disguise, covered by a *chlamys*, the short cloak worn by young Greek males and secretly attended Vassilios' performances.

She wanted to act. She wanted to burrow her way into body and soul of mighty if flawed characters. As they rehearsed lines, her tongue wrapped around styles of speech, little mannerisms; her limbs contracted and expanded altering her from arthritic to athletic, cramped to languid, young to old. Her stride might be mincing or light, her eyes open wide or squinting, hairstyle, mask, dress infinite and varied. Her breathing slow, broken, or rapid; her attitude haughty or meek.

So, it was in her many lives: she morphed through the ages and marriages, flowing from one type of woman to another. The one constant was her womanhood and sensuality, despite her masquerade as a man in life with Vassilios.

He explained to her that homosexual practices were simply part of *aphrodisia*, love, which included men and women alike. "An older lover," he said, "the *erastes*, courts a boy, the *eromenos*."

She looked at him dismayed. It had not occurred to her that he might have other lovers, men or boys among them.

"Oh, Tyche! If you could see your face!" he laughed.

'What of it?" she replied. "You are not my first, either."

He pulled her into his arms. "You're right. You are not my first. But, you are my last."

Mollified, she asked, "Tell me about this *erastes*."

"All right," he began, "often the erastes has a beard and plays the active role, especially of mentor. The adolescent is too immature for a beard and remains passive. *Paiderastia* means "boy love." The man educates, protects, loves, and provides a role model for this *eromenos*."

"What does the boy receive?"

"The reward for him lies in his beauty, youth, and promise. The older lover acts as some sort of substitute father, there to help his beloved one on his way to manhood and maturity, and to initiate him in the customs of grown-up people."

"Enough!" she commanded. "I am tired of *Paiderastia*. Now I want some *gynephilia*."

"You mean you want some 'girl love'?" he teased, and pulling the *chiton* off her shoulder, he kissed her fully on her naked breast.

Walking together one evening, Vassilios said, "The ideal woman, you know, does not go out in public or interact with men she is not related to." Mothers educated female children in the skills of running a household. They married young, often to much older men. When they married, women had two main roles: to bear children, and to run the household.

"I know. I was a wife, remember?" she asked. "I hated having my freedom restricted! In the country, I was free. I loved Amfissa. Here I know women often live in separate areas from men."

"The other day," Vassilios responded, "I heard a philosopher pronounce that women are deformed, incomplete males, designed to be subservient to men."

"What?" she exclaimed.

"Yes, he said he views a woman as a passive conduit of male fertility, on long term loan by her father."

"When I was married, we were not equal, even though my husband was kind. I was glad not to have children, as my husband would have owned them like they were slaves."

"Men don't have the same obligation of sexual fidelity that wives have," he added as a taunt.

When she and Vassilios went to the market as a couple, he acted as the mentor and bought her small gifts typical of an older male lover to present to his beloved boy. Sometimes a pet hare, others a caged rooster, or a white duck. Sometimes he gifted her publicly, as part of their deception, with a garland, a bottle of oil, or a few *drachma*. Once, on a stroll on the outskirts of the city, they came upon a nursery where he chose a myrtle tree.

Looking at her, he said, "We'll plant it in our courtyard where it will receive rain and afternoon sun. I have always wanted a myrtle tree."

"Why?" she asked, unaware that its flower symbolized love.

"Aphrodite wore a wreath of myrtle when she emerged naked from the sea. Then, to hide her nakedness, she hid behind a myrtle tree, and later adopted it as her favorite. I want this tree to grow like our hearts, lingering together with roots of a lasting love."

As with this gesture, he was full of surprises. One morning robed by the sun, she awoke to find a ring on her finger.

"What is this?" she asked, pleased.

He turned the band around her finger saying, "this finger holds the vein of love, you know, the *vena amoris*." He pulled her finger to his lips to kiss the ring. "You see, this ring is a circle with no beginning and no end. And, most importantly, it is open in the center. Do you know why?" She shook her head. "Because, this opening is the open door to our future."

The difference in their age did not really matter in society as it was not youth, but rather beauty that was important, although Tyche did not fit the ideal of male beauty. She did not sport broad shoulders or a large chest; nor was she muscular. Fortunately, she did have a wasp's waist, and when they walked the streets, she pushed out her buttocks in the favored protruding style. Her thighs were big, but her calves were not long. A man's forehead was not supposed to be too high, his nose had to be straight, and he had to have a projecting lower lip, a round chin, and hawk eyes. She tried to perfect a penetrating stare. She rubbed dirt into her lengthening hair, rolling wads of it in her fingers to create a mane like a lion's as was the fashion. She never went naked in the public baths like most men and boys. Vassilios worried that someone she knew might recognize her and put an end to their charade. She kept her name, Tyche, as it suited a man or a woman. No one ever guessed her true gender. Though time passed, she and Vassilios did not marry. She did not want to draw public attention to herself as a woman, choosing instead to live with him pretending to be a homosexual. She did not want to risk losing her male privilege.

Fellow Athenians did not distinguish sexual desire or behavior by the gender of the participants, but rather by the role that each participant played in the sex act, that of active penetrator or passive penetrated. This active/passive polarization corresponded with dominant and submissive social roles: the active, penetrative, role was associated with masculinity, higher social status, and adulthood, while the passive role was associated with femininity, lower social status, and youth.

She and Vassilios patronized a *taverna* that offered wild game. Many hunters earned their living from hunting and trapping, allowing a trade in pheasant, wild hares, boar, and deer. Peasants sold chickens, geese, and eggs from their farmyards when they had an abundance. Tyche never cared for the acidic *retsina* wine so typically served, preferring the subtler reds. Vassilios was wild about the fruits of the sea. He ordered an appetizer of anchovies or sardines with garlic and oregano, followed by a main course of fish or mollusks such as squid, octopus, cuttlefish, prawns, and crayfish from the Aegean. When short on funds, he satisfied himself with olive oil fried sprat, the cheapest of the fish.

For breakfast at home, they typically ate barley bread so hard they soaked it in watered wine before trying to chew it. Or, she prepared *teganites*, pancakes topped with cheese or honey. They occasionally drank *kykeon*, a thick combination of barley gruel, herbs, and goat cheese.

For lunch, they ate figs, salted fish, cheeses, olives, bread and watered wine. They ate the eggs from quail and hens and when in season, plums. She grew radishes, turnips, and carrots along with lettuce, cress, arugula, and cabbage in the southern side garden of their house where she also planted lentils, chickpeas, and other legumes not only to eat but also to replenish the soil in her garden. Vassilios had a bergamot orange tree on one side of his house and an almond tree on the other. A quince bloomed beautifully each April, and later provided a delicious fruit. Often neighbors shared harvests of pears and apples, which were plentiful. They bought walnuts and jujubes, a delicious red date, from market stalls. There they found squash or marrows and many herbs for seasoning like coriander, dill, mint, oregano, saffron, and thyme along with purchases of salt and pepper. They grew fond of asparagus, artichoke thistles, celery, fennel, garlic, and leeks.

In the *plaka*, they purchased *loukoumades*, a deep fried honey pastry and *petimezi*, a grape syrup made from grape-must she used in one of Vassilios' favorite puddings: *moustalevria*.

The little meat they had, they smoked, dried, sometimes salted, or soaked in syrup. She had learned to cook as a child from her mother in Amfissa, and over her fire she boiled, fried, roasted, or stewed whatever was available. Her mother had eaten dried vegetables and acorns. Tyche used vegetables in soups, boiled or mashed, seasoned with olive oil, vinegar, herbs, or *garon*, a type of fish sauce.

She and Vassilios spoke often of what might happen to their relationship should she bear a child. Occasionally, he teased her about the weight she was adding to her waist and hips. But, she told him it was only the food and not a growing baby. Though she wanted one, she wanted more to enjoy the freedom she had found masquerading as a man. They took precautions. Infant mortality was common, with perhaps one out of four babies dying at or soon after birth. In addition to the natural risks of childbirth, infanticide was widespread and not challenged. Girl babies were more likely killed than boy, and she knew several parents who had lost a child or two in this manner. If they survived, children were named in a ceremony called *dekate* ten days after birth.

"Are you trying to tell me something?" Vassilios teased.

"No, no!" she protested. "I am most definitely not carrying a child."

Vassilios put his finger to his lips to shush her. "You make me think of a female character I played once, Macaria, who sacrificed herself for the safety of Athens in the *Heracleidae*. She claimed that 'for a woman, silence and self-control are best.'"

"Surely, you don't believe that," Tyche said, feeling a bit chastised for her outburst.

"That philosopher we heard in the square the other day," Vassilios replied, "declared that females must possess love for infants. He fears that women are irrational, too full of religious fervour and of sexual passion. Even Socrates says portraying 'inferiors like women and slaves in drama is morally harmful.'"

"Oh," Tyche asked scornfully, "is he also worried about 'womanish' emotions in tragedy? I think the declaration 'that a noble man ought either to live with honour, or die with honour' should apply to women, too."

"You do?" Vassilios asked. "I think tragedy displays universal human experiences, ones that inspire terror, sorrow and rejection. The plays make women visible and vocal."

"But, the roles of women are performed by men," Tyche protested. "Exclusively!" In a society that valued women's silence, their predominance in the most public of Athenian art-forms constituted a paradox she couldn't understand. "Didn't you tell me that female tragic choruses play larger roles and are in more plays than the male choruses?" Tyche asked. "Doesn't the chorus speak for the public conscience?"

Vassilios answered by sharing a remembrance. "A few years ago, I was performing in Aeschylus' *Eumenides*. There was the usual screaming from the crowd. On one afternoon, some frightened woman in the audience went into labor and miscarried. After that, the theatre banned women and children from attending performances. The Assembly excludes women as well.

"Look at the tragedy that resulted when a self-willed woman took matters into her own hands," Vassilios continued. "Clytemnestra took power in Argos, while her husband, King Agamemnon, fought at Troy. On his victorious return, Clytemnestra murdered him."

"He sacrificed their daughter, Iphigenia at the war's start," Tyche defended. She knew every line in Aeschylus' *Oresteia* trilogy. "Clytemnestra wanted revenge. And, she killed him in public."

Vassilios interjected, "In the second play, Orestes forced his mother, Clytemnestra, into the house where he killed her out of the public eye. Look at Alcestis," he went on. "She represented the 'perfect wife' who sacrificed her own life, so her husband, Admetos, could live," Vassilios added apparently supportive of such a woman. "Dramas were set in public, outside the private sphere of the home, until Euripides wrote *Hippolytus*."

"What do you mean?" Tyche asked.

"Euripides put tragedy in the bedroom. It is only in the public eye when Phaedra is carried out of the house by her servants, to declare her love for her stepson," Vassilios said. "Oh! I almost forgot! I have some news I want to share. Euripides asked me to play Medea."

"The sorceress?" Tyche asked, surprised.

"Yes, the daughter of Circe and granddaughter of the sun god, Helios.

I am in a state of elation and fear. I read the script. This Medea is an even better role than Antigone was!" he said. "You must read it with me." He handed her his copy drawn from his satchel. "Medea is so strong. I do not understand her. I have never known a woman like her," he admitted.

As Tyche read the script, she understood it was jealousy, yes, jealousy and betrayal were the issues her sweet Vassilious could not comprehend. Not only Medea's jealousy of Jason's new bride in the play, but also a jealousy of Tyche's own which she tried hard to hide. She was jealous of Vassilios' opportunity to receive such a role, a role she wanted to play, but wasn't allowed. She was invisible as all women were. Fury ignited to burn in her. She was playing the role of his male lover in real life, was she not? She knew how to act, all right. She wanted her time in the theatre, the recognition, the glory: none of which were to be hers. Frustration and discontent added fuel to the fire in her heart.

Yes, she helped him with his lines. Yes, she explained what a jealous rage and fury at betrayal felt like to a woman. Yes, she described the feelings boiling so furiously inside her, all so he could be more realistic on stage.

Medea broke marital conventions in the beginning of her relationship with Jason, when she herself, instead of her father, chose him as her husband. She was a princess, a foreigner, coming to Greece as his bride, a stranger in a strange land. Later, after she had borne him two fine sons and when he wanted to leave her for a new and younger wife, she reacted to his infidelity by breaking her oath of loyalty.

Her name, Medea, meant cunning and was also the word for the hated Persians, the Greek's greatest foreign enemy. Yet, Medea displayed attributes that the Greeks held as positive—for males only—possession of courage, intelligence, decisiveness, resourcefulness, power, independence, the ability to conceive and carry out a plan effectively, as well as the art of rhetoric. The nurse in the drama likened Medea to a rock of the sea.

Women became tragic figures in drama when men were either absent or mismanaged the marriage, reflecting life. Most commonly, society perceived women as full of fear, too weak to defend themselves or to bear the sight of a steel blade. But, if a woman was wronged in love, hers became the blood thirstiest heart of all.

Heinously, to take revenge for his betrayal and to destroy him, Medea went on a killing binge. She killed their two young sons, Jason's bride-to-be, and her father, the King of the Corinthians. But, the Greek credo "that a noble man ought either to live with honour, or die with honour" did not apply to women. And, in this drama, Euripides did not portray Medea, a woman displaying traits of the heroic Grecian male, in a positive light.

O, Tyche wanted to play that role. She understood the hypocrisy of hiding the true self; she understood the red-heat of betrayal from the Pythia's stories of the priests who impregnated her only to throw her out of the temple. Tyche understood Medea well.

Ten years after meeting Vassilios, Tyche's world was thrown into disarray. She found herself pregnant. How could she bear a child? How could she bear to lose the freedoms she had come to cherish?

Tyche did not want to let go of the freedom she enjoyed as a man. She did not want to confine herself to the house, no matter how familiar and comfortable it was. She did not want to make new friends as everyone she met knew her as a man. Yet, this was her lover's child and therefore precious.

Torn, she decided to keep her pregnancy secret from Vassilios. She visited an herbalist, asking for the seeds from Queen Anne's lace, whose poison was known to abort a child. The herbalist gave her the seeds with instructions for how to prepare them and what to expect. The herbalist also gave her a deadly hemlock plant, which Tyche placed in a back corner of her vegetable garden, hoping Vassilios would not recognize it, and wondering if one day she might have to use it for herself.

The Queen Anne's lace sickened her more than the nausea she experienced in the first trimester of her pregnancy. In the afternoon as he arrived home early from a canceled rehearsal, Vassilios found her on the floor holding her belly, moaning from cramping pain. He lifted her only to see clots of blood oozing between her legs.

"I'm sorry! I'm sorry!" she cried.

"For what?" he asked.

She confessed, sobbing, to what she had done.

"Tyche! No! No!" he cried in disbelief. On hearing her desire to abort their child, he felt betrayal for the first time. He unleashed a fury she had never seen. He ran outside growling in his grief. There in the garden, he grabbed an axe. And, swinging round, he chopped down the myrtle tree, their tree of love. Chopped it into dozens of pieces. And, he wept.

She was too weak to stop him.

Vassilios' grief over the loss of their child came as a surprise, surprise as great as the discovery that she was pregnant at all. That she did not tell him! And, that she killed it as it grew in her womb, their child! His disappointment overwhelmed him. The bitter taste left in his mouth from this betrayal never left.

As she recovered and the child was no more, a rift grew between them. Vassilios stopped taking her with him into the streets. He stopped asking her to run lines with him. He destroyed her *chitons* and one day laid for her to wear on their bed what he found of her women's clothing from her trunk.

He stopped rolling the ring about her finger when holding her hand just as he stopped holding her hand altogether. He stayed out late, drinking wine at the *taverna* in the city. He made excuses, and then he didn't make excuses. He could not look at her, this woman who was like the Medea he had played, this woman who killed their child, thinking only of her life and not of theirs together. What had he done wrong? He had not betrayed her like Jason had Medea. He had only loved her, protected her, befriended her, cared for her with all his might. And a child? How he would have loved their child!

Tyche considered continuing pottery and grave sculpture, but she had little energy for it, though she did make a *stele* to honor her aborted child, crying the while. She cooked, but she found she had no appetite. She sewed, but she had adequate clothing, even though she long before gave away most of her women's attire. She neglected the garden. She neglected herself.

Over the next months, she sank ever deeper into a depression. She felt like a fallen god, like a female Prometheus, tied by her failed motherhood to a rock at the edge of the sea, her guts devoured by a ravenous eagle each day as punishment from the gods, not for giving mankind the gift of fire, but rather for failing to be a woman and giving birth to Vassilios' child. All seemed lost to her.

She left him that time. He found her lifeless on their bed, the arthritic Molossus beside her body whining while licking her face, the remains of the hemlock she boiled and drank in a cup on the floor. Vassilios, in his rage and grief, threw the cup onto a compost mound at the side of her neglected garden where the myrtle he had chopped lay rotting.

BLIP EIGHT

Warp and Woof

Again, they met when she was a child, only this time in a different land. And, they married when she was a child, a child of thirteen. That was in Morocco, oh, sometime in the fourteenth century. She remembered Morocco, of course, and the weaving of rugs. Ibn was there, she was absent. Or, she was there, then Ibn was absent. She married Ibn, a Muslim Berber, at least she thought he was Ibn, in the year 1360 near the end of the Marinid Dynasty and when he was fifty-six. He was always fifty-six, or almost always. Her parents married off this girl, their eleventh child, a girl they named Hiza, meaning lucky, when she turned thirteen to this prominent visiting scholar from Tangier, Ibn, who came to their shop in the medina accompanied by his dog.

The sloughi was of medium size, short-haired, smooth-coated, and athletic, a sight-hound developed in the Berber world of North Africa to hunt game: hare, fox, jackal, gazelle, and wild pigs. He was of this ancient breed, treasured for its hunting skills and endurance running over long distances, a robust pursuit dog.

Normally a quiet and withdrawn child, this dog drew Hiza to him. "What is your dog's name?" she shyly asked, standing behind her mother, and peering around her side.

The sloughi, bestowed with class and grace, looked somewhat aloof, the expression of his dark eyes gentle and melancholy.

"It's an odd name," Ibn warned, smiling, "one I chose from his way of moving."

"What is it," she asked.

"Woof," he replied.

"Woof? Woof is the sound of his bark," she corrected in a whisper, her own eyes downcast at her sudden outburst. Yet, she persisted. "I asked, what is his name?"

"You are a weaver, are you not?" Ibn asked, bending down to her.

Her mother elbowed her. Keeping her head bowed, Hiza murmured, "I am learning."

"When you weave your carpets, is there not a warp and a woof? Do you not wend your thread through the warp?" She nodded. "My dog moves like your woof, undulating until it finds its resting place."

"Oh," she shyly smiled. "I see." And, summoning her courage, she looked up to ask, "May I pet Woof?"

Woof's head was long and elegant with drop ears. He lifted his eyes to hers. She stroked from his gray crown, down his ears, along his back, and to his tail which was long with an upward curve at its tip. She beamed at Ibn, who nodded in satisfaction, as Woof moved closer to the child, wanting more caresses. Ibn, in turn, felt drawn to the girl, compelled by a sudden desire to protect this child, this innocent who looked like a boy, slim of body, no budding breasts or bloody changes altering her. What she knew of men was from her brothers, seven of them, who still included her in their games of *dinifri* which they played, whenever they could, together in the street.

Calling her to come, the eldest boy drew a square with chalk measuring at least one meter on the ground. Smaller squares he drew within the original square; one in each corner, and one in the middle. The other brothers gathered five flat pieces of stone. To win, a team stacked the stones in the center square.

"Hiza! Hurry! We need you!"

Begging her mother with her eyes, Hiza was freed to go as Ibn watched the play commence.

The children divided into two teams; each team got a rolled up fibrous bat. The eldest's team got five chances to throw the bat to knock the stacked stones in the center over. Succeeding quickly, they became the attackers, and the other team became the defenders. The attackers raced to the center square to gather the stones and then raced to the corner squares, placing one stone in each.

But, while the attackers were placing the stones, the defenders got to throw the bat at them! Hiza didn't shrink from playing though her bruises were plentiful and a disturbing shade of purple. She eliminated one attacker from the game when she hit him. Her defending team went on to victory after all five of the attackers were pushed out of the game before they could place their stones in the squares. Ibn watched, impressed.

A new game began called kick and catch. Hiza started by kicking a rag ball into the air, while two teams tried to catch it. One of her brothers caught the ball, kicking it up and over the heads of the other players, aiming the rag ball at one of his teammates. The winning team made ten catches before the other team stole the rag ball away. The elbowing and shoving were rough and rugged. She ended the second game with a blackened eye and a bloodied lip.

While this bout of mayhem filled the street with shouts and cries, Ibn inquired of the parents if the girl was *khafd*, circumcised, a rather new custom among the Maliki Sunni who considered *khafd* to be *makruma* for a woman, a noble choice as opposed to an obligatory custom. In that Moroccan incarnation, Lucky could not remember being stitched. Or cut. As Hiza at thirteen, she had never seen a naked person, so she didn't know what a man or woman, a boy or girl looked like. If she'd been cut, she didn't know what was removed, if anything. If she was stitched, well, stitched was the way she was. She was content, cut and stitched, or neither cut nor stitched. She was simply herself. In her understanding of Islam, husband and wife were each other's protector and comforter, and that was all she needed to know.

She didn't know what her parents told him, as, in the end, whatever she was or wasn't hadn't hindered their wedding. He wanted to protect her from other men, from possible abuse, from pregnancy at too young an age. Married, he knew she was safe from assault or from other courtships and need not fear for her while he traveled afar. And, whatever she was or wasn't had definitely hurt when he finally mounted her, but hurt in the best way possible, as it set her ablaze. Whoever she was before, as a child, as a girl, went up in flames. What came down was burning desire for this man, for his lips, for his long, slender fingers crawling lazily inside her, stitches or no, and an appendage she had never before seen, his glorious, untiring stretch of pure pleasure tread within her folds on a highway leading to heaven. He was a man of much experience and was thoughtful and careful with her, training her in ways to love him, as a fine horseman fit his horse to bridle and saddle, to trot and to canter, knowing patience in the beginning brought years to come of pleasurable riding, from the softest touch on a velvet muzzle, to the whispered endearments on her neck just below the ear, to the gentle prodding at her hips to keep pace with him, done expertly without the dig of a spur or the crack of a whip.

Or, had he not. Ridden her. Bridled her. Entered her. Then, when she was a child, or ever? Or, was it later, when he returned from his travels? Or, did he travel before they wed and settled quietly with her in their *dar* forgetting about travel after their marriage?

Her mind, her mind. Memories leaking out, seeping like wet dreams into the thirsty sands of time, so much time, so many centuries to sift, to try to find herself, her children, him, not sure what was real, what happened, and what didn't. Her rings of memory, like those revealing the growth of a tree, circled around her own heartwood making her dizzy, bringing her nowhere closer to the truth.

She remembered living in the old capital. How proud she felt as she walked with her parents and Woof past the University of Al Qarawiyyin, proud because a woman founded it in 859, and Ibn lectured there. Vast Al Qarawiyyin University and mosque with its ornate cupola tiled in vivid cobalt glazed ceramics, while the towering R'cif Mosque overlooked a lively market square. Fez El Bali was the older medina, an ancient walled market with narrow streets and the ornamented entryway, Bab Guissa. Souk vendors specialized in perfumes, spices, lamps, and leather. Food stalls filled the streets with the aroma of steaming kebabs.

She had not worked in the 9th-century old Fez el Bali but rather in the adjoining 13th-century new Fez el Djedid, whose gardens, squares, and imposing palace show-cased Marīnid aesthetics and urban planning. Fez el Djedid extended from Bab Lamar Gate near the Royal Palace to the Blue Gate entrance to Fez el Bali. The Marinid dynasty from 1248 to 1465 ruled the Morocco she knew.

Her grandparents passed down stories they heard from their grandparents who in turn heard them from their grandparents of the Marinid overthrow of the Almohad dynasty in 1244. Now, in her young life, the Marinids controlled all the Maghrebin of North Africa and were also known as the Moors. They supported the Kingdom of Granada in Al-Andalus and attempted to gain a direct foothold on the European side of the Strait of Gibraltar. But, again, the stories handed down told of their defeat at the Battle of Río Salado in 1340 and the consequent Castilian conquest of Algeciras for the Catholics.

Fez was home to over one hundred dye workers and thousands of artisan embroidery and weaving studios located in the *medina*, her family among them. The *medina* she loved was an unpaved space transmitting a life-style of skills and culture within architectural and archeological splendor. She felt a romantic, child-like pleasure in getting lost in this low-rise urban tangle with its multitude of cafes where she liked to rest and watch the people pass, even though she never went there alone. Her mother or an aunt or one of her many brothers held tightly to her hand as they passed through the streets and stalls. She begged to rest for a moment at its monuments: ancient mosques and elaborate *madersas*, religious colleges with stunning, decorative courtyards, or discreet old-school *hammams* and crumbling *fondouks*, or the *caravanserais* that housed travelers. She especially coveted visits to Chemmaine-Sbitryine *fanadiq* used by caravans on the Rue Quaraouyine. There were *souks*, or markets, tomb-shrines, and even the remnants of an enigmatic water clock. Wedged, almost furtively into the heart of it all, stood the Mosque.

As soon as she could weave, she created a prayer mat in a brilliant shade of pomegranate. Prayer rugs needed to be large enough to kneel above the fringe on one end and bend down and place the head on the other. Hers was rectangular with a niche at the top for the *mihrab*, which was the niche in the wall of her mosque, pointing to Mecca. Before praying the required five times each day, most often at home, she performed *wudu*, ablution, and always prayed in a clean place where she could prostrate or sit on her rug directed at Mecca, the *qibla*. Next to her loom, stood a broom and a rag which she used religiously to keep the floor under her mat spotless. Her prayer rug had a symbolic meaning, and she took care of it in a holy manner. It was disrespectful to place a prayer mat in a dirty location, and she showed respect to Allah through cleanliness. She neatly rolled it and never cast it about in a disrespectful manner.

Within the rug's rectangle, she wove green geometric symbols. In yellow wool, she wove two mosque lamps, a reference to the *Verse of Light*, the thirty-fifth verse of the twenty-fourth *Sura* of the *Quran*, *Sura an Nur*. She loved this verse's remarkable beauty, perhaps more than any other.

Allah is the Light of the heavens and the earth.
The example of His light is like a niche within which is a lamp
The lamp is within glass, the glass as if it were a pearly star
Lit from the oil of a blessed olive tree,
Neither of the east nor of the west,
Whose oil would almost glow even if untouched by fire
Light upon light
Allah guides to His light whom He wills.
And Allah presents examples for the people,
and Allah is Knowing of all things.

The decorations she wove on mats were sometimes aids to memory. On a prayer mat for a man she might include a comb and pitcher to remind the supplicant to wash his hands and comb his hair before performing prayer. Most of her rug patterns, dyes and materials came from family traditions. For newly converted Muslims, she stitched decorative hands on the prayer mat where the hands should be placed when performing prayer as the supplicant knelt at the base of the rug and placed his or her hands at either side of the niche at the top of the rug with the forehead touching the niche.

Salah meant to pray or bless. It also meant contact, communication, or connection. It was the second of the Five Pillars in the Islamic faith, and an obligatory religious duty for every Muslim. She knew its primary purpose was to act as a person's communication with Allah, and purification of the heart was her ultimate religious objective, a physical, mental, and spiritual act of worship she observed five times a day at prescribed times. She performed *salah* in its time unless there was a compelling reason to prevent doing so. While facing towards Mecca, the holy city of Muslims, she stood, bowed, and prostrated herself, before sitting on the ground. During each posture, she read certain verses, phrases, and prayers, *rak'ah*, a sequence of prescribed actions and words that varied according to the time of day.

When at a mosque with her parents, she sat in the children's rows between the men's and women's, with her father at the front and her mother at the back. Sometimes, the men's and women's rows were side by side, separated by a curtain or other barrier, with the intention being for no direct line of sight between male and female worshippers who lowered their gazes.

She practiced the *fard*, obligatory prayers every Muslim recited, if healthy. She knew prayers were *fard, wajib, sunnah,* and *nafl,* which she recited at a prescribed times measured by the movement of the sun: between dawn and sunrise *fajr,* after the sun had passed its zenith *zuhr,* when afternoon shadows lengthened *asr,* just after sunset *maghrib* and around nightfall *isha.*

She found it hard to remember Ibn, his face, his hands, if he had ever made love to her...No... Yes, of course she remembered him. It was coming back to her. How she squinted through the carved screen in her parents' home when he visited to ask for her. His once dark hair turned pure white and fell in unruly waves like a stormy sea from his head, as though agitated not by the wind but rather by the energetic thoughts moving beneath his scalp. He emitted electricity through this wild hair, his gold-flecked eyes seemed to spark as though struck by flints, his graceful, dancing gestures as if he spoke not only with his voice but also with his hands, carving wordless gestures on the air.

It was harder if not impossible to remember having children, if she had children with Ibn. She must find him again, ask him. Only the designs she wove into her carpets held clues to her life with him at that time. He was gone, he was often gone, he was almost always gone, a traveler. He left her to travel the medieval world. Or, did he? Over a period of thirty years, Ibn visited most of Islam and many non-Muslim lands, including Central Asia, Southeast Asia, India, and China. He was not faithful. He took wives. He took sex slaves. Ibn was a man who ate life whole. And, his singular interest in Hiza was one of protection and not propagation.

Their wedding planners, *Neggafates,* surrounded her for days, since no wedding ceremony could occur without them. At first, she felt excited by all the fuss. Then, she became cranky when not allowed out to play with her brothers, care for her goats, or wander the *souk*.

Her marriage began with signing a contract. Only the couple and the *wali*, or guardians, of the bride attended the actual wedding ceremony. Hiza and Ibn, the *wali* and her parents went in front of an *imam* to sign the paperwork finalizing the wedding. Her family and Ibn decided the terms of the marriage contract ahead of time, so this part was a short formality. There was no ring. Men did not wear gold, whether a ring or anything else. The Prophet forbade gold for the males of this *ummah*. Nor did Ibn present Hiza with a ring.

Their wedding celebration lasted seven days, starting with the *hammam* day for women. Her mother gathered all her female family, friends, neighbors at the public bath, the *hammam*, which she rented. The women washed Hiza's hair with clay called *ghassoul*, then scrubbed, massaged, perfumed, and waxed her body in preparation for the wedding night. A henna ceremony followed the next day.

It was hard for her to hold still while the women decorated her hands and feet with henna tattoos, signs of fertility, beauty, and optimism. Hiza hoped the henna masked the orange and red so deeply imbedded in her skin and under her nails from the wool dye baths. The henna was not permanent and faded with time, but it was very beautiful and did a good job of hiding the other dyes staining her hands. All the female friends and relatives got tattoos. They giggled *fal,* a wish for lots of luck in married life. Then, everyone danced and chanted for her. She felt hot with embarrassment and a bit damp with fear.

While the women reveled, the men gathered for their own much more demure party. They shared a meal and recited verses from the Quran to celebrate the groom's upcoming nuptials. Ibn, being a scholar and blessed with a rich speaking voice, recited many verses and some poems of his own. His family belonged to a Berber tribe known as the Lawata. As a young man, he studied at a Sunni Maliki *madh'hab*, a school of Islamic jurisprudence. Maliki Muslims, a smaller group of Sunni, honored Ibn with a request to serve as their religious judge in Fez, as he came from an area where it was practiced, in addition to his work at the university.

Ibn came alone as most of his Berber relatives remained in Tangier; the rest stayed in the lower part of the Atlas Mountains to the northeast. He wore a *djellaba*. It was beige, like the sands of the Sahara. It was long and loose with full sleeves, whose hood, fallen back below his broad shoulders, came to a point called a *qob*. Ibn preferred the *djellaba* with a *qob* as the *qob* protected his face from the sun and his body from the cold by keeping heat in and protecting his face from falling snow. His dark skin and thick hair were set off by the neutral color, and he looked extraordinarily handsome in a wary but knowing, almost wolf-like way. For this special occasion, he also wore a red *bernousse* or *fez* on his head.

On the day of the wedding, Hiza tried to rest but failed, overcome by fear of the unknown. She attended three of her brother's weddings, but her own was different. She was to leave her family to live with an old man of fifty-six.

In the afternoon, the women came to begin her makeup and hair. Her mother-in-law was supposed to welcome her and offer dates and milk as a sign of welcome and affection. But, as Ibn's parents did not come to Fez, if they were even still alive, her sisters welcomed the wedding guests with dates and a little glass of almond milk flavored with orange water. Then, they presented appetizers of cake and sweets and different sorts of juices.

Everyone waited for Hiza's entrance. She wore a *kaftan* decorated with ornaments and *balgha* on her feet, soft leather slippers with no heel, dyed yellow. She begged off wearing the high-heeled silver-tinseled sandals her aunt brought, too afraid she might trip and look foolish or snag the hem of her *kaftan* with them. She sat with Ibn in an elegant roofed *amaria* carried by her seven brothers to an elevated and decorated couch. Guests gathered round to offer congratulations while an artist painted their picture.

She was changed into a second outfit for the dinner where she and Ibn sat at a family table with her parents and close family. Her parents spared no expense on this wedding of their youngest daughter to such a prestigious scholar. Dishes of grilled chicken with saffron sauce and lamb tagine with prune and almonds sat next to a platter of short noodles called *seffa*, sweetened and served with cinnamon and grilled almonds. A pastille of puff pastry stuffed with a fricassee of pigeon, almonds, sugar, and cinnamon was also served, this on a bed of couscous. The interplay between sweet and savory flavors, as exemplified by *tfaya,* a mix of caramelized onions, butter, cinnamon, sugar, and raisins delighted the palate.

Ibn surprised them with a whole sheep cooked *mechoui* style and served at each table. Hiza realized he enjoyed making the grand gesture. Cookies and cakes like *ka'ab ghazal* and *ghriba* followed, accompanied, of course, with mint tea and coffee.

They danced a few times during the evening with all the guests gathered around them. He danced like the wind, fierce, smooth, relentless. Her legs hurt, unused to dancing though adept at running and kicking, and unused as well to his speed. Her back arched and twisted, pushed, and pulled by his long fingers. She smiled, pretending to enjoy the show, although suddenly frightened, no not frightened, terrified, by thoughts of the night to come. The guests clapped and swayed, their hips moving rhythmically from right to left and left to right, the music carrying them all to joyful rapture.

The dancing over, it was time to change again into a beautiful but heavy *labssa fassia* covering almost every part of her body except her face. Her mother had worn it for her wedding ceremony, refreshing it by adding new ornamentation encircling the hem for her daughter: small silver sequins in a third-eye diamond motif to ward off evil. Hiza wore this outfit for the tour on the *mida,* an open platform. For it, Ibn changed into another *djellaba.* There was a *mida* for each of them. Her brothers, father, and Uncle Farouk lifted them up at the same time. Ibn leaned across to kiss her forehead.

After the procession, there was the wedding cake. They changed clothes yet again. Ibn ate the cake, swirled her in a last dance, and departed the group for the wedding night.

No, she remembered, they didn't depart.

The wedding started late, as was customary, around nine p.m. It finished at dawn. Her cousins prepared breakfast for everyone: white *harira* soup, *beghrir,* pancakes, and *msemmen,* flatbread, all served with *atay,* Maghrebi mint tea. Ibn kissed her three times on the cheek and once on her forehead, and it was then that they left. She remembered most the trembling.

His house, now her house, like most Moroccan homes, adhered to the *Dar al-Islam,* a series of tenets on domestic life. From an Arabic perspective, symbolically, the exterior represented a place of work, while the interior represented a place of refuge. Consequently, the *dar* exterior was devoid of ornamentation and windows, except occasional small openings in secondary quarters, at stairwells and service areas, as these piercings afforded light and ventilation. The *dar* walls were high and thick, as protection from thievery, animals, and other hazards. The interior, in contrast, was lavishly decorated. Ove the next years spent there alone, she added many, many of her weavings.

Ibn did not wish to take her away from her family and Fez; nor did he plan to include her in his travels, which were to be many and far, far from home. Or, did he finish his travels and was there to stay, to teach and to write? She did not remember. What she did remember was that this, her new home, was next to the *medina,* the walled urban area of the city she loved. Upon entering the *dar,* the wedding guests moved through a zigzagging passageway that hid the central courtyard. The passageway opened to a staircase leading to an upstairs reception area, the *dormiria,* the most lavish room in the home. It was adorned with decorative *ziliij,* colorful geometric mosaic tile work, painted furniture, and piles of embroidered pillows from India and silks from China collected by Ibn on his journeys. Affluent, he had a greenhouse and a second *dormiria,* accessible from a street-level staircase. Service quarters and stairways sat at the corners of the structure.

A small, open-air patio commanded the center, surrounded by the rooms which blocked direct light and minimized the daytime heat. Intermediary triple-arched porticos led to four symmetrically located rooms. These rooms were long and narrow, because the regional resources and local construction allowed for joists no longer than thirteen feet. Beautiful and comfortable as the home was, it could not assuage Hiza's loneliness after Ibn left her soon after the wedding when she was still but a girl.

He left Woof as well. Ibn saw that Woof had grown to love Hiza who was also sensitive, intelligent, and conscientious. Woof played in her games of rag ball with her brothers in the streets back then when she could leave the home safe in their company, quickly becoming the fastest and best catcher of all. As Hiza matured, she grew to depend on Woof as her closest companion and friend. If a stranger came near, Woof emitted a low, warn-ing growl, devoted as he was to protecting her. With the passing of years, she wanted a child, but Ibn was far, far away. She tried to remember their lovemaking, if there had been any. She saw her brothers' many children come into the world, and she cared for them. The laughter of her nieces and nephews in the courtyard often filled her ears.

The dog lay beside her for long hours as she wove, listening even as he dozed, eyes half-lidded, to the soft sound of her knotting of the threads. Sometimes, she took him to the roof where she did her weaving under lavender skies as the evening cooled, and the moon rose to light her work. The dog's dark eyes never left her.

As evenings drifted into night, the stars lit her loom before she rose to light candles. What if the sky split, she wondered, separating the stars like curtains, to reveal absolutely nothing, nothing but blackness to the eye? She answered her own question. To a faith-filled spirit like hers such nothing revealed everything.

She wondered on those nights about the residing place of the soul when the body died. Where did the soul go? She imagined space, infinite space, dotted with souls like the specks of stars she saw from earth spread in ever deepening layers across the sparkling night sky. She tried to imagine Ibn in lands far off, farther than her experience carried her.

There was once an occasion, the single occasion, when she called him, called him from the depths of her despair as his wife, alone. It was when her mother lay dying. He came; he came in spirit anyway. He came as a brilliant chrysanthemum of gold light, expanding as he neared, and then appeared in silhouette in his familiar posture, seated, elbow on knee, head on hand. He told her mother, who was suffering greatly, that it was not her time to die, to go back from death, to return to life. Her mother pushed against brown robed spirits from all faiths whose arms linked to form a fence preventing her from entering death's dominion. Hiza's aunts, father, grandparents, so many loved ones who had already passed, and unknown others, stood resilient under their hoods and held her mother back. She could not cross over, and she lived for another year.

When Hiza, on those lonely nights, thought of connectedness, she saw an infinite spider's web strung across space. At first, only Ibn and she were there, one the spider, the other…caught, not certain which of them was which, the spider or the prey. Then she saw that though she was connected completely to him, they were connected to others as well. The web held his father, his grandparents, his friends. And, it held her parents and families and friends. And, theirs. And, theirs. And, soon she saw that this gigantic web held all souls.

And, what, she wondered, sat at its nexus? Allah? A spider? Or, was there anything at its center at all?

Loneliness permeated her body. Her tongue felt coated by the tannin of tea long drunk leaving its parched residue, making her thirst for him, for him, and finding nothing to cleanse her yearning year after year as she waited. As she waited, she wove.

After Ibn left, she needed a trade and took up weaving seriously with her family. Typically, their designs related to fertility, sexuality, survival, protection, and the natural and agricultural world, with most rugs being hand woven by women and sold by the men in their stall in the medina.

Her mother taught her to source her dyes from local vegetation or minerals as had her parents and generations before them. Some, like Tyrian purple and the rich red from cochineal, came from shells. She utilized indigo to create deep shades of blue and purple. Traditional dyes were all natural: ocher and madder for red; henna for orange and brown; saffron, turmeric and sumac for yellow; indigo for blue. Using this palette, she employed a technique called *abrash* where she made sudden, dramatic shifts in color.

She began to place the spider or the sun at the center of her carpets. The spider secreting its threads was like the sun spreading its rays. After all, the spider was the greatest weaver of all. The spider's thread symbolized that strong yet invisible link between the creator and his creature. Hiza felt the threads she wove connected her to Allah.

She also copied Berber carpets to honor Ibn's traditions. Probably the most important motif in Berber carpets and the main female symbol, alone or as a network, was the lozenge. The chevron, the M-shape, and the X-shape also represented women. While a large, single diamond was a watchful guardian warding off evil, it also represented female attributes and fertility. An X was a body with arms and legs spread out. A dot might indicate a pregnancy or child.

She wove straight lines, some like sticks, others like ribbons, some like twig-and-ladder symbols. She placed these male motifs on the outer edges of the carpets, containing or protecting the female motifs within their confines. Long, straight motifs had phallic signification, and she used them to border female symbols, indicating sexual union. The cock was a popular, stylized symbol, because its voice announced sunrise. Islam employed this symbol, because it awakened people to pray.

Hints of henna, indigo, saffron and madder root dyes made their way into the rug's motifs and fringes with their own tales to tell. She knew in Berber culture a rich pomegranate red represented strength and protection, blue wisdom, yellow eternity, and green peace. She knew this and perhaps used these colors to please Ibn. But, being neither Berber nor traditional herself, as she gained confidence, she began to use colors as she saw fit. She wove in the flat weave style, using weft substitution which required handwork. She learned from her mother to create complicated patterns from the back of the loom. There, she used different colored weft threads in the same line. On the surface, a tight design showed with no breaks in the weft. On the back, she allowed the threads to run, creating a padding of longer, floating threads on the underside of the carpet. Some weavers preferred to clip the floating threads, which left short, loose ends on the back of the rug. They varied patterns with the addition of knotted or embroidered sections, and colors ranging from vivid hues to undyed natural whites, off-whites, grays, browns, and blacks.

Most urban weaving was based on geometries that were symmetric and gave birth to shapes that repeated themselves endlessly, usually in the form of medallions whose center evoked *Al Kaaba*, the prophet's tomb. The animating lines suggested the flux and reflux of Muslims who engaged in ordered and rhythmical processions invoking Allah.

Her symmetrical borders she made of two thin strips and two arcs, although prayer rugs had only one arc. The centers of her carpets were ornate with a medallion surrounded by geometric and floral motifs, like leaves and plants reminding Muslims of the promised life in *Jannah* after death. Her favorite border was a measured motif of lion paws in saffron threads. She wove this border for her lion of the desert, Ibn, and prayed for him to return.

She worried about Ibn, gone so long. Had he other wives, other loves? She used dyes to remind her of his flashing eyes, golds and hazels and greens. Had Ibn wandered? She incorporated snakes and scorpions more frequently in her rugs to ward off dalliances while he lived abroad. Would he return? Was she to be fertile or barren? These were the questions she asked year after year as she matured into a woman, a beautiful woman, in his absence.

Her marriage to him prevented pursuit by other men, protecting her but leaving her isolated and lonely as well.

To design a carpet, Hiza dreamt of its entire composition, allowing its rhythms, harmony, geometry, colors, and symbols to dance through her head. Through symbols and signs, she expressed herself. She wove gardens that symbolized eternity and paradise according to Sufi mystics. Paradise had four gardens: the garden of the soul, the garden of the heart, the garden of the spirit, and the garden of the essence.

She became a storyteller narrating past events or stories about the people of her tribe, and her carpets acquired a dimension that elevated them from mere decorative objects to a repertoire of recorded events, habits, and traditions.

Hiza wove her carpets flat and light as to suit the hot climate of the Sahara. Some were bed coverings and sleeping mats, some saddle blankets for camels and horses, some for self-adornment, others for burial shrouds. Stained rose from the orange and red dyes, her fingers grew gnarled with large arthritic knobs on the knuckles and joints not from age, for she was young, but rather from the arduous, repetitive work of knotting. She more she missed Ibn, the more she yearned, the tighter she drew the knots, as though clutching at a life she did not have.

Lucky thought it quite bizarre to have lived in that place with a man, Ibn, with no memory of togetherness. She remembered their courtyard with the square pool in its center, the geraniums in mad orange profusion spilling over their terracotta pots into the turquoise water or beyond to the florid tiles of the floor. She did not remember him being there. She remembered so many afternoons, sitting on the side of the pool, dipping her wrists, one after the other, into its cool water, and dribbling it into her beloved Woof's open mouth where he lay panting on the tiles next to her feet.

In her Chinese life, four hundred years hence, Lucky met and married Ibn again, this time he was a Chinese Han named Sultan Du who had converted to Islam and led a revolt against the Qing. And, odd as it may seem, they reunited quickly that time, for only two years earlier, her husband, the Englishman called William Merrill, had died of consumption en route to London from Canton with his boss, the merchant Jardine.

As the weaver, Hiza, Lucky unveiled an intimacy of herself in entire compositions on her loom., Her patterns about birth or fertility appeared as a mirror of femininity and of the phases of her life as a woman. Childhood and virginity, bridal state, union, pregnancy, birth pains, birth, and the newborn child, though she didn't remember ever having one, one or more that she must find, must traverse the landscapes of the past for traces of her progeny, if there was any progeny, ever. The geometric motifs were female patterns based on the triangle. The diamond represented a vagina or womb. A diamond with extended lines represented a woman ready to conceive, and the small element between the "legs" indicated birth. Hiza wove diamonds within diamonds within diamonds. Often, she added lines next to the long sides. Sometimes she used crossed lines like the letter *x*.

The spider, snake spine and lion's paw protected the owner from harm. Often the patterns had lines and diamonds representative of the evil eye. She wove the crab and the spider to ward off evil. Little birds or their feet symbolized the land's fertility. Floral patterns banded by solid borders came from Arabian weavers. Her large rugs held abstract images of animals such as lizards, snakes, scorpions, and turtles as they were associated oddly with both fertility and preventing adultery.

Her flat weave involved strands of weft yarn laced in and out of the warp threads and beaten down to make a close, even textile. Some from the hot lowland and desert areas of Morocco used this technique. There were no knots, so flat-weave rugs lay thinner than pile carpet but many featured intricate designs. Stripes and chevrons were common, but fine weavers created rugs that almost resembled tapestries in their complexity.

A knotted pile rug was fluffy and trapped air between the yarns to be warmer than the thin, flat-weave carpet. She laid a few rows of weft threads across the warp and tightened them to make a secure base for the raised-pile knots. Then, she slipped extra weft yarn around the warp, catching at least two warp threads, and knotted the extra yarn across the width of the textile. She continued weaving with weft threads added across the vertical warp threads, interspersed by rows of knotted yarn. The design and the intended thickness of the rug determined how many weft passes she made between rows of knots. At the end of the carpet length, another border of plain weft weaving secured the knotted design. She clipped knots as she worked, or trimmed the pile to an even height before removing the weaving from the loom. She always finished the carpet herself, not leaving her work to a finisher.

Over time, she gained many clients not only from Fez but also from afar. Often, she herself transported her work distances accompanied by her brothers. Camels were the mode. She slung her rugs on one side of a beast and she on the other and across the desert or mountains or plains or coast they swung for days and perhaps weeks at a time until they reached their destination. The camels carried up to a thousand pounds although three hundred and fifty was a far kinder load. She didn't want to simply send off her work; she wanted to see as much of the world as she might be allowed, and so she traveled with her menfolk, carrying their merchandise to the imperial cities, from Fez to Marrakesh, Meknes and Rabat, always on the lookout for Ibn, asking for him in every corner of every medina. Hiza wondered if he fathered children on his travels or spread the word of *Allah* in those far places.

In truth, Ibn was a man of the world, a traveler, soaking up culture wherever he went, leaving semen in his wake. Throughout his journeys, he acquired for himself sex slaves. He also wedded several women, divorced at least some of them, and in Damascus, Malabar, Delhi, Bukhara, and the Maldives begat children by both his wives and his slaves. Ibn detested Greeks, calling them enemies of Allah, drunkards and swine eaters. Yet, in Ephesus, he purchased a Greek girl to hold in his slave harem as he traveled through Byzantium, Khorasan, Africa, and Palestine. It was two decades before he returned to Damascus to find out what happened to one of his wives and child there.

In Calcutta, Ibn came across thirteen Chinese junks built in the cities of Zaytun and Sin-Kalan. He described their sails and even briefly how they were constructed in his journals. He noted the junks were equipped with oars as big as the masts and took tens of men to wield them. When Ibn traveled west to Delhi and Damascus, as the commander of a magnificent Chinese trading vessel, the people greeted him as a great Emir. When he landed, the archers and the Ethiops marched before him bearing javelins and swords, with drums beating and trumpets blowing. When he arrived at the guesthouse where he was to stay, they set up their lances on each side of the gate, and mounted guards to protect him throughout his visit to their cities.

It was long before he returned to Fez, if he left at all, where he found a woman more beautiful than any he had met during his wide travels: his wife, his child bride now a mature woman of great stature and allure. When he recognized her at thirteen as his true, soul wife, she was yet a child, and his desire was to protect her, and protection from other men was his reason for marrying her. Hiza felt it was her good fortune to have married such a man. He never once explored her body, never once saw her naked.

It wasn't true. He did explore her body. He tamed and rode her bareback to arrive at their own shared Garden of Eden, or *Jannah,* on earth, had he not?

BLIP NINE

Lullaby and Good Night,
Thy Mother's Delight

In that next life, her father hired Guillaume, a man of about fifty-six with a huge head of wavy white hair, to tutor her in science, literature, mathematics, Latin, and Greek. The mill in southwestern France provided the perfect place for La Chanceuse, as Lucky was known there, to learn. On warm summer afternoons, the tutor read Voltaire's *Candide* aloud to her great delight under a magnolia tree in full bloom by the mill, where the sound of its water falling soothed her ears while her imagination raced with adventure. He helped her conjugate Latin verbs and write the Greek alphabet. He shared Newton's theory of gravity and spoke of the social theories of the day. He did his best to dramatize the ancient tragedies of Euripides. He read the Greek text in his magnificent baritone. She begged him to stop reading *Medea*, however, when she grasped enough of the plot to be horrified.

"*Arrêtez!*" she cried, shaking all over. "I cannot listen to another word! How could a woman do such a thing?" she moaned. "How could she kill her own children?"

Guillaume turned from drama toward art, convincing her father to let him accompany them on excursions to Paris to preview the latest exhibitions. In the city of light, they feasted on chocolate truffles in small bags from the chocolatier as they walked between museums and artists' studios. Guillaume was right: on seeing the work of sculptors like Edgar Degas and Auguste Rodin, La Chanceuse determined to study clay and modeling, wanting to learn how to create delicate porcelain figurines like those she saw in the artists' studios. Chinoiserie was all the rage. The monarchs of Europe considered porcelain to be as precious as gold for a time. From a small antiquities shop on one such trip, Guillaume gifted her with two small pieces of carved jade. One was a green dragon holding a golden pearl in its jaws. The other was a pendant carved of lavender jade, of a Chinese junk with its small sails and two figures on board wearing conical hats. She set the pieces on her bedside table and dreamt of what life on a Chinese river was like, if it was anything at all like her beloved mill stream?

She married Guillaume despite her father's displeasure, who said Guillaume was his employee and too far her senior. He allowed them to stay on at his home on his many hectares of land, unhappy about their difference in age, but died soon after their wedding. When her sorrow at his sudden loss abated, La Chanceuse began working in earnest in porcelain. Guillaume took over managing her family's land, instituting a new style of farming on the hillsides fronting the stream. He took quickly to the work, reading the latest agriculture texts and improving the yield from the land in many ways.

Guillaume spent a great deal of time with his men in the vineyards. He had a keen nose and routinely lifted the grapes to inhale their fragrance. He perpetually worried about the vines getting enough sun, enough water. He kept rabbits both for the stew pot as well as for their droppings, which he spread in the winter months as fertilizer to provide nitrogen for the vines. He also spread manure from the cows they kept for milking and whose tender offspring they slaughtered for veal.

Late afternoons or early evenings, Guillaume amused himself by playing an antique single action harp inherited from his great-grandfather, Pierre. The harp was magnificently decorated with relief carving of cherubim and lavishly gilded. He kept it in the downstairs parlor, cushioned on a stack of Moroccan carpets. He often played Bach's *Sonata for Harp in G major*, which she loved, or a rendition of Beethoven's *Six Variations on a Swiss Song*. She smiled and hummed along while he pulled the taut strings with near expert aplomb. On such happy evenings, Guillaume playfully dubbed her his "heureuse Chanceuse."

But, she was not truly happy, for she was barren. She wanted to blossom with life like her beloved crab apple trees outside the bedroom. She wanted to give Guillaume a child. She waited season after season for her body to respond to their love, falling into moodiness each passing month when it did not. Her focus was inward, not outward. She wanted a baby, and that was all. Over the centuries, she wanted a child, and she didn't want a child. She knew she had curbed her pregnancies. And, though she thought she had given birth, she could not remember raising any children.

"Perhaps it is me, Ma Petite," Guillaume consoled. "I am old and stale! You are young and fresh! It is a waste of time to ask why."

"It is the only thing I can do," she replied. She attended mass asking God to grant her most fervent prayer.

On evenings after he played, she told him stories she heard as a child about the family's rugs. How each symbol carried meaning either for the weaver or the owner. She showed him the evil eyes woven on borders.

"These ward off danger," she explained. "Grandpere said there is a widespread belief among North Africans in the evil eye, which they say is an envious force that covets the belongings of another." She pointed to some small and large diamonds on the first carpet on the stack. "See, this?'" she asked, touching a deep blue "S" on the edge of the carpet.

"Ah," Guillaume interrupted, "I know! A dragon and it represents strength."

"That is in China," she corrected. "Here, in Islam, on this rug, it symbolizes good and wisdom. This 'S' is a dragon and the guardian of hidden treasure."

"How vivid is the color of your heart, Ma Heureuse!" he declared often, not expecting an answer, loving her stories. "How do you know so much?"

"Grandpere said his family collected these rugs and sold them all over Europe, some to the grand houses in England, even to Hardwick Hall. He saved some of the finest for himself."

"But, what about this shabby, old thing?" Guillaume asked, pulling the ragged, red edges of one low in the stack. "Look, see this one?"

"It is my favorite!" Guillaume lifted the pile to let her unfold the rug. "Grandpere told me it was a very old prayer rug made by a child long ago, probably in Fez. He knew it was made by a child because of its size and the rudimentary weaving. See?" she asked, touching places where the woof was not pulled tight enough to the warp. Look, see this?" she asked, caught by his interest. "It's a frog! Frogs were associated with fertility and magical rites. And this? It's another fertility symbol: a seed."

"I cannot see what you see," Guillaume said, throwing his hands into the air. "All the symbols look geometric."

"Yes, they are. The Muslims never depict people in their art. Only nature and geometric shapes."

"But, you know how to interpret them?"

"Yes, my love. Grandpere taught me. Look, the five linked boxes are a bird, the cross is scissors, the triangle is for religious trances and dizziness, the snakes and fish skeletons of triangles and lines are for magic and medicine."

"And, this, this most elaborate notched square with lines and markings inside?" he asked, touching a saffron yellow pattern woven around the entire edge of a large carpet.

She smiled. "That, my dearest, is the lion's paw! A great symbol of strength. The claws symbolize protection. Just like your big paws!" she laughed, drumming her thin fingers atop his fleshy hand.

They lifted off the carpets one by one until she came to one which she opened fully on the floor. Sitting back to gaze at it, she said, "This one has the most important symbol of all, the cross."

"Why," he wondered. "Isn't the cross a Christian symbol?"

"Of course, but not to Muslims. You see," she pointed, "this cross contains four elements: the triangle whose superior point symbolizes fire and the masculine, while the inferior point represents water and the feminine. The left point of the triangle symbolizes air and that of the right, earth. The cross creates a relationship between the center, the circle, and the square. The four basic points of the cross symbolize the totality of the cosmos. On carpets, the cross undergoes many variations and takes several forms whose significance a non-Muslim," she teased nudging his ribs, "might not understand."

As a sort of consolation for their childlessness, she worked in porcelain, creating paste figures she posed in romantic postures. It was messy work which she did outdoors on days warm enough. She removed her pearl wedding bands before dipping her hands into the moist and sticky clay. Guillaume told her that a white pearl was a tear shed by the gods.

"When I was a child in catechism, a nun told me the tears Eve cried when she was banished from Eden turned to pearls." As LaChanceuse turned her face to kiss Guillaume, he placed his finger on her lips, saying, "Like a pearl, Aphrodite, the goddess of love, came from the sea. And, you, La Chanceuse, came, whether from the sea or from the garden I do not know, to be my love."

She sold the little figures at first to a local chocolatier's shop where they made popular gifts on Valentine's Day, her favorite holiday, surpassing even Christmas and Easter. Valentine's Day became a day for the celebration of love in the Middle Ages. In fact, it was a political decision by the Church as it corresponded to the pagan celebration of Lupercalia, an ancient celebration of fertility, celebrated every year from 13th February to 15th February.

For her projects, she needed clay but not just any clay. They took excursions to local caves searching for signs of feldspathic rock to quarry. At Saint-Yrieix-la-Perche, she bought samples of feldspathic rock to mix at the mill with the kaolin gathered at Limoges. She washed impurities from the raw porcelain clay with the water running through the mill from the stream, taking away pebbles and impurities from clays quarried locally, creating the "hard paste" needed for her sculpting. The mill wheel crushed the rock to a fine powder before she mixed it as an essential ingredient in her hard paste. Such materials, already quarried in France as early as 1768, were used to produce porcelain similar to Chinese porcelain, which was very expensive and very much in vogue.

Petuntse, meaning "little white bricks," referred to the form in which it was transported to the potteries. It was a category covering a wide range of micaceous or feldspathic rocks subjected to geological decomposition processes that resulted in a material which, after processing, was suitable as an ingredient in ceramic formulations. *Petuntse* was an important raw material for Chinese porcelain called *cishi*. There were large deposits of high quality stone in Jiangxi province in south-eastern China, which became the centre for porcelain production, especially in Jingdezhen. La Chanceuse didn't know how or why she felt an affinity for the pure white clay she mixed with kaolin in proportions varying according to the grade of porcelain to be produced; equal quantities for the best and two thirds petuntse to one third kaolin for everyday ware.

It was a day's carriage ride through orchards of walnuts and pastures of sheep to Saint-Yrieix-la-Perche near Limoges to meet the miners. Guillaume's calash had a folding top, and a horse, a roan they named *Femelle,* jauntily pulled it. They rode with the top down as the day was warm enough despite it being early autumn. Though the drive took half a day, at noon they stopped to explore a grotto and to picnic. On a cloth, she set out a dish of foie gras she had made from the livers of a few of their geese, a small jar of preserved cornichon, crusty bread baked in the predawn hours that morning by Madame Roncher, and a variety of cheeses including her favorite, Rocamadour. Belonging to a family of goat cheeses known as Cabécous, this small, velvety disk lent its name to the sacred village of Rocamadour and was one of the oldest cheeses produced in the Dordogne Valley where they lived. The region's chalky soil grew few vegetables but rather hosted herds of goats ever since the fifteenth century when cheese had a monetary value between tenant farmers and landlords.

Sometimes, she and Guillaume planned a roundabout route, going from their home east to Fossiac to see remnants of prehistoric life in the caves surrounding that area. They slept overnight at small inns where she could stock up on the local cheeses before traveling on to Saint-Yrieix-la-Perche. Bleu des Causses, not made from sheep's milk, was a milder variant of Roquefort and shared the same distinctive veins of blue penicillium. Like most blues, Bleu des Causses was delicious with its astonishing mild flavor and aromatic ardor when paired with a sweet, white wine and pears. From the vineyards of Bergerac and cheese stalls of Bretenoux to the truffle farms of Martel and the saffron festival at Carjac, as residents of the Dordogne, their mealtimes weren't to be ignored.

The Abbaye Notre-Dame de Bonne Espérance produced the celebrated Trappe d'Echourgnac cheese. Driven by a mission to help the people, its monks created a cheesemaking facility and purchased milk from neighbouring farms. They produced Bleu des Causses using the milk from cows that grazed on the limestone plateaux of the Dordogne Valley. It matured on oak shelves for three to six months in the natural caves of the Gorges du Tarn. Nature controlled the temperatures in cellars responsible for the cheese's maturing which imparted it with a special aroma. Its flavor differed depending on the season in which it matured. Ivory-yellow summer cheeses were milder than the stronger-tasting, white winter cheeses.

Whether as Lucky sculpting in the tropics or creating at Rufford, or as Tyche making headstones beneath the myrtle, or as Ying Yue glazing in her warehouses, or her many other selves, La Chanceuse spent hundreds of happy hours sculpting her delicate porcelain into figurines under the shade of the crab apples in spring, the magnolia tree in the summer, or the golden rain tree in fall which stood near the mill.

At the top of a lovely square overlooking the historic center of Bergerac sat tiny, old Saint-Jacques church. Romanesque in style, built in the twelfth century as a chapel on the pilgrim route to Compostela and enlarged in the thirteenth century, it became the medieval town's church. It underwent many alterations over the centuries with the nave completely rebuilt in the 18th. But now, it was deemed too small for its large congregation.

A new church, the Eglise Notre Dame, was to be consecrated. It had the typical longitudinal, cruciform plan with a long nave crossed by a transept. If viewed from above, which no one could, it looked like the Latin cross lying on the hilltop.

One of the priests she confessed to on numerous occasions as she prayed for a child came by to watch her work on Saturday afternoons. As the church was nearing completion, he suggested she create miniature creche tableaux for its first Christmas celebrations. The priest asked if her creche might be ready for display at the first mass in December in one of the completed naves. Throughout the spring and into fall, she worked on several creche scenes and small boxes topped with the individual animals from the manger like the donkey or the cow. For them, she sculpted from hard paste miniature cows, sheep, donkey, angels, wise men, and a stable, in addition to the doting Mary and Joseph. The Christ child himself was cherub-cheeked and swathed in white porcelain sheeting with a gleaming halo of gold leaf surrounding his head. Once on display, the scene delighted the parishoners' children, who wanted to pick up the pieces, cradle them in their arms or stuff them into their pockets to take home. The nuns had to keep vigil. If a piece did disappear, generally a sheep or cow, sometimes an angel, the priest summoned La Chanceuse. She made many replacements and was overjoyed to bring in new ones as it meant the town approved her work.

After the holidays, in the heart of winter cold, the priest came to her again, this time to ask if she could make the center piece for the cathedral: the Christ child of the Virgin Mary.

His request astounded her. She knew it was a sign from above, the sign that meant she was to be a mother, if not in the flesh, at least in her art.

"Why not let me make the whole statue?" she asked. "The virgin mother and the child?"

"Can you really make something so large?" the priest asked in great surprise.

"Yes, I shall do it!" she exclaimed.

Energized with life by this commission, she set about listing what she needed. A new kiln was obvious, as she never made any larger than life-size, human figures. Then, she needed to create saggars large enough to encase the figures. She used wood to heat the kiln to high temperature. To prevent the ash falling from the wood firing and marring her glazes, she needed to make saggars. A saggar was like bottomless a lidded casserole made of fire-clay large enough for her sculpture to fit inside. She needed many of these saggar rings to stack to accommodate its height. She needed quantities of chemicals to mix to make enough glaze and colorants for the clothing and facial treatments. She also needed gold, much more gold for the young prince of light than she had needed for the creche scenes, for a halo above his head.

She visited the church often not only to pray but also to study the space where her statue might stand, take measurements, monitor the light for the best spot to place the Christ child for illumination.

"Guillaume! Guillaume! I need your help," she implored. "I need a new kiln. I've drawn it. Can you find some men to bring bricks and mortar? I need metal struts for an arch and to hold the bricks for the door."

"You are on fire, my darling!" he laughed. "Of course, of course, whatever you need."

"I need chemicals. I have the list. And, wood, cords and cords of wood, for the firing. Oh! And, clay! We must return to Saint-Yrieix-la-Perche. I must create a new porcelain body, something that can be large, not the hard paste I use for my figurines. I must have many clays to mix and test. I cannot let the Virgin crack!"

"It sounds like this project will take months," he remarked.

"Yes, perhaps even years. It will be my life's work," she proclaimed. "The church won't be completed for some time to come. By then, I should be ready."

She did not know from whence her knowledge came. Without thinking, she formulated a clay body that neither shrank nor cracked. She requested kyanite from the miners, the element that allowed her porcelain to withstand the rigors of drying and firing. It was to be ground to a powder and mixed with the clay. In her French life, she had forgotten her Chinese experience dealing in porcelain. She had imported porcelain from Jingdezhen. She brought it down the Pearl to Canton, where she glazed and fired it before storing it in her warehouses for export. The British merchants waited there with payments in silver to take these teapots, cups, vases, and figurines back to England along with the tea, porcelain, and pearls she brokered.

She sketched for hours sitting under the magnolia near the mill. How the virgin would stand, or would she sit? How tall? How to place her so every parishioner could see her. Where the light from the glass windows fell to best illuminate her face and the child?

Located ideally by the river, the mill and house attracted guests. Chanceuse and Guillaume's friends were many; they enjoyed the company of artists, farmers, vintners, and artisans alike. Guillaume's vineyards stretched in neat rows for hectare after hectare, spread over a large area on both sides of the Dordogne River, divided between alluvial terraces on the right and limestone plateaus on the left bank. Guillaume's wines and brandy gained steady clients not only in Paris, but also abroad in England and as far as Russia in the court of Alexander III. Occasionally, she accompanied Guillaume on the sales trips, as Paris was among her favorite destinations. But, she did not travel as far as Russia.

In his Bergerac rouge, Guillaume used at least two of four prescribed varieties: merlot, cabernet sauvignon, cabernet franc and malbec. In Souillac, he kept in buildings called *chais* a smooth plum brandy called La *Vieille Prune*, in wooden casks. In the *chais* were also stills, presses, filters, and pots. His brandy grew highly refined as it matured slowly in oak barrels. He brought home the dark bottles, uncorking one or perhaps two in the late afternoon, under the magnolia tree where Chanceuse was finishing her porcelain work and guests were lounging on the grass, relaxed, or rolling a heavy ball from their game of boule. Theirs was a quiet and rich life, smooth as his brandy, as romantic as her sculpture. She did not rail at lack of public acknowledgement of her work as she felt divinely inspired.

Each evening, Guillaume poured his wife a glass of wine, surprising her anew with the vigor and smoothness of his blends. They spent many hours enjoying conversation, relaxing in this manner, glass in hand, warmth on tongue, dog near the hearth, love deep in heart, creativity flowing, often leaving their wine glasses unwashed in the sink, eager to heat the cool linen sheets with each other.

Guillaume warmed to see his wife so happy. He invited the priest for a celebratory toast, uncorking one of his best wines. Suddenly, Guillaume, too, gained a commission, as the priest, delighted with the wine, asked him to provide the sacramental wine for the church and mass. Fortunately, Guillaume had several rows of the requisite *Vitis vinifera* grapes and was delighted to accept this profitable commission from the church.

He traveled occasionally without her to England where a lucrative market waited for his wine and cheese. He returned home with the latest fashions and songs. She laughed when he sang "Home Sweet Home" with the lines, "'Mid pleasures and palaces though we may roam, be it never so humble, there's no place like home,'" and felt her eyes prickle with his rendition of "Auld Lang Syne," which resonated pleasantly somewhere in memory.

She had the kiln built of local brick, iron struts from the iron monger in the village, and fired with wood dried for months from the trimmings of their cherry and apple trees. She fired several small loads to test the altered clay body, the glazes she formulated, and the saggars. After a few months, she was ready to fire the eight-foot tall virgin holding the Christ child. She placed stacks like donuts of the large saggars around the virgin, reserving the smaller saggars for the child. She planned to cradle the babe in the virgin's arms later, once she safely installed the sculpture in the cathedral.

She summoned the priest to bless the kiln and its sacred contents. He brought a vial of holy water to sprinkle on the bricks and prayers to utter for safety. The firing took over three days, feeding the kiln wood to heat it to temperature, and five more days to cool before unbricking the door to see the results. Almost nine days later, the kiln was ready for her to unload. For this, La Chanceuse wanted to be alone. This commission meant almost as much as life to her. She wanted her eyes alone to see it, whether they beheld a success or dismal failure.

She began with the top brick of the door, sliding it out with a gloved hand and setting it on the ground to her right. A lantern flickered providing just enough light for her to see. Guillaume brought her white wool shawl, silently draping it over her shoulders and walking away without a word, understanding her need to be alone.

Once open, the kiln revealed in the dim light the short saggars holding the Christ child in front of the much taller saggars containing the Virgin. A long, jagged crack ran from the top half of that larger stack of saggars to its base. She sucked in breath through her teeth. A possible disaster. The small saggar was cool, and she lifted off the lid. Holding the lantern above it, she could see that the child was unblemished and intact. She stood back to gather herself, debating whether to look at the Virgin's cracked saggar or to wait until morning to do so. She sank to her knees and recited ten

Hail Mary's. Finished, she rose and walked to the house without hesitating or looking back.

The next morning, she asked Guillaume to bring his workers to the kiln to lift away the saggars for her as they were heavy. She waited in the house all morning. Around noon, the men arrived and went to the kiln. Guillaume strode up to the house, a large smile on his face, and without a word, took her by the hand to the kiln.

There, revealed in soft colors and folds of seemingly life-like porcelain fabric, reminiscent of the draped clothing Phidias sculpted on the Parthenon's caryatids, stood an immaculate Virgin and, at her feet, the Christ child. La Chanceuse rested her head on Guillaume's chest and wept. She went back to the house and slept. When she regained her strength over the next few days, she ordered gold leaf and applied it to the halos. She thought a tiny amount of paint might brighten cheeks and highlight the eyes. Guillaume summoned a cart, workmen filled it with hay to nestle the statues for a safe journey to the Eglise. The same workers carried the statues inside for the installation. The parishioners gasped when they saw the statues unveiled at the Sunday mass, astounded that La Chanceuse captured chaste beauty almost transparently in clay. They laid bouquets of roses, iris, peonies, and more at the statue's feet, and left some bouquets on La Chanceuse's doorstep as well.

With the commission completed and consecrated, La Chanceuse stayed in bed for weeks, exhausted. She could not understand why she had no appetite yet felt bloated and nauseous. Guillaume worried that she had ruined her health working so tirelessly on the commission. And then, there was the blood. She wept, inconsolable.

"I didn't know! I didn't know!" she cried. "I only thought I was tired."

Guillaume tried to calm her. "A baby will come, my darling, if it is to be. It is you I want. Only you." Concerned for her health, Guillaume was desperate for her recovery and ordered every sanitary precaution taken. He knew that Voltaire's dear companion, Marquise du Châtelet, a French natural philosopher, mathematician, physicist, and author died after childbirth. Châtelet was in her forties and had many lovers, but succumbed to a mad passion and became pregnant. In a letter to a friend, she confided her fear, "I may not survive this pregnancy due to the ignorance of the doctors!" Sure enough, her baby, a girl, was born in what at first seemed an easy delivery; but the physician washed neither his hands nor his implements. Châtelet contracted a fever and died.

La Chanceuse did recover, and a few weeks later, Guillaume presented her with an eight-week old puppy, a Chinese Shar Pei full of wrinkles with a soft purple tongue jutting from its jowls. She was delighted.

"Where did you find her?" La Chanceuse asked.

"In London. Queen Victoria has one, and they are all the rage. People think they are teddy bears! I asked around on my last visit. One of the wine shop owners knew of a litter and promised to send one with his man when he came to pick up the cases of my Bergerac. The housekeeper has taken care of her while you've been recovering."

"What shall we call her?" she asked. "*Belle?*"

He looked at her and laughed. "How about *Le Dindon?*" he asked.

"Turkey?" she replied, confused at first. "Ah," she realized remembering Huo-ji, "Turkey, so the gods won't be jealous!"

"Absoluement!" And so, Turkey, it was. Or rather, *Le Dindon*.

That winter as she fired her wood burning kiln, both hardening her work and keeping her warm as ice lay on the ground, Le Dindon was her constant companion. The dog accompanied Guillaume in the vineyards, kept rats at bay, and took special care herding the sheep. He curled at their feet on carriage rides or chased the ball thrown by the boule players. La Chanceuse occasionally fondled his back as he lay on the Moroccan carpet of pomegranate, decorated with many deep ochre diamond shaped evil-eyes and straight black masculine lines while she listened to Guillaume read, sing, or play his harp.

Happy with their new pup, her sorrow at the loss of their child began to diminish. Inspired to create again, this time she designed a line of dolls, babies, her babies. These she made of bisque-fired porcelain heads and hands from the clay left from the batch she had mixed for the Virgin. The parts were sewn onto soft bodies made of stuffed cloth. Her baby dolls with their life-like faces and hands became popular beyond her hopes. Needing help to fill orders, she found a girl from the village to sew and stuff cloth bodies for them. Other women in the village were eager to help this artist who had created the Virgin. They fashioned wigs for the dolls from real hair and stitched dresses from silk and lace. A milliner made hats in the style of the day festooned with ornamental flowers and small jewels.

Sometimes Chanceuse painted her dolls' faces after they hardened enough in a bisque fire. Other times she glazed the faces with ceramic materials and fired the colors in the kiln. Later, she left holes for the eye sockets and commissioned a glassmaker to make the eyes. Blue-eyed Victoria was on the throne in England and much admired. Chanceuse ordered the glass maker to create blue eyes for her dolls, both the baby and the fashion, *poupe'e de mode,* dolls.

She also designed and made adult fashion dolls, gaining a wide following when Guillaume sold them through Francois Gaultier near Paris. She could not market her goods in France under her own name as it was not acceptable for a woman to be an artist or sculptor in her own right. Guillaume took credit for her work to gain such a contract with Gaultier, where he sold her dolls wholesale in Paris.

On the outskirts of the city, they stopped at the house of the sculptor, Auguste Rodin at Meudon as they had when she was a student. Once in the city, she went to Rodin's other studio on the Rue de Varenne called the Hôtel Peyrenc de Moras where Camille Claudel was working.

When Camille's physical relationship with Rodin ended, she was not able to get the funding to realize many of her own, more daring ideas. The art critics of the day expressed sex-based censorship, damning the sexual element of her work. Camille had become dependent on Rodin financially, especially after her loving and wealthy father's death, which allowed her mother and brother, who disapproved of her lifestyle, to cut her off. They controlled the family fortune and left her to wander the streets dressed in beggars' clothing.

"She is as a revolt against nature," her brother said. "Working is a right reserved for men."

Claudel thus had to either depend on Rodin or collaborate with him. And, if she did collaborate, like La Chanceuse did with Guillaume, Rodin got credit for her work, despite her genius, lionized as he was as the great French sculptor. La Chanceuse far preferred Claudel's work to Rodin's. Though similar to his in spirit, hers showed an imagination and lyricism quite her own. As a consequence, La Chanceuse felt a kinship with Camille, as neither were credited by the art community as creators of their own art. La Chanceuse wanted to befriend the sculptress, but the passionate artist had no time for friendships. Even the composer Debussy's overtures of love were rejected by Camille.

At Camille's studio, La Chanceuse became enamored of a piece called *The Waltz* and begged Guillaume to buy her a plaster copy. Debussy was one of the few, like Chanceuse, who admired Camille as a great artist in her own right. He kept a copy of *The Waltz* in his music room until his death. Of her disavowal of his affection, Debussy wrote, "I weep for the disappearance of the dream of this dream."

Lucky wondered how she as La Chanceuse died in that French life. Did she outlive Guillaume? Die of old age or disease? Or, as she was young, did she die during childbirth? Or, get sepsis after delivery? O memory! Return! Infant mortality was as high for the mother as the newborn. Did she as La Chanceuse finally get pregnant only to succumb after the birth?

Oh, if only she could return to that home in France, to the village to peruse the gravestones, checking for names, dates of birth and death, to find Guillaume, to find herself, to find their child, if they had one. Did she finally receive the blessing of a child only to die like Voltaire's mistress, Châtelet?

Lucky remembered burying *Le Dindon* under the magnolia where he spent many hours watching her sculpt in its shade out of one semi-opened eye or the other. Perhaps her own grave was there?

Guillaume had left, she knew not why, through death or disappointment. He went east to Russia on one of his sales' trips and did not return. It was Russia, wasn't it? And, she? Did she leave as well, going west, past America, into a new incarnation, to an island, a paradise somewhere in the Pacific? How else must she have gotten here, she concluded, as she looked out her window at the breeze softly combing the fronds.

BLIP TEN

Song for The Broken-Hearted

The fragrance of plumeria in the air bowled her over. She had found a place to live, a beautiful house, on the edge of a cliff above the ocean and next to a spectacular waterfall. She loved the soft caress of the air almost as much as she loved the changing colors of the sea. She learned of beaches and trails unknown to tourists where she trekked to swim or hike alone.

Enchanted by the new landscape, she took to photographing elements of the tropics new to her but not in any professional way: the sunrises behind the island painting the sea a glowing rose, the sunsets beyond her beach staining the clouds in pigmented layers stacked like trays of golden apples, oranges, and tangerines. She photographed the night sky when the stars sank so low they scraped the sea floor, bathing the coral heads there in skeletal light. She captured the wetted greens of the forests, the rainbowed blossoms of the flowers, the filtered sunlight as it danced across the blackened rocks.

Lucky disliked spiders, although she respected them. They were fellow weavers after all. The tropics held huge ones, the largest known as cane spiders. They thrived in the acres of sugar cane fields cultivated on nearly every island. A big one skittered across her field of vision with a soft rat-ta-tat on the woven *lauhala* mat in her living room. The usual revulsion shuddered through her body as she gingerly walked by it to the kitchen to retrieve a sieve. Plopped over the spider, it imprisoned him until morning when she could see well enough to let him loose. Sure enough, the next day, he waited, trapped, while she tuned in radio news reports of missile launches followed by jihadist retaliation. She slid a plate from the kitchen under the spider and bore him, under the protective dome of the sieve, outside. She let him run free in the garden under the *haupu'u* fern amid red anthurium blooms. She didn't harm him this time.

Lucky punished herself, instead, afraid of life, afraid of living, horrified by the mistakes she made, costly mistakes, what some might rightly call "murder and mayhem." She fled to live her current incarnation as a hermit, on an isolated dot of volcanic rock in the middle of the Pacific, a prison of sorts, not unlike Elba or Alcatraz, where she let guilt run rampant through her soul before her attempts at personal metamorphosis. Over time, she succeeded in raking away some of the misdeeds and regrets from her many lives. What she couldn't rake, she jerked out by hand, not minding the dirt or mud or self-recrimination.

Despite her clean-up efforts, she found she couldn't weed out guilt. That was rooted too deep. She did not rest easy. Guilt made a hard and cruel mattress. She tried to drown her guilt with a poison of choice—alcohol. But, it only increased the height of unwanted weeds crowding her soul. The *Round-up* of a hundred woulda-coulda-shoulda's, shoulda's like saving a life—her baby's, her husband's, her mother's, her children's, and more—had been drunk, but could not kill her grief over their losses. She understood she failed in grand form to take off her self-absorbed blinders in time to come to the aid of her faltering loved ones before they were gone, gone perhaps forever, as she'd never found them again, neither to return nor resurrect.

She relied heavily on sleeping pills, hypnotics, and, felt lost, not wanting to recognize herself. Seeing old photos but not quite remembering who she was or how she got to be who she was now, that old woman in the long bathroom mirror, that wrinkled, white face and gobbler neck, those tight lips, those querying eyes, those lashes faded and thin. Who had she become? No longer beguiling, no longer imbued with boundless energy, no longer physically able to run or skip or even go down steps without holding a handrail. Where were her pelvic bones which used to march ahead of her flattened belly? Her stomach protruded with gases as her mother's did. Had she somehow become her own mother without knowing it? Where was her flexible spine which contorted in every direction, turning her upside down and inside out like a pretzel in the yoga classes she once taught? Where was her liquidity of form learned from the *qi gong* she practiced? Leaning back, arms outstretched above her head, she could move scarcely a degree or two. Was it age? Inertia? Depression? Probably all three, if she was honest.

Post seventy, she became sedentary, moving from bed to computer to dining table to couch with little or no actual exercise inserted into the day. And, depressed, having lost a marriage. No, how could she? She didn't marry. At least, she didn't remember being married this time around. Losing children, whose children? Hers? No, no children without Merrill. Losing multiple friends and a few family members, made her sad, of course, but now, without clay, loom, or camera, the tools of her livelihoods, she was slowly losing her marbles. Yes, she was depressed, and her marbles were rolling across the deck to fall through its slats into the sands of time.

Headaches like morning alarms wakened her. Startled by pain, she lifted from her pillow, surfacing with a whale-like, partially lidded eye to see the scarlet flush of dawn over a still sea, before she re-submerged into the cool of a deep, second sleep. The sky continued to blush a rouge of sweet nectarine across the surface of a world burnished within by the gentle breathing of its many submerged and sleeping souls.

As the day opened its eyes, no sun lit the land. A storm stealthily approached, and, warned by its thunder, birds scattered uncertainly to quaking branches of trees. She awoke, too, at the piercing crack of pain in her head and chest, in her lungs, the repositories of grief, reminding her not to move quickly, not to roll to the left, but to lie still. She had much to do, but she'd leave it undone this morning.

She heard Turkey give a soft bark. She waited for a more serious alert. When the dog barked not twice but three more times, she knew she must roust herself from bed. Her knees as usual refused to cooperate when she tried to rise. She sat on the bed's edge, her head down, breathing deeply and begged her knees to come to attention and support her.

She rose slowly, one hand on the bedside table for support, the other pushing on the thick back of the black and white hunting dog who had come to her aid. Together they walked to the sliding glass doors at the deck above the sand, her other hand pulling her nightdress away from her legs. She didn't want to trip. There, Turkey growled again. Lucky couldn't see a thing; the only thing she could hear was the wind as it whipped the fronds made bitter by its torment.

She lived alone; no neighbors nearby to call or to hear a call, if she made one. There were a few native seabirds, the pink-legged stilt called *ae'o,* the *kolea,* a seasonal plover, an occasional heron or cattle egret. Once a green turtle drowned in an errant net blown to shore on the trades. She hadn't yet spotted a monk seal, though she swam with them on the more westward beaches. Throughout the winter months from her wind-blown deck, she intently watched the antics of humpback whales through high grade binoculars.

Turkey barked rarely. Perhaps, she thought, it was a deer come to drink the brackish water from the pond fronting the reef or to escape the battering of trees in the upper forests.

Why hadn't Merrill or Ibn or Vassilios arrived? Her love always came. Where was he? Why was he taking so long this time? What if she had forgotten who he was by the time he made it to her? This eternal waiting created nothing in her soul but misery. Her fragmenting memory was like the loosened, network of a delicate dandelion blossom strewn suddenly by a breeze.

The blue of her eyes, clouded by tears, yearned to see Merrill, again. She watched the sky through its many dawns, noons, sunsets and nights. She knew the sky felt her longing as it built clouds of its own beneath its aching belly to slip as underskirts of rain to the earth at her feet. It frightened her to lose her pasts. She lived so often, died so often, always knowing for certain she would come back. But, even that certainty was eroding. Would she know Merrill, Ibn, William in her next life? Was her memory to evaporate before her body expired? Would this death of so many before be her last, leaving behind an entire life lived without him?

She wondered if spring was coming. She dwelled on this island without seasons, and without her daughter, her son, her children, her husband, the season for her was always winter. How she wanted spring with her family and flowers!

She sank back into bed. What time was it?

Her mental faculties suffered small, short-term memory lapses the day after taking *zolpidem* for insomnia. Faces recalled but names lost, that sort of thing. But, names soon came back; the lapses only transitory. Her grandchildren accused her of repeating herself, telling them stories they heard before. She laughed them off. She reached across the bed for the empty bottle of *zolpidem*. How old was the prescription? No, she hadn't been able to sleep since they died. Since he died. No, since she died. Her children. Her daughter. But, no, stop. She didn't have any children or grandchildren.

"Mom! Mom!" Lucky opened her eyes. It was that woman again. "Mom, you haven't answered your phone! You had me so worried!" Lucky looked about. She sat up in her bed and saw about her sheets, white sheets, white sheets tangled everywhere.

"Did you do a laundry?" she asked the woman.

"No, Mom."

"Why are there white sheets everywhere?"

"Mom, get up. You're wearing your old wedding dress. That's your veil across the bed. It looks like you've torn it this time, and you've got the train wrapped around your legs. Here, I'll help you get out of it."

"No! Don't touch me!"

The woman retreated.

"Now, look," Lucky cried, pointing to a broken necklace strewn over the gown, pearls dropping one by one from the bed to the floor.

"Oh! Your Chinese pearls! What a shame," the woman said and bent to gather them.

"I am waiting for him," Lucky said.

"Who?"

"Him," Lucky repeated, annoyed at the broken necklace and further annoyed at the woman's incomprehension.

"Oh, Mom. I'm sorry. He's not here. Dad's not here."

"I'm talking about my son, my boy," Lucky said angrily. "Go away."

"Mom!"

"If you must stay," Lucky relented, "help me with my hair." As she got up, she saw her wedding bouquet. Someone put it in a yellow Chinese cloisonné vase beside the green jade dragon on the table next to her bed, a lovely bouquet of long-stemmed white roses with sprigs of baby's breath.

At the wedding, she remembered seeing the bride and groom face one another. And, *she* stood, *she*, a woman, was it her daughter who stood? *She* stood between them adorned in a dress of claret. *She* faced the groom, *her* back to his bride, and *she* wore a dress not of white but rather of claret. Lucky saw *her* clearly, though perhaps no one else did, for *she*, her daughter, was his true bride, her daughter, the woman, the bride of his heart, the bride yearning to bear his children, to sleep in his arms. Her daughter died, a suicide in that love triangle. But, *she* stood there, at the wedding, between them.

She was not alive, too frail for the savagery of this world. A photo journalist. Was *she* killed, her work so dangerous? Lucky remembered fear, so afraid for *her*. And, yes, *she* did die. It was in Kuwait, it was Kuwait, wasn't it? Something about being too close to the fumes of the burning oil fields. They were never sure. Maybe a sniper. Maybe a roadside bomb. Lucky suspected it was a broken heart. After all, *she* left her fiancé to shoot the war, and while *she* was gone, he married her best friend.

Lucky's memories swirled like eggs cracked in a bowl, at first separate, then whisked into goo, scrambled.

It was her daughter who loved him. Her daughter. Lucky's daughter. That was coming back to her, wasn't it? And, it was her daughter who loved her own best friend's fiancé. And, he proposed to *her*, her daughter, and her daughter was glad, her daughter was sad, her daughter loved her best friend, and worst and most, her daughter felt guilty. *She* told her best friend *she* loved the fiancé but was giving him up. *She* told the fiancé *she* was giving him up. And, give up *she* did: *she* flew to Kuwait to cover a war where *she* died, not by bomb or bullet but rather by swallowing a very large bottle of *Tylenol* and falling into a coma. And, about a year later, *she* died, didn't she? And, the best friend married the fiancé, and they did not live happily thereafter. For *she* was there, always there, standing between them, as Lucky, her mother, clearly saw.

The dead were never dead. Although they disappeared from both sight and sound, she felt their presence through her skin, in the muscle of the heart, or the pathways of her mind, in the ear of memory. The dead acted upon her, sometimes with violence, sometimes with beneficence, but act they did. The living and the dead rolled together down roads of dust in her soul like tumbleweeds tossed by the wind.

What was her name, this daughter? Blue eyes, yes, *she* had blue eyes, still eyes that observed the world but revealed nothing, nothing of her own reflections. Scraggly ponytail, yes, ashen hair gathered into a scrunchy behind her head. Blonde, yes, *she* was blonde, so blonde, her hair often glowed like her father's did as white as the full moon. Like a rose pricked by its own thorns, this daughter was born without skin. Life hurt her. Even the air hurt, the bedding, clothing, all. This daughter had skin, of course *she* had skin, which was thin and a porcelain white despite hours surfing and swimming. Her mouth a rosebud, rich Valentine red against that white of her complexion. White was Lucky's favorite color, like a prism, all colors in one. She had never taken off the rope of moon-like pearls she wore around her neck, until it broke, pearls adrift over the bed covers and rolling across the bamboo floor.

A photo journalist, this daughter revealed truth not in words, for she spoke little, but in pictures. *She* documented wrongs; *she* unveiled secrets. She even found beauty in war and in death.

Yet, *she* felt, deeply and powerfully. *She* stood behind life armed with a camera, her eye behind the lens, recording events, friends, places, flowers, water. Beauty was everything to her. Her mother, Lucky, yes, she taught her that. Nudity, bare bones, the whiteness of bones, whether from dead livestock or antlers of deer taken after a kill, fascinated her. *She* photographed funerals, the coffins most often, favoring black lacquer with white roses or lilies atop. And then, abruptly, *she* abandoned this strange whitened landscape of shadows and turned to photographing death itself. The dying, the dead, some cadavers, but only if wrapped in bandages looking like the mummies of old. *She* went to war.

Too sensitive for this world, *she* grew fascinated by the world beyond this, the world of death and afterlife. And, so, *she* chose to leave and took her own life.

Lucky remembered sitting on the small plane, flying back to her island home, a small sack on her lap with this daughter, this daughter inside the sack, her daughter's remains, ash and graveled bits of bone. Not heavy, quite light in fact, yet the heaviest burden Lucky ever bore, this child, this dead child.

Her body or what was left of it, and was it even her body? burnt, mangled, arrived in the U.S. on a military flight from Kuwait. Lucky flew to Washington to identify her, although that proved an impossible task, as the body presented looked nothing like her daughter looked in life. Lucky signed papers, allowed a cremation, waited until the health department approved release for the little sack of ashes to travel again, this time, to the island. Lucky sat numbly holding the precious bundle on her lap, flying above clouds and over oceans. At home, she rested it on her mantle, where she passed it several times a day as she walked through her house, trekking back and forth on the hardwood planks, digging ruts of regret, deep regret, and sorrow. Months went by before she scattered the remains of her daughter off a cliff below her house, a gift to the winds and waters of time.

Did she sing a lamentation then as she had for the Greek oil trader? Did she lament high above the waves as her child's ashes showered down?

No. She contemplated in silent solitude as she stood in the wind, how those ashes might recombine. Would they resurrect as the petals of the white roses *she* loved? As the soft fur on a newborn pup? As the vegetables in the garden? Matter once created was never lost. But, what about her soul? The invisible? Was it partaking of heavenly feasts or perhaps wandering the ether seeking salvation?

She didn't pass alone. *She* took others with her when *she* died, as if punishing the living for the normal offenses like ignorance or self-absorption. *She* walked as a ghostly presence through their lives as memory, rode with the living in their cars and swam with them in the sea, bathing them in loneliness, and blanketing them with regret before they slept. Yet, her face would be reborn like an angel's on the faces of generations to come.

Lucky looked at the silver gelatin prints on the wall taken by this daughter, the daughter with the long, ashen ponytail, who fell in love with death, photographing cadavers and whitened bones on backgrounds of black. The one that hung over her bed was of discarded ivory tusks poached from a beast long dismembered in some far-off land.

BLIP ELEVEN

Time Goes by So Slowly
Wait for It, Wait for It

Lucky arrived at the station just before eleven. It was quite dark, and no one was on the platform. This dream trip was not ideal. It was a scouring of the soul, a "scraping of the last shreds of meat from the bone" trip. She approached the track with luggage unreasonably heavy and saw no one on the other side. The train master's office looked deserted; the ticket window closed. She rechecked her ticket, and yes, her train was due at eleven, departing Athens for Istanbul at eleven fifteen. She was heading east for the first time.

The wind was sharp; her clothes too thin; her camera leaden; the loneliness at the station palpable. It was Christmas Eve, she the only soul traveling and not toward family. She wasn't sure why she had come; looking for something or someone; but had found nothing in four days except ruins and closed shops. It felt cold enough to snow, but that close to the sea, the wet and icy weather slapped her unshielded skin.

He wasn't there, her husband. He wasn't in Athens. Sometimes she was lucky, and he turned up as she haunted ancient sites. But, not this time. Her fragile wings felt more like claws, clinging to the mire of their entanglements through the centuries, of retribution, of guilt from their mortal failures.

And, she missed him. She missed him so much. She pushed down the prickly sensation in her nose and throat of tears about to flow, pushed down the disappointment, pushed down the missing. Maybe this wasn't the right century. Or country. Or place. She would plant herself elsewhere, catch a train, and hope for the best. She hoped he would catch up with her, grab her suitcase by the handle, and lead her home. She wanted to reach up on tiptoe to place her arms around his neck, how she missed that stretch, when he pulled her into a tight and lengthy embrace.

She left him, her most recent entanglement, a self-styled guru of sorts, the very frank and ascetic, Josh, who was a much-admired practitioner of *A Course in Miracles.* He was a celebrity of sorts in the eyes of those following the path of new-age style enlightenment. Though he had a full mane of wavy white hair, baritone voice, and sparkling eyes, he was a mistake. Sometimes she erred, thinking a new love was her husband, only to be disappointed on getting to know the new man better.

Before they met, Josh spent most of his adult life like the Biblical Joseph, a carpenter, and lived in communes all over the world. He fathered a few children from brief liaisons with various devotees, as he was joyously polyamorous, remembering his children on rare occasions, just as Ibn had occasionally remembered one or two of his. When this Josh became a self-styled mystic, he changed his name, choosing Joshua as it meant salvation. Lucky, too, changed her name. He chose Arbella for her, meaning yielding to pray, or maybe simply, yielding to him. It was then they had married by the temple, holding hands in a ceremony with hundreds of others, outside a hippie communal geodesic dome in the heart of a distant rainforest, somewhere tropical and humid.

She wielded a hammer like other commune members to build domes for meditation, covered pavilions for cooking, and huts for sleeping. There were no telephones, no mail, no paved roads, no internet. There were lots of drugs. The group was a polyglot of nationalities, although most were American and all spoke English. They were young, hopeful, and amoral. Lucky come Arbella helped in the vegetable gardens, scrubbed laundry on the rocks near a waterfall, and took care of Josh's every personal need and desire.

His beard was Jesus length in varying shades of gray, his head topped by that shock of curling white she so associated with her true love, though Josh wore his hair quite long and unruly. He was ascetic-thin, living on air and religious fervor, more attentive to his notion of God than to food or to her. She was young then; her blonde hair draped to either side of her soft, often naked buttocks, her small breasts rarely clothed lifted upward toward her lips, above which her blue eyes shone with the light of naïveté and hope.

He levitated. It was marvelous to see. He sat in a lotus pose, eyes closed, breathing deeply with audible frog-like exhalations. Slowly, his body began to rise until it was about eighteen inches above the floor. He remained suspended while deep in his self-induced trance for varying periods of time.

She was jealous of his practice, of his devotion to God. She wanted his attention on her. He, on the other hand, wanted her to drop acid, drink the toxic and hallucinogenic *ayahuasca,* eat magic mushrooms, snort cocaine, shoot heroin, smoke peyote and marijuana, swallow ecstasy whole. Then, he said, she might loosen up enough to leave her body, to astral travel, to enjoy the shamanic insights which he so regularly did. But, she did not indulge in pills, drinks, or smoke.

She tried *kriya* yoga instead. She let her breath ride the down escalator from her nostrils to her pubis, down her spine and back up, through every one of the seven *chakras,* down and back up until she felt fully charged. When her body vibrated like an electrical circuit board, she opened the long-closed fontanelle at the top of her skull to let her soul fly out on electric volts of energy. The excited air took her on a magic carpet ride through time and the cosmos.

How shocking it was. Bits and pieces of people she knew, actual body parts or whole cadavers, flew by like birds seeking their nests against galactic winds. But, there were no nests in space. She saw babies, a fetus even, drift by, quite out of reach, though reach for it she did. She saw her mother, the Pythia from Amfissa; she saw her dog, Molossus; she saw her headless husband, Sultan Du, and many others from the corner of her eye. Her out-of-body experiences completely unnerved her. Wedding veils, white roses, and children traveled through the galaxies like asteroids nearly colliding with her, above and below her path. Magnetized as though iron filled her marrow, she attracted them to her, as if to no other.

Out there, it was not silent. She heard music. She thought it was the celestial spheres, but the chords were too familiar. Bach, Beethoven, the plucking as Guillaume did of harp strings, and of her own old songs played on the lute and pipa, her fingers striking the keys of the virginal. The old sounds filled her with longing to find the players, find the singers, find her husband whom she realized, whom she knew, was not this present Josh. He was not her true love. He was a misadventure of sorts, a wrong turn in her search.

Disappointed, she returned to her body spent, her spark of life waning. Needing rest, she stayed abed for long, drowsy days, until she remained immobile long enough to feel herself refreshed.

Joshua needed the help of drugs to attain heights before unimaginable. She did not. Her free spirit rose and traveled on its own vehicles of transport wherever she wished to go, even when the destination was unknown. Drugs frightened her. Her inner life was beyond vivid. His was not. Like many of his followers, he needed external stimulation to unleash his mind to unknown realms.

She wanted to gain an ecstatic state with Joshua through orgasmic love-making instead of taking her *kriya* astral travels, which were so melancholic, the solo magic carpet rides, hurtful to her energy and spirit. She wanted to attain ecstasy in the mindless union attained through her body joined to his, her spirit merging with his. That carnal connection was how she experienced God.

Lucky's eyes dimmed with disillusion; their marriage had not succeeded. It might have produced a child or two, she could not recall, but no lasting happiness. They were accident prone. When, a year or so later, a daughter was born, all seemed well, and the little family left the hospital for the drive home. But, perhaps discharged too soon, as a new mother, she began to hemorrhage. Blood flowed from her womb as expected, but there was too much. It flowed into the upholstery of the car seat. Her head grew light. She fainted while holding the baby in her arms, and hit her head on the console. In a panic, Joshua turned the car back, returning, racing to the emergency entrance of the hospital they just left. They scraped her uterus; Arbella, wait, was it Arbella? almost died from loss of blood; three days later she was able to go home with a mild concussion. She didn't know where the baby was.

He sought the thrill of speed and rode a big Harley. She thought him part guru and part Hell's Angel. He had an accident, one where his face was torn, teeth ripped out, jaw smashed, skull bored through by the handle bar of his motorcycle. A car hit his motorcycle on a rainy road. He tumbled under the car's weighty tires which also drove the handle bar of his bike through his mouth and out the backside of his skull, narrowly missing the medulla. He lay in critical condition when she arrived, but conscious. She gently wiped road grit from his one unscathed eye with a damp white cloth.

He warned days later as she ministered to him, his words barely audible, "Careful around my wounds."

"Of course," she replied. "You're not cut right here," she said, touching his temple, "just dirty. There's a tear at the edge of your mouth. I can take a picture of it for you."

He cut her off. "I don't want to know. I don't want to see. I don't want a picture or a mirror. I don't want to see myself."

How true, she thought, chastened. He never really wanted to see himself or acknowledge the flamboyant ego he possessed. He pretended to seek Truth, but she saw he was fearful. He demanded his followers engage in trust exercises. He ordered them into a large circle, shoulder touching shoulder. One person stood on a platform or diving board with his back turned to the group. Then, on Joshua's command, the person fell backward into the open circle, trusting to be caught and held aloft in the outstretched arms. Everyone participated, except Lucky.

This was not an exercise she could do, nor one she wanted to do. She would not risk injury in order to be part of a group. She did not trust her well-being to others. She did not engage in random acts, of what she would term, idiocy. She sought love, took risks, and was brave. She faced truth, sought it out, even, and dealt with it. She owned her actions. She felt no need for group approval. Joshua did. He lived in a dimly lit, mystical cavern of lies supported by followers all seeking god and devotion, a place where they could avoid truth as he invented a bright, new reality for them all.

She wondered if she was to live her entire life dissatisfied. Why did she not accept Joshua's love and move with him in his groupie togetherness? Why did she wait for a state of perfection and distrust the validity of his love? Why did she suspect the love mightn't last or be supportive or quite good enough for her? She knew the answer: it was uncertainty on her part: uncertain that he was worthy of her love and full attention just as she was uncertain he was her true husband returned.

"I was the one who said no, who did not join hands and go through the circle into a future together. I waited. I hesitated. I stayed outside." She remembered the group wedding where dozens of his devotees got hitched at once.

In a year or two, healed well enough from his accident, Joshua got up to his old tricks of seduction and engaged in a tryst. Then another, and then another. She remembered those years when free love was in the air and on everyone's lips and tongues. She remembered Joshua ushering loosely amorous young things into her world, into her bed, demanding she share him, expand her consciousness, drop her morals.

She seemed to remember a child, children, rooms filled with children, unsure of whose they were. And rooms, so many rooms, some she built, others she forgot were there but found herself in anyway. Josh was there, and he was not there. She found other women in the rooms she thought she built, she thought were hers. It was all so dream-like, and the dreams recurred: the children, the boys, the girls, the rooms, the women. Faces recalled but names lost, that sort of thing. But, names soon came back; the lapses only transitory at first. Her grandchildren accused her of repeating herself, telling them stories they heard before. She laughed them off.

All the freedom Josh demanded for himself cost her love, worse, it bankrupted her heart and her hopes. She grew disenchanted, no, she grew disgusted, by Joshua's endless pursuit of other women, his polyamorous attitude of "the more the merrier," spreading enlightenment to the spread legs around him. She tired of Joshua's growing need to be a mystic, a guru, a leader enlightened and worshipped. His cerebral, spiritual epithets, the endless, pretentious drivel of gratitude, the host of holier-than-thou mantras, the mumbo-jumbo he muttered to his adoring followers wore her.

She stopped loving him. She left him. He wasn't hers, anyway. She moved out, leaving the child, the children, were they hers or his, she wasn't sure. They were quite strange. They didn't know how to laugh.

After a failed search for her husband that winter in Istanbul, she flew back to an island on the other side of the world where she thought she had last lived.

An encounter with a well-dressed island couple at the tiny inter-island airport amused her. It was unusual to see a woman in heels there, equally unusual to see a man in blazer and tie.

"Where are you headed?" she asked.

"A marriage encounter."

"What is that?"

"It's a sort of *Come to Jesus* meeting for relationships," the man said.

"He means we volunteer to help couples with religious questions about their marriages," the woman clarified. "We help couples reconnect in healthy, constructive ways that can deepen their intimacy and understanding of their union after they die."

"What kind of questions about relationships?" Lucky asked.

"We are talking about their eternal life," the woman clarified.

The man pointed toward a row of metal chairs against the terminal wall, where they moved to sit. He leaned forward intently, pressing his elbows onto his knees. He explained, "Once a month we fly to neighboring islands to hold weekend retreats. Two or more couples and a priest join us as we examine ourselves, our behaviors, and attitudes within our relationship with our spouse and God. This weekend the topic focuses on what to expect in the afterlife for widowed and remarried couples."

"Yes," the wife interjected with great verve, "our question for discussion is: 'when you die, which spouse meets you in heaven, your first spouse or your second?'" She paused, smiling, as though expecting Lucky to answer.

Instead, Lucky posed a question of her own. "Do people really worry about this?"

"Oh, yes. It is a very big subject. It's about everlasting life."

"Well, what do you tell them? I mean, is the assumption that both the first and second spouse have gone to Heaven?" Lucky amused herself by what she didn't ask, "What if the spouses aren't there? What if they went to Hell instead?"

The man responded, saying, "We contend that the first spouse meets you in the afterlife."

"What happens to the second or third spouse, then?" Lucky asked. "Are they left out in the cold with no one to love them in heaven?"

The couple appeared flummoxed and fell silent. When her flight was called, she excused herself from further conversation.

She hadn't told this couple what lay on the other side of death, and it was not the majestic Heaven of their dogmatic dreams. It was rebirth, resurrection, and reincarnation. If she told them, she knew they would just brush her off as a crack-pot and continue their fantasy. Yet, she understood religion very well. She was at least once over her life-times a pagan, a Muslim, a Protestant, a Buddhist, a Catholic, an agnostic, and an atheist. Yes, she knew a thing or two about religion, which may have started from nature worship, superstition, and ignorance, but grew to be a sham, she thought, contrived by the rich and paid for by the poor. In her view, it was a cosmetic painted on life by those who sought power, to conceal life's ugliness and exert control. Religion covered humanity's natural state of nakedness to mask, and even justify, the horrors men wrought on themselves and the physical world.

How many museums, housing relics of dead and bygone eras, she wondered, did the rich fund to feed their bird's eye view of culture to the public, often intravenously through the megaphones of social media, music, film, books. Purveyors of culture told people who they were and who they should aspire to be, while simultaneously castigating and punishing any deviant or free-thinker. She saw religion and culture keeping people in a bondage to play strict male and female roles, domestic and economic. If humans lived in their original state of nakedness like the plants and creatures did, well, she stopped, that was not possible, as humans did not live solo, unless marooned like a Robinson Crusoe or a monk, for people were never without tribes and the mores that grew firmly within them.

In museums what she saw rendered into art, with the exception of portraits, was mundane: a little fishing boat bobbing in the harbor, sunflowers in a vase, fields of hay, farms, rooms, landscapes, beds, boots—articles of daily life. The boats at Arles painted by Van Gogh, century after century of still life, iconography. Crowds poured into museums to see the paintings of what anyone could see anywhere with their own eyes: real life. Objects that meant nothing per se. Yet, painted by a master, voila, they were everything, and the world flocked to gaze and copy and gaze some more, their daily reality captured and transformed by the hand of the master, the painter, the poet whose act of transformation created beauty, giving the ordinary an exalted sense of meaning and value.

Lucky's imagination ruled her powerfully. She believed more in myth than in history. History only told half a story, she thought, written as it was by the conquerors rather than the vanquished. Her own dreams felt like a second reality.

She allowed hoped-for dreams to triumph over the disappointments she endured. Her laughter acted as a salve to bandage grief, and her love outlived death by far, as she knew from experience that true love was everlasting. When she occasionally heard the celestial spheres laugh at her whimsy, she wept. So, it went, her many lives teetering and tottering between hilarity and despair like a child on a carnival ride.

BLIP TWELVE

The Twelfth of Never
And, That's A Long, Long Time

Was it the moon, she wondered, drenching her in memories as she lay in her hammock or in her bed watching its reflection dance on the night waves? This moon promised her nothing more than a future alone. Artemis, the goddess of the moon, should be my ally, Lucky thought, but she's not. She has not brought Merrill back to me. This moon was her enemy. Its white, a color she once coveted, she mused in discontent, felt sterile and cold. And, above all, it was remote, rotating far, far from reach.

Perhaps it was the tropical sun that kept her alive in glorious hope on its rise each morning. After all, it was Apollo who lit the day and lingered in a dying wake at dusk, trailing his cloak of velvet, purple embers into the night. Or, was it Gaia who offered a sanctuary of calm in the island's rainforest with its deep, cool shadows dappled in liquids of green and gold?

Lucky woke, heavy lidded, to a world emerging from shadow and bathed in lemon, pre-dawn mist. She lifted her head fractionally from her pillow like a whale eyeing the surface of the sea as if, perhaps, contemplating a breech. The world looked the same, though dark, the palms silhouetted erect, the sand sloping first upward into dunes, then downward to the shore, where the water tread tentatively without creating waves. Beyond were deeper waters held by corals and creatures small and large, waters not yet turquoise nor blue nor navy as if not ready to catch the light. And, beyond this barely moving and silent sea rose islands, islands large yet diminished in size like the great pyramids seen from a plane window rather than from the land-locked eye of a camel.

She had seen this world many, many times on many, many such mornings.

And yet, this world, her world, was not the same.

She was patiently waiting for him to show up. She was independent, earning her way as an artist, making clay dolls and graveyard statuary, weaving wool rugs, trading in pearls. She knew there were whispers, "She's gay. She must be gay. I've never seen her with a man." Contradicted by, "But, I've never seen her with a woman, either." Or, the accusations she bore from insecure wives that she was bedding their husbands.

She wasn't celibate. She housed a forceful libido and sought pleasure regularly and often from a range of lovers. As too much time passed, and he didn't show up, this husband of hers, she wasted. At least, she felt she was wasting, lingering in a state of stasis, doing nothing.

"My god," she said to herself, "I am sitting on a speck of sand, a broken and blistered fragment of volcanic ash in the middle of nowhere." Waves washed on the shore, quietly but steadily eroding the fragile crust protruding above the sea where she tentatively perched, and she let her body and mind erode as well. Like a large blue whale, she submerged back into the deep comfort of her pillow and bed, failing to breach that morning at all.

What did it matter if she was seventy-three or nineteen? What was she to do? What did she want to do? Search for him instead of waiting? Time, time, ticking and tocking, moved at a steady rate while she sat, stewed, and mused, all the while twisting round and round the old pearl ring on her marriage finger. She still wore his ring, the gold-banded gimmel with two hands. What if she waited and dawdled, and her heart gave out or worse threw a stroke, leaving her truly incapacitated, as if the dawdling wasn't stagnating enough? She felt horrified by her paralysis, yet paralyzed she was, for she could not move, or rather she did not move. Neither drydocked nor adrift, she bobbed at random anchored by a deep inertia.

She had waited, waited for over seventy years on this western shore, watching and waiting, yearning for him. He did not come. Time for her was not linear. It was a carpet she wove back and forth through centuries and in and out of relationships. Like a spider weaving its delicate web, surprising even the mightiest engineers with the tensile strength of its threads, Lucky wove her many lives, connecting her love through life and death, on nearly invisible threads, unbroken, throughout time, the bonds of love the strongest in creation.

In the golden morning light, she saw her life as she had not until that moment. She felt grateful for this new home by the water. She guessed she was there to stay and only needed to wait for him, her husband, to arrive, like the gift of a pristine shell washed to shore at her feet.

She fantasized that after the last dinner-cruise ships came to port on the island, and the last pasty-fleshed tourists finished the *luau* at the resort, tossing *Styrofoam* cups of their untasted, purple *poi* in the rubbish, after the last drunken sailors fell comatose on their beds, and after the last bunch of visitors got their skin fried to a deep crimson at the beach, he would join her, to feel the soft trade winds, to watch the lingering sunsets, to smell the intense fragrances of plumeria and *pikake*. She wanted him to ride horseback over the trails with her. She wanted Turkey to shake sand and salt water in their laps in the annoying yet endearing way he did after retrieving his ball from the sea. She wanted to play among the grass shacks of times gone by, letting the images of each day together emulsify afresh on the surface of their souls.

She perused dating sites for seniors, even though she used an online service unsuccessfully for her DNA search. When his photo opened on her screen in the international section, she pushed back from her computer in surprise. There he was, her husband, well, there he was in cyberspace, anyway. His name, this go-round, was Merrill.

"Ah," she sighed, "Merrill, again." But, there was no full name, as the site did not allow full names. To reach out to him, she signed onto the site, paying a one-month membership fee, and she was free to scrutinize his profile. Where did he live, what did he do, what were his hobbies? He lived in London. Again. He was an obstetrician with the World Health Organization. A wine connoisseur.

"Ah, Guillaume," she sighed. He liked beaches and theatre, noting he was particularly fond of Greek drama, hence vacationed in Greece often to attend the summer festivals at the ancient theatre of Epidaurus. She smiled remembering Vassilios.

He requested hearing from women from ages thirty-five to fifty-five, he being, as always, fifty-six. At least he didn't lie about his age, she laughed. But, she was over seventy in her present, near senescent incarnation. With age the first obstacle to meeting in front of her, she debated whether to lie about her own. Perhaps sending an out of date photo…

She sought a way other than the dating site to find him. She "googled" "Merrill, London" and "Dr. William Merrill" but got nowhere as there were far too many entries.

She returned to the site to expand her own profile, to add places and experiences he might recognize. In every life there had been art, dogs, seas and rivers, trade, porcelain, food, carpets, and wine. When they parted, he went east, she west.

As she was living on a tropical isle, she decided to cheat on her profile, adding an address in Hampstead, where she claimed to live part of the year, as she showed her art in a gallery there.

She posted an old photo of her dog, Turkey, reminiscent of the dogs they had over their lifetimes together in the hope he would at least recognize the dog. They almost always gave their dog the same name, "Turkey." She remembered the beautiful "Le Dindon" when they lived in the Dordogne, and the others, Woofie, Molossus, and Huo-ji.

Bingo! A cryptic note from him. Was she in Hampstead at the moment? If so, would she like a coffee?

She bit her lip as she typed, "I suspect we have met before, you seem familiar to me. Yes, I want to meet, but I won't be in Hampstead until the twelfth." She laughed at "the twelfth." What? "The twelfth of never? And, that's a long, long time." Considering the eons that already passed, the twelfth felt like a blip.

When he agreed to the date, she booked a ticket to London.

She wrote reminders on her palms, on her wrists, and even up her forearms. She couldn't allow herself forget her plan, her flight, the date. She spoke to herself, repeating aloud her plans, printing them onto her memory, inking them onto her skin. She packed a bag and wrote the dates and reminders on a sheet of paper as well which she taped to the top of her bag.

How she longed to continue the journey of love they promised each other. She knew their bodies might let them down, as they had so often through death and betrayal over the centuries. But, their minds? She never imagined losing him by losing her memory.

She swung in the hammock a long while before pulling herself up by holding the railing with one hand and steadying the strings of the hammock with the other. She must get the other letter from the morning mail that woman put on the side table. She sought her reading glasses. Postmarked "London, 1974" it held a folded sheet of velum. Her hand shook slightly as she opened it. The words she made out were about marriage and eternal love and the value of patience and the little things. Moistening her dry lips, she read it through again, aloud this time.

"What is important, my Darling? What will make our love last forever?"

Who wrote this, she wondered, not recognizing the handwriting. And, who was 'my Darling?'

She got up to riffle through her lingerie drawer, seeking the vows she and William once pledged. She pulled out a small cinnabar chest. From inside, she lifted a red silk bag. It housed a tiny braid woven of black and white hair. Next to the bag, a parchment lay, rolled and tied with a white satin ribbon. Unfurling it, she saw vows, written in English, modern English. She paused. The vows were not written as she anticipated in the antique, olde English tongue of William nor in the foreign tongues of Ibn, Guillaume, Du, or Vassilios.

Returning to her bed, she sat down on its edge to read:

"Let our love be an illumined circle like the ring that we share, with no beginning and no end, open in the center to hold the future." Words, these words, echoed through the hollow chambers of her mind.

"Ah," she thought, "that sounds like something William said." She looked at her hand, holding the parchment. Yes, there, on her finger, was his pearl ring. She slid the ring off, and it fell apart. On the inside of one band was inscribed an infant, on the other, a skeleton.

"Let our love be like the phoenix, rising anew on wings of love from the ashes of the past."

"William didn't say that." She thought, "Merrill." In her mind's eye, she watched that English merchant beneath a porcelain blue sky practice *qi gong* in the shadows falling from the broad sails of her junk.

"Let our love transport us on a magic carpet through time and place, each lifetime we share shining like a star upon the blanket of heaven." Ibn she guessed, for no other man she knew spoke like that or had traveled so far.

"Let our love, like a good glass of wine, fill this world with pleasure. Let there be beauty, in work and in play, in our garden of love, serenaded by the splashing waters of the mill."

"Guillaume," she murmured, "my wise and kind vintner."

"Let us dance under the bright gaze of the sun and moon." Was that William entreating her at the Tethys Festival? Or, perhaps it was the distant voice of Vassilios from another festival, that of Dionysos?

"Let our love be a gentle call to prayer, a reflection of the joining of our souls with faith and fidelity, kindness and respect, and above all, with the gift of patience for one another."

"Du," she sighed.

As her husband's many voices rose like a chorus in her heart to join her own, she heard the duets they sang through the ages.

She nodded her head to their music. It was heavenly. She was remembering. She had not forgotten. Yes, thankfully, she was remembering them all. As she rolled the parchment, she saw at the bottom an "L" on the left, a burnt umber kiss—was it ink or blood or perhaps lipstick? —she wasn't sure, and on the right, an "M." She tied the parchment again but did not return it to the drawer. Instead, she put it next to the red silk pouch in a special compartment within her travel bag to accompany her on this journey.

The wild shrieks of pink-legged stilts skimming the waves below her house shook her from her thoughts. Did he know the volcanic island where she lived? Her husband? This "maybe" husband she was going to meet in London?

The threatened psychic tornado, the loosening of her sense of longing, of deep loneliness and fear of never joining him again, gave way instead of to that turbulence, rather to calm, to a sense of embarkation, like a gentle and encouraging breeze nudging at her back. She jumped over the cusp of regret to leave the past. Something shifted, like the tectonic plates of her decades, moving not up or down but rather sideways, a sliding over and under. Her life felt like a zipper, the tines on each side, neatly meshing to zip all her desires together: love, marriage, home, family. Her many lives cruelly unzipped when the betrayals began letting love fall out, the marriages broken, children lost, the homes abandoned, and the families imploded.

She felt a surety that a new paradigm was about to begin. A fragrant air of sweetness infused her thoughts.

In the interim before the scheduled coffee date in London, they corresponded by email under her assumed name, Muriel, filling in gaps and learning anew to their mutual delight.

anon. Merrill:

Wow, what a nice match.... your profile is quite similar to mine.... searching for a soulmate, another true romantic, a person who feels that this is not a dress rehearsal so it better be good, and who feels strongly that "what goes around, comes around." Your profile ignited me.... I used to travel to the Pacific several times a year, delivering babies or helping set up hepatitis prevention projects in Samoa, Guam, Palau, Saipan....Thank you so much for your response, and if you don't mind a superficial note, I must ask, are you pretty? I like the photo of the dog, but I want to see you as well!

As to myself, I'm English-French-Russian. Not many people know Krupinin Island where I live part of the year. It's off the Kerch Strait between the Black Sea and the Sea of Azov. The other part of the year, I live in my father's residence in London. He is long dead. He came to Krupinin as a French medic during the Crimean War and married my mother, a nurse. I was born in Russia. My mother called me her Crimean pearl floating in a bowl of borscht!

anon. Muriel:

You've probably gotten my photo, so we'll see who's laughing now.

Muriel (Valiantly Holding on To Her Vanity While There's Still Time)

P.S. I can just see that pearl in borscht bobbing to the surface for air, struggling to stay afloat. I know nothing except what you tell me about the region where you live, never having been or explored there. I can't even find it on the Atlas (what good is Atlas anyway, if he cannot lift me to new heights?)

She wanted to ask how many girlfriends he had, but she refrained.

anon. Merrill:

I got your photo. You are as lovely, as I expected. Let's meet over a fine merlot, some sharp cheese, Greek olives, and fresh figs. I am rather tired of my diet of kilka, the most common fish in Crimea.

What day might suit?

anon. Muriel:

I won't be in London until the twelfth. Does the thirteenth work? Ha! I see on the calendar it will be a Friday!

anon. Merrill

Let's avoid Friday the thirteenth! To be on the safe side, rest after your flight and possible jet lag. Meet me on Saturday, the fourteenth around eleven, if that suits, and I'll be there, if Lady Luck allows.

A reality jolt hit her. Her old nickname, "Lady Luck" bounced off the screen. She wondered if he could already sense this "anon. Muriel" was her, Lucky, his eternal love? It boosted her helium supply of hope. She felt dizzy with relief. She cautioned herself to keep her equilibrium, despite the lack of gravity in this burgeoning cyberspace adventure.

anon. Merrill

I am wondering if you like chocolate? I have a favorite: the cocoa-powdered dark chocolate truffle; I often get them from L'Atelier du Chocolat at Saint Lazare when I am in Paris. That being said, I am also a sucker for dried apricots dipped in dark chocolate. Here I am talking about favorites. So, let me ask, what is your favorite cheese? Mine is a French goat cheese from the Dordogne called Cabecous. My French father introduced me to the region's most delectable foods.

One day perhaps we can share a bottle of Domaine de Canton liqueur. Do you know it? It's ginger-flavored and hard to find, as it is no longer produced in the Pearl River Delta near Macau. I must have been Chinese in some other life as I love it!

Meltingly, Merrill

anon. Muriel

Chocolat? Moi?! Je crois que je suis fait du chocolat. Translation: I believe I am made of chocolate! As to cheese, I really like an unusual cheese I tasted on a farm visit to France called *Trappe d'Echourgnac*. As to wine, I like a cold *Vouveray* mid-day and the wines from Bergerac, as they are pressed and aged in oak. When I can, I like to indulge in a small glass of a very special plum brandy from Souillac.

anon. Merrill

Now I not only hear but feel tiny bubbles of delight as I drink your words off the screen... *Tiny Bubbles* (remember the Don Ho song?) came to mind on reading your note: I failed to mention my affinity for champagnes and fine wines. You mentioned *Vouveray*. I, too, much prefer the wines from Bergerac. And, to my surprise, you know them! Not only that, but the plum brandy that is simply the best!

What are you doing for New Year's? I'm hoping you're virtually a free woman (which does not mean without cost) who will stay in England through January, as I suspect I shall want to spend time with you.

anon. Muriel

I have wanted to shed my routine and travel the world as a camera. And, a sponge. Yes, a sponge! The camera is me recording and interpreting artistically what I've seen incognito, and as a sponge I absorb it all.

The camera I use is one I got from a woman who works for me now and then, doing small tasks like bringing the mail and lunch from the deli. It's an old *Leica*. I worry about mildew or mold getting into the lenses as so easily happens in the tropics.

anon. Merrill

Your desire to "be a camera" is noteworthy and worthwhile. I hesitate to respond as photography holds a dear place in my heart for the following reason.

Did I mention I have a daughter who is a wonderful photographer? She specializes in black and white, silver gelatin prints, photographing skin and bones, mostly animal bones and skulls, which I know sounds morbid, but her compositions are extraordinary. I'll show you her work when you are here. Sadly, you won't be able to meet her, as she's not in London.

This revelation startled Lucky. So, there was a daughter! Was this child hers? Theirs? She wanted to ask, the sound of fireworks going off inside her head, but she could not. She had to be patient and wait.

anon. Muriel

I am sorry to miss her. She must be lovely. May I ask about her mother?

anon. Merrill

That is a long story, full of sadness and deceptions. My wife told me I was her one and only. And, I believed her. Then, I found out she'd been married many times. She told me she couldn't have more children after our daughter was born. But, I discovered she had abortions without ever telling me she was pregnant. Suffice it to say, as both husband and obstetrician, I felt betrayed and deceived. We drifted apart, my fault really. I left her and went east, to the Crimea. My wife, I heard, went west, past America to some island. I kept our daughter, who was young at the time. I warned her, "If you tell a lie to Daddy, I won't be able to find you, because I won't know who you are. And, my love will go away. Just like Mommy went away." My daughter never told a lie, but her mother, my wife, did. I don't know if she suffered post-partum blues or some sort of mental breakdown. All I do know is she was lost to me.

Liars bothered Lucky as well. They were as dangerous as quicksand. If she came within earshot of one, like Maggie, the ground sank beneath her feet, and she felt herself slip perilously. Lucky learned that love could not survive lies. Yet, she told them, lies, mainly of omission: like the times she was pregnant. Or, when she lost the baby. Or, when she aborted the baby and lost the husband, Vassilios and possibly even Guillaume. And, what about that baby she birthed on the Pearl or was it Hong Kong, after Merrill sailed away from China and from her? Or, was it in the Thames? some river anyway? when William failed to save her?

anon. Muriel

I am sorry. That is a sad story.

anon. Merrill

It is a sensitive subject. I prefer to speak to you in person or by phone. Tell me the best time, if you'd like me to call.

Meanwhile, soft trade winds to you, Muriel My Marine Moon ...uh, I'll save the Goddess for later, because romance is so delicate. Know that I await you in London.

At the airport in San Francisco, she bought appropriate city clothes for the English climate that early spring and some high heeled boots along with a broad brimmed white wool hat and white mohair neck scarf, white remaining her favorite color no matter the season. She also purchased a proper handbag, warm gloves, new bronze lipstick, and lots of body cream, as she knew her skin lost hydration away from the tropics. She worried he would run when he saw how old she really was, despite her porcelain complexion and eyes shielded by dark glasses. The only jewelry she wore was her old gimmel ring and a pair of pearls on her ears. She wanted to wear her pearl ropes, but left them behind as they had broken.

She bought a kennel for Turkey and booked him in the cargo hold on her flight. As her island was rabies free, it shared a reciprocal relationship with England, also rabies free, for animals to travel freely into and out of the country without the usual delay of a quarantine.

On the eight-hour flight, she sat in a window seat, reading and re-reading her itinerary and plan. Her name, address, even social security number and return flight she penned on her arms in case she suffered a lapse. Her carry-on held a few long-sleeved blouses to wear to cover her tracks, conscious that while she might need to read her notes to refresh her memory, she did not want anyone else to see her arms.

She watched the clouds piled like duvets tossed about after lazy love below her. She thought all her lives were as insubstantial as clouds—full, beautiful, voluminous, and, in the end, ephemeral. Clouds formed then evaporated, traveling through time like a clock, as its marked minutes disappeared into hours, hours disappeared into days, days disappeared into months, all the while re-forming and circling the globe. Her loves rose, billowed, blew away. Her lovers brought joy as lofty and full as the cumulus clouds over the sea, roiling her in jubilant waves of pleasure. She knew there were storms, but she refused to entertain those turbulent times. On this flight, she wanted happiness, to imagine herself with him, her love, in the clouds, not in a bed but sitting on a bench of cloud, their legs dangling, laughing, floating, delighting to be together again, free of gravity.

It took a while to find a cabbie willing to accept Turkey as a passenger. On the gray drive from Heathrow, she saw an urban landscape that looked like it suffered industrial anorexia nervosa. Skeletal power towers loomed over the carved and chilled low hills with wire tentacles stiffly outstretched to grasp one to another, dragging cities together as they obliterated the countryside. How depressed she used to feel in the overcast light and damp air of England when she did absolutely nothing but waste away, starving, in the Tower or after the unsettling, ghostly encounters at Rufford.

Before leaving her hotel two days later, she deliberately donned tight tummy tucking pants, sprayed a goodly dollop of *Worth* cologne at her breast bone, and settled on a leopard patterned blouse hoping to exude subliminal animal allure.

She and Turkey arrived about ten minutes late at the Curled Leaf Café at Perrin's Court in Hampstead. She liked it from her stays in London before she headed north to Rufford, the art centre where she created large clay sculptures for international exhibition. She liked Hampstead's charm, its heath, and the cottages where the likes of Coleridge, Freud, Lawrence, Orwell, and Constable once lived. She showed her sculpture with an excellent gallery there on Flask Walk.

When she arrived, Merrill was sitting outside on a little wrought iron garden chair at a matching wrought iron table for two beneath a small, blue umbrella. There was a nip in the air, but, unusual for London, the sun was out. As she paid the cabbie, Turkey lurched from his lead and nearly knocked Merrill over when he stood to greet this virtual "Muriel." The dog leapt up to lick his face, mewling in sharp staccato tones of joy. Startled, Merrill gently fended off Turkey's advances and sank to his knees to settle the dog nicely at his feet while prodigiously stroking his head and back.

She stood watching them. "Will this man fall to me like an apple falls from a tree?" she wondered.

Then, Merrill turned his gaze to "Muriel."

He was all smiles, proffered a long-time no-see obligatory hug and light kisses on each of her cheeks. He gestured for her to sit.

She said, as she placed the white wool hat to the side of the table out of the breeze, in a rather curt manner unsuited to her, "Beautiful flight, restful hotel, beautiful day." Her nerves betrayed her.

He said, gesturing in a wide circle, "You've chosen a comfortable cafe."

She said, "Yes, I always like coming here. It's close to the gallery where I show," she said, pointing to a small cobbled alley. "There, on Flask Walk."

Without looking in that direction, he said, "I am seeing someone."

Did he really say that? Slide that bit of information into their first parlay? Had she heard him correctly? Who? Where? When? How? She didn't ask.

How rude, how amazingly rude and insensitive of him to mention another attachment. Her sense of self, along with her profusion of in-flight phero-mones, sank. Did he see how old she was and gave himself an easy "out?" Was she no longer a viable woman, single, self-assured, even if fadingly, in an old-world sort of way, beautiful? If he was seeing someone, why did he invite her to come? She turned away, as tears of self-pity welled over her high cheek bones to join the sudden puddle her nerves were making on the stone pavers beneath her feet.

"Coffee?" he asked, unaware of her discomposure. She nodded.

"A double espresso," she murmured, adding a formal, "Thank you." She removed her gloves and loosened the new mohair scarf from her neck to brush the tears discreetly aside as they fell from her cheeks. She watched him walk to the counter, elegant as always in his relaxed carriage, tweed jacket, cashmere turtleneck, slacks, expensive loafers. He ran his fingers through his wavy shock of white hair a few times as he waited at the counter to pay before returning to the table.

"Ah, well then," he began but stopped. He sat. She looked into his gold-flecked, hazel eyes. She did not speak.

"That was quite a greeting from your dog!" Merrill finally said. "What's his name?"

"Turkey," she answered. They looked quizzically at each other, and both began to laugh.

"That's the dog's name, but you're a turkey as well!" she teased a bit roughly through her anger. She took a risk, seeing him, flying half way around the world on the half-baked hope he was her love, her Merrill, Ibn, Du, Guillaume, William, Vassilios. She set her heart on open. And, there he was, tall, handsome, aged, skin reddened by small keratoses from too much Crimean sun on that thin British hide. She knew him. She knew him well. She had known him forever.

The espresso came. She blew on it, then opened two packets of raw sugar, stirring them into the small cup. She drank it in one gulp as he watched her, nonplussed by her remark, occasionally stirring the cooling remnants in his own cup.

"And, what should I call you?" he asked. "'Muriel,' as you wrote on the site?"

"Yes. No. Lady Luck. Lucky. Lucky is my nickname. That would be fine." He was looking at her bemused. She went on, flustered. "My given name is Emily. My brother calls me Em. Everyone else calls me Lucky. And, you? Merrill?" He nodded in assent. "Is that your first or last name?"

"It's William Merrill, but my friends call me Last."

"Last?" she questioned, looking puzzled.

"Last name. You asked first or last," he smiled. "They call me Merrill." Then, when she smiled, he went on, "You mentioned you thought we'd met before?"

She nodded in assent.

"You look tired," he said, changing the subject. "The flight was long?"

"I am only surprised," she said, her hopes continuing their downward plummet. She was feeling trapped and exposed, as if her panty hose clumped about her ankles, and she was unable to move. A possible reunion seemed most unlikely.

"Surprised?" Merrill asked. "About what?"

"You just said you were seeing someone."

"Ah, so that's it." He took a last sip of coffee and wiped his lips with the starched linen napkin. There ensued an uncomfortable silence. Merrill began to hum, thrumming his fingers on the cast iron rim of the table as though it was a piano keyboard or a harpsichord.

She looked at him, flummoxed. The tune he hummed was familiar. It was, of all choices, *Auld Lang Syne*. "Should auld acquaintance be forgot..."

There was a mystery and power in music, a power able to reach into unseen places to bring back a memory that might part the darkened sea of remembrance, if for only a moment; but a moment that was worth everything. The whole of their life-song eventually became their end-of-life song. When nothing else was heard, and all else faded away, the song sang itself over and over from a far away, quiet place, singing back the lives they had lived, and singing them forward into the new life they were entering.

"The someone I am seeing is... you," he said. "And, yes, we have met before. Many, many times." She saw her own reflection begin to dance in the gold of his eyes.

"Ah, Lucky," he went on, "you really are Lucky, aren't you?" And, as the dog rubbed his muzzle against Merrill's knee, Merrill added softly, "Shakespeare has anything I might want to say to you now, in this moment, beat." He reached down to pet the dog, who wagged his tail and turned in circles around the chair, returning each time for another embrace. The breeze blew the mohair scarf back from Lucky's neck as though it was an eraser clearing her head where something new could be written. And, as though a teacher holding the chalk to draw a quotation on her memory, Merrill took a deep breath, looked at her, and continued, "But, I seem to remember, and you bring to mind, these lines." He slid his chair closer to the table and took both her hands in his. They were thick hands, like the paws of a lion, showing age spots beneath the light dusting of reddish hair that poked from the cashmere edge of his sleeve. In a husky voice, he whispered slowly, his baritone quite hidden, "'Age cannot wither her, nor custom Stale her infinite variety...'"

There is a certainty in love, invisible perhaps to the eye, but clearly remembered by the heart, a unity across time and place, sometimes requiring patience, a great deal of patience, in awaiting its revival. For her, for him, time, all time, became as one pulsing heart, whose crimson liquid circled a body of love interconnecting all the lives they lived in its widespread web of veins.

Her eyes were shining above her softened lips when his phone rang.

Picking it up, he said, "Yes, yes, Darling, she's here. Yes, Turkey made it, too," he chuckled. Pointing to the phone, he whispered to Lucky, "It's my daughter."

Lucky smiled and nodded. A daughter.

And so, they began again. Or, perhaps, she wasn't certain, they already had begun? Was this the new beginning she had journeyed so far to find or an ending to a life she scarcely could conjure in her fading mind? No matter how hard she tried to remember, she did not know if it was a first or the last.

But, she wasn't alone any longer. He was there. And, there was a child! That she knew now for sure.

At least, she thought she did.

THE END

Post Script:

"I hope you don't mind that I put down in words how
wonderful life is while you're in the world."
Elton John, 'Your Song'